Readers love Amy Lane

ChrisMyths

"As usual, Amy Lane gives us everything we didn't know we wanted. …this story is a breath of very refreshing air."
—Love Bytes

Late for Christmas

"Amy Lane finds those who are beaten down and in need of a hug and makes theirs and our lives better."
—Paranormal Romance Guild

Freckles

"I have major kudos for Ms. Lane in creating relatable, realistic and fun characters and breathing some real life into this story. I absolutely enjoyed it and would strongly recommend it."
—Long and Short Reviews

Homebird

"It'll make you feel good and leave you as warm and gooey feeling as a warm sugar cookie right out of the oven!"
—Diverse Reader

Christmas Kitsch

"Sigh. I had a hard time even sitting down to write this review, because you guys, this book is just so good. Easily one of the best I have read all year. I just loved it, and I just want to tell you that you will love it too,"
—Joyfully Jay

By Amy Lane

Published by DREAMSPINNER PRESS
www.dreamspinnerpress.com

Published by DREAMSPINNER PRESS
www.dreamspinnerpress.com

By Amy Lane (cont)

Published by DREAMSPINNER PRESS
www.dreamspinnerpress.com

THE 12 KITTENS OF CHRISTMAS

AMY LANE

DREAMSPINNER PRESS

Published by
DREAMSPINNER PRESS

5032 Capital Circle SW, Suite 2, PMB# 279, Tallahassee, FL 32305-7886 USA
www.dreamspinnerpress.com

The Twelve Kittens of Christmas
© 2023 Amy Lane

Cover Art
© 2023 L.C. Chase
http://www.lcchase.com
Cover content is for illustrative purposes only and any person depicted on the cover is a model.

Trade Paperback ISBN: 978-1-64108-689-9
Digital ISBN: 978-1-64108-688-2
Trade Paperback published November 2023
v. 1.0

Printed in the United States of America
∞
This paper meets the requirements of
ANSI/NISO Z39.48-1992 (Permanence of Paper).

To Mate, of course, and Mary, who saw this one first. To Jason, who gets random manuscripts and is like, "Hunh—what car was he driving?" and to Steve, Nebula, Dewey, and Jelly, who every night turn my kitchen into *West Side Story*, the Sharks vs. the Jets, stalking each other to music in their own minds.

ACKNOWLEDGMENTS

THERE'S LOTS of Easter Eggs in this one—thank you to everybody who will join the hunt.

Author's Note

My daughter—grown—keeps adopting cats and then realizing that she lives in a tiny apartment and giving the cat to us. To this end, we have one cat—Steve—who we adopted twelve years ago and is the most feared animal in the house, and three male cats under five years old who range from psychopath to mouth breather to "I think I'll pee here." During the pandemic, when we were all scared and forced to endure each other's company for way too long, those stupid furry poop-machines saved our lives. When we couldn't talk about being afraid or being frustrated or being depressed, we could tell wild stories about whether Nebula the bird-murderer caught his quota today, or how many breaths Dewey has to take while gazing at the sky before he just flops over. We may have watched every miniseries on TV, but our house animals were a never-ending source of entertainment for us. Animals give us so much. It is an honor to be able to give them a place in the home.

LAST CALL

KILLIAN THORNTON wiped down the varnished wooden counter in front of him and fought the first yawn of the night. It was the Friday after Thanksgiving, and the rush had been fierce—lots of people celebrating their "friendsgivings" anywhere but in their own homes this year—and he was ready to clean up and go home.

"Don't do it," Suzanne, his night manager, ordered.

"Don't do what?" he asked, yawning.

"Don't do that, you bastard!" she responded with a yawn of her own. "Dammit, I still have to count drawers!"

Suzanne had been hired ten years ago straight out of college; she had an MA in history and no interest in teaching. She was smart, could talk customers down off a drunken soapbox and count a drawer at the same time. She also didn't hesitate to break out the baseball bat underneath the bar if things got rough, although they didn't often get rough in Catches. Catches was a chain bar—you could find one in most major cities in America, although usually they were found in big malls and shopping centers, along with BJ's and Cheesecake Factory. This particular Catches, though, was deep in Sacramento's midtown, maybe three blocks from Lavender Heights and sitting cheek by jowl between a mom-and-pop Mexican food place and a designer thrift shop—but right across from a Starbucks. There was enough unique and personalized business going on around them for the place to have grown a little character of its own, and for people to need the reassurance of a brand name while pub crawling through midtown.

"Go ahead and start," he said, moving on to polishing the brass fixtures. "Then we can go home."

Killian loved this area—lived less than two blocks away, in an old square apartment building with five units, vintage wood frames and floors that swelled and stuck in the summer, and wrought iron that had been painted over often enough to obscure the filigree patterns on the stair rails and the sconces in the upper apartment. He had a car, but he could walk anywhere: the laundromat across the street, the bodega a block down, the comic bookstore five blocks away, even the place he bought his shoes. All of it was close enough for a brisk walk under the Sacramento trees. What was left of them, of course, after the storms the year before.

Killian had been visiting a friend who'd worked at Catches, after he'd done two tours right out of high school. He'd come home rootless—his folks lived in the Midwest and had been happy to see the back of him—and lonely. The Army hadn't sucked entirely. Three squares, a salary, a daily goal. If it hadn't been for being in a war zone, it might have been great. But the war zone thing had been... frightening. He'd seen some action, and he'd hated it. Hated the casual disregard for life, hated the moral grayness, hated not knowing if he was going to be woken up by trumpeted reveille or mortar rounds. Hated seeing the civilians hurt, hated hurting the soldiers, felt like he had no business there to intervene but no choice but to help keep the civilians safe.

And then he'd just... left. Time served, sir. Go back to your business, go to school, get a job, nothing to see here, folks.

It hadn't sat right—guilt, anger, depression, the whole weight of it had rested on his shoulders. And he'd just come out to himself, if not the world. Going back home when he hated *everything*, including his own shadow, had not filled him with joy. Well, nothing back then had filled him with joy, but in particular going back to his fundamentalist family in the Midwest who wouldn't understand his feelings about the war or the military or other men—*that* had filled him with everything from horror to irritation to disgust. So he'd taken Jaime, who'd been stationed with him briefly in Kabul, up on his offer to come visit Sacramento in the spring, when Jaime said the sun was pleasant and not destructive, and there might be flowers on the hills.

He'd fallen in love with Sacramento—and briefly with Jaime, although that had been more of a starter relationship than the real thing. Before their sad but amicable breakup, Killian had gotten the job at Catches, and after it had gotten his own apartment nearby. Jaime had taken his savings and started his own bar up in Folsom, where he kept promising to ask Killian to come work, but Killian kept thinking that he'd miss the big sycamore tree in front of his apartment in the spring, or the way the breeze off the river could cool the whole place down in the summer. He'd miss the thick, honey-dripping light in the late afternoons in the fall or the boozy happiness of the pub crawlers on a warm Friday night. He wouldn't hear the women preening about their new looks as they left the nail boutique next door or be torn between the Starbucks across the street and the indie coffee place a block and a half down that he liked better. What if he never ate a dessert at Rick's again? All of these things, these moments, had rescued him when he'd come to Sacramento eight years before—they'd anchored him, filled him with quiet joy when he'd thought that was the impossible dream.

He couldn't leave them now. This city, this job, they'd served him so well.

And loneliness was such a small price to play for a little bit of peace.

But it meant that closing time at Catches had the same melancholy feeling as the Semisonic song. Nobody was ready to go home, but they couldn't stay there.

Tonight, though, things had cleared out rather quickly, with the exception of the kid in the oversized white sweatshirt and the skinny pants with the big denim jacket and trout-fishing hat sitting on the barstool behind him as he played one more spectacular round of darts.

Thunk. 25. Thunk. 50. Thunk. 100.

The kid with the slender, lithe body and the vulpine little chin with a wide gamine mouth—not usually Killian's type of face, but it was an *interesting* face, wasn't it?

Thunk. 25.

The kid who looked borderline familiar?

Thunk. 50.

"You got the drawer for me to count?" Suzanne asked, suddenly standing right next to Killian. "Don't you want to go home?"

Killian had been staring at the kid—twenty-two, twenty-three, maybe—throwing darts at the board with astounding precision.

Thunk.

"Wha—oh, yeah." Killian went to the old-fashioned register—a Catches staple—and hit the No Sale button, popping out the cash box along with the receipt he'd generated with all the night's transactions on it, as well as his first drawer count, done after the last—*thunk*—or, well, almost last customer had left.

Bullseye! Killian remembered who this kid was.

"Here's the drawer," he told Suzanne. "I'll polish some brass and wait until you count it out."

She snorted. "Puhleeze, Killian. Like your drawers are ever more than two bucks off."

Killian inclined his head modestly. He did like a clean count at the end of the night.

"Well, then," he said, "I'll wait to walk you to your car."

Suzanne was fit—as was Killian—but she also wasn't stupid. "How very gallant," she said. "I accept. I'll be back in a sec after I get this in the safe."

Killian nodded, because why use extra words when you didn't need to, right? And then turned his attention to Lewis Bernard, his upstairs neighbor's little brother.

Thunk. "Lewis?" he asked, timing the name carefully so as to not break the kid's stride.

Lewis, apparently, could multitask. "Hey, Killian." He yawned before bebopping to the dart board to pull out his latest round. "You almost done?"

"Yeah," Killian told him. "You weren't… were you waiting for me?" *That* seemed unlikely.

Lewis gave him a sheepish look that indicated the unlikely was true.

"See," he said with a sigh, "Todd wanted to, uhm, have some time with his girlfriend tonight—you know, Aileen?"

Killian nodded because he did know her—and Todd. Todd had been his neighbor for about four years—had been to movie nights and was, Killian thought fondly, a friend.

"Yeah, well, Todd never gets a night off—you know that-- and he didn't want his twinkie little brother around while they got their thing on. I guess it was true romance. Anyway—" He shrugged. "—I didn't want to go up until he texted me, and, well, I knew you lived in the building. I figured I'd walk home with you, you could let me in, and I'd hang in the stairwell until he remembered I didn't have anywhere else to go."

Killian squinted at him. "Did he just… *forget* you were here?"

Lewis made one of those faces where he squinched his lips together until his top lip touched the bottom of his almost hawklike nose. Killian wondered if he ever put a pencil in the space when he was a kid, bored at school, and then he put a dart in there and tried to make it balance, and Killian didn't wonder anymore.

"Lewis?" Killian prompted, and Lewis turned his head to the side with the dart caught lengthwise between his lip and his nose and smiled.

The smile changed the curvature of his upper lip and the dart slid off, landing point first into the scuffed wooden floor with its own *thunk*.

"What?" Lewis asked, bending to pick up the dart.

"Did your brother forget you were here?"

"Mm… forget?" Lewis tilted his head, his shaggy blond hair falling into place with his every movement. "That's sort of a harsh word, don't you think? I, uhm, may have mentioned that he's already involved."

Killian squeezed his eyes shut. "Your brother forgot you need a place to sleep tonight," he said on a sigh. "No worries. You can use my couch."

Killian's place was small; all of the apartments in the building were small. The building was a large blocky rectangle with a peaked roof, and the two bottom apartments were built like crooked shotguns: The front door opened from inside the foyer, and the apartments consisted of long skinny front rooms connected to long skinny kitchens that led to a hallway with a bathroom and bedroom on one side and some storage cabinets on the other. Killian had never been in any of the upstairs apartments, but given there were three of them and a flight of stairs, he was pretty sure they were even longer and skinnier than the ones on the bottom floor, and two of them shared a bathroom.

"Really?" Lewis asked, eyes enormous. "That would be amazing. My brother's apartment is *small*."

Todd lived in the unit that *didn't* share the bathroom, thank God, but it still wasn't big enough for a guest. Particularly if….

"Does Todd even have a couch?" Killian asked, horrified.

Lewis shrugged. "He's got a nice recliner," he said, as though making up for his brother's shortcomings. "But you know the best thing he has?"

Killian stared at him, at a loss. "No idea."

"An address not in Texas," Lewis said, nodding sagely, and Killian sucked air through his teeth.

"Is that where you went to school?" he asked apologetically. Lewis's pretty, angular face sported two yellowing crescents of old bruises under his brown eyes, and he was half afraid to ask where those had come from.

"Don't get me wrong," Lewis said. "There are a lot of great things about Texas. Barbecue, nice people, country music, wide-open spaces. You know what's not great about Texas?"

"Fox News and bigots?" Killian asked, pretty sure this had been the reason Lewis had shown up to sleep in his brother's recliner.

Lewis put a finger to a still-swollen nose, looking glum. "Yeah. Got out of college, tried to get a job—had three different companies outside of Houston tell me they 'didn't hire my kind.'" He sighed. "I've got a degree in software engineering." He paused. "A *master's*."

Killian sighed. "Well, I wish you luck. You may have a better time finding a job here."

"And my parents' neighbors will quit signing petitions to evict them from the neighborhood," he muttered.

"Oh God," Killian said. "I'm sorry. High school must have been a *drag*."

Lewis nodded and touched his nose again—gingerly. "Bingo."

"Well, I can't solve any of that, and politics depress me. But you can sleep on my couch."

The way Lewis's face lit up right then, like Killian was his hero? Killian rubbed his chest, surprised at the warmth that look generated. It felt… potent. And *dangerous*. Like the opioids he'd taken sparingly when he'd fallen three years ago and broken his ankle. Like if he wasn't careful, he'd crave *more* looks like that. And *more*, and—he couldn't think about it.

It didn't do to need people like that.

"Thanks, Killian. That's kind." Lewis's voice had this sandpaper purr when he said "kind," and Killian had to fight that uncomfortable, needy sensation.

"I need to finish my closing shit," he said shortly, spinning away on his heel. "We'll leave when Suzanne's ready to go."

IN THE COLD AND DARK

LEWIS WATCHED as Killian stalked back and forth across the bar, stacking the stools up off the floor, giving everything a final sweep. He even took a cloth to the windowsills and then got some Windex for the insides of the window itself. Lewis was pretty sure that the place had a deep-cleaning service that came in the morning—most bars and restaurants did—but Killian Thornton moved with a sinuous grace and self-assurance that said he'd rather he see it done right than rely on somebody else to do it.

Mm... muscles.

Lewis tried not to drool at his brother's downstairs neighbor, but it was hard. Lewis had shown up on Todd's doorstep the week before, after Glenda Dupree had discovered he'd blown her husband in the backyard when Lewis had been visiting his parents over spring break. Granted, Lewis hadn't known Richie Dupree, his brother's old friend from high school, had been married, and it hadn't been their first blowjob among friends, but this time another neighbor—a friend of Lewis and Todd's mother—had spotted them and apparently brought it up over the neighborhood pre-Thanksgiving potluck after Glenda had bragged about her Kitchen-Sink Hash Browns.

Glenda's shrieks had apparently burst eardrums across the neighborhood, and Glenda's best friend's husband, who had always carried a bigger torch for Glenda anyway, had led the charge across the Bernards' lawn to scream things like "pedophile" and "child molester" in Lewis's mother's face.

Lewis loved his mother. Glenda's best friend's husband had needed to have his nose set and to use the steaks planned for the day before Thanksgiving on his two black eyes. For that matter, Lewis still had a crooked nose and a couple of shiners himself.

As Lewis retreated into the house, more to get away from the hysterical screaming than to get away from the fight itself, his mother had given him a sympathetic look.

"Lewis…," she'd said helplessly, and he'd read everything right there in her face. She loved him. She and his father had supported him through his coming out, through his turbulent adolescence, through his Fuck yeah I'm gay! T-shirt wardrobe. But the political climate in their part of the country had gotten too damned violent for him to stay there while he looked for a job.

"I swear, Mama," he said, taking a towel from her and putting it to his bleeding nose, "I didn't realize Richie had gotten married."

She sighed and went to get him some ice. When she returned, she held it tenderly to his nose as he sat on the couch and then ruffled his hair. "It was Richie's fault for not telling you," she said, kissing his temple. "But that doesn't mean this place is particularly healthy for you right now."

Property values had sunk so low in their state they couldn't afford to move.

"Think Todd's got a couch?" he asked.

No, in fact, Todd *didn't* have a couch, but he still opened up his tiny apartment to his little brother. Todd worked nights at a movie theater and mornings in a book store and was on call as a special ed tutor, so they often ended up sleeping on Todd's queen-sized bed, just at different times. Todd would be gone in the morning, and he'd come home to sleep while Lewis was out looking for jobs and an apartment of his own.

The chance to see his girlfriend—take her out to a dinner, have some uninterrupted time with her—had meant a lot to Todd, who had grown up string-bean thin, with the lion's share of acne in high school. His skin was mostly clear now, and he'd grown into his height, but mostly he'd developed that kind of confidence that people got when they survived a miserable adolescence and were perfectly happy with themselves and therefor made the people around them happy too.

Todd didn't have much, but he'd opened it up to Lewis with a hug and a peanut-butter-and-banana sandwich and a "Hey, little bro, missed you." He didn't even bat an eyelash when Lewis told him about Richie. "Heh heh—shoulda known. He always *was* sorta crushing on you. I was too dumb to spot the signs."

That was Todd—laid-back in the extreme. If he'd forgotten to text Lewis after his date, it was probably because he'd fallen asleep, because the multiple jobs thing was exhausting. Lewis *probably* should have led with that when he was talking to Killian but….

But Killian had black hair with brown streaks from the sun, stunning blue-gray eyes with thick lashes, abs, shoulders, arms and thighs (abs and thighs!) of the muscular variety, and a rather sardonic, tight-lipped regard for other human beings. This was Lewis's third night in the bar, and he'd seen Killian be gallant to all the patrons, polite to the drunken come-ons aimed his way, and kind to the people who seemed to be in the bar because they were genuinely distraught. On Lewis's first night— Todd had brought him in as a sort of welcome-to-the-neighborhood— he'd inquired solicitously about Lewis's black eyes, had given Todd a reserved if friendly "Hey," and then had comped them both a drink as a rather sweet "welcome" gesture—after he'd checked Lewis's ID of course.

Lewis and Todd had snagged a table and sat with their beers while Todd gave Lewis the lowdown of the city and what he might be able to do with his degree. And generally? It had been a better hello than Lewis figured he deserved.

And watching Killian, brooding, polite Killian, work the bar had been the highlight of his night.

He'd almost swooned when he'd run into the man in the hallway the next morning. The aloof, polite nod, the "Let me know if you need anything," although it was clear Killian expected Lewis to be fine on his own, but still…. There was a sort of innate courtliness to the man that Lewis responded to.

He'd always wanted to be courted.

Lewis had an entire block-and-a-half walk home to make Killian Thornton think about courting *him*.

He kept playing darts, thinking he had to bring out his best game, and then it occurred to him that this man lived damned near in Lavender Heights, with its rainbow crosswalks, out-and-proud clubs, and happy mass pub crawls. If Killian Thornton played for Lewis's team, odds were good he'd seen *real* game, and not just the boy most likely to deflower jocks in the dorm of his state college.

Ugh. Jocks. Most of them didn't respect the equipment, and too many of them thought playing for the other team gave them a pass for not knowing the rules.

Someone like Killian—all of that repressed chivalry, that kindness, that *having his own apartment and a job*. Yeah, Killian might actually be out of Lewis's league.

All too soon, Killian's boss was clicking out of her office, dressed in her warm wool coat, with a hat. She had Killian sign the deposit slip for the night's take, which she tucked inside the cash register for the day manager, and together the three of them walked into the misty autumn darkness, the smell of woodsmoke thick in the air.

Suzanne sighed. "I know it's bad for the air quality, but I still love the smell."

Killian let out a chuckle. "Yeah, but now only rich people can afford fireplaces in the city, so that cuts down on emissions."

Suzanne gave a short bark of laughter. "You guys be safe on the way home." She looked at Killian meaningfully. "You hear?"

Killian nodded, and Lewis realized that bartenders got tips and the man next to him was walking home with a wad of cash in his pocket.

"Does that ever worry you?" he asked as Suzanne drove away.

Killian shook his head. "Naw. I've been mugged twice, and both times I just handed over my wallet and kept going."

Lewis gaped at him, and Killian gave a faint snort of laughter, like Lewis was too precious for words, and gestured with his shoulder for them to continue down the street. The silence was pleasant, but at the same time, Lewis racked his brains so as to not waste this perfect opportunity.

"I feel like I have to correct an impression here," he said, as their footsteps rang hollowly against the concrete.

"Hold up," Killian said softly, holding out his arm to direct Lewis away from a patch of wet leaves. "Those get slippery."

Lewis refrained from jumping him right then and tried to stick to the subject.

"My brother's a great guy," he said. "I mean, I know he forgot me, but God—he's so sleep-deprived I'm surprised he remembers to get up most days."

"Three jobs is a rough gig," Killian said, surprising Lewis because he obviously knew something about Todd's life.

"He needs to find one that can pay the rent," Lewis agreed. "But, you know, he deserves a night off. I was…."

"Also being a good guy," Killian said. "I get it."

And that was that. They kept walking, their apartment house looming nearer while Lewis almost hurt himself trying to think of a better subject to talk about. C'mon, c'mon…. Lewis was just about to try "Are you getting a Christmas tree," because wasn't *that* exciting, but when he opened his mouth a squeak came out.

Lewis stopped, and Killian stared at him.

"No!" Lewis said hurriedly. "That's not what I—"

They heard the sound again.

"What the hell is that?" Killian asked, sounding rattled for the first time.

"That's—"

And this time it was unmistakable. Crystal clear into the night came a pathetic little "Mew."

"Baby kitty?" Lewis asked, staring at Killian.

Killian looked around frantically. "Oh no," he said.

"Yes! I heard it!"

"But no," Killian told him, a hint of panic in his voice. "No. There is no kitten—"

"Yes, there is!" Lewis said excitedly. He listened again, turning toward the parking lot they were crossing in front of, where the sound came from. There was a retaining wall between the lot and the converted business building next door, and Lewis ventured into the shadowed area, the part cut off from the streetlight that sat in front of the bar half a block away. Lewis pulled out his phone, hit the Flashlight button, and swept it along the mess of wet leaves until he saw it.

"Mew."

"Aw," he said. "Baby. C'mere."

The light revealed a midsized marmalade kitten, maybe twelve weeks old. As he reached for it, he heard another "Mew," although the orange kitten had only regarded him with peaceful eyes as he reached for it. With another sweep of his phone, he saw the electric green flash. Huddled behind the orange kitten was a *black* kitten, blending in so thoroughly with the leaf mold that if the kitty hadn't been caught looking at the light, Lewis might have missed him again.

"Aw, guys!" he murmured, tucking his phone back in his pocket and reaching down to grab them. "Look at them!" he turned to Killian and without asking thrust one into Killian's arms.

"Wait a minute," Killian said, staring at the little black kitten in surprise. "Kid—"

"I'm twenty-three."

"And I'm thirty-two, and I don't have anything in the apartment."

"Do you have meat?" Lewis asked. "They're totally weaned."

"I've got turkey burger and tuna," Killian began, "but I was going to—"

"Great!" Lewis said, taking his own kitten and tucking it under his denim jacket to keep it from the cold. He noticed that for all his seeming reluctance, Killian had done the same with his black kitten, his arms wrapped around the creature protectively.

"But what about a litter box?" Killian asked unhappily.

"You've got a sandpit behind your building. Don't worry. I can rig something up." Lewis had seen some flat cardboard boxes, the kind they used for four sixpacks of soda or beer, hanging around his brother's dumpster that morning. He had a plan.

Killian puffed out a violent breath. "Okay, but kid—"

"Lewis."

"Lewis, we can't keep them forever. You've *got* to find a place for them, okay?"

Lewis grinned at him. "Oh, of course. I mean, you're just letting me crash on your couch, right? It's not forever. I'll totally have some place for these guys to go before I leave."

Killian stared at him. "Wait...." His brows were knit and his unflappable aloofness had been somewhat damaged, but he seemed to be trying to hang on to it with both hands. The kitten in his arms meowed and curled up, burrowing into his shirt, and he swallowed.

"Okay?" Lewis said, nodding like this was a done deal.

"Sure," Killian muttered helplessly. "Yeah. You'll find a home for them—I mean, there's a shelter not too far away, right?"

"Absolutely," Lewis said, nodding some more. Oh God. Oh God. This was gonna happen!

Killian looked down at the little black kitten, who was rubbing his whiskers against Killian's finger. "Kitten," he said, casting Lewis a baleful look, "I don't know if either of us knows where this is going."

The kitten started to nurse on the end of his finger, making biscuits against Killian's chest.

Lewis grinned at them both.

Kittens from heaven! Who knew?

Strange Awakenings

Killian awoke with a warm motorboat sound in his ear and little pinprickles in his hair.

Oh God. Was that thing nursing again?

They'd arrived home, and Lewis had run out to find a makeshift sandbox while Killian set up an old bath mat in the corner of the bathroom, with a few towels in an old shoebox, figuring he'd give them a bed, a place to poop, and some food and they'd be fine until Lewis found them homes.

He broke open the turkey burger, browned it without seasoning like the internet said, and then, after putting most of it into a plasticware container, added an egg and scrambled it in with the rest of it. He figured that these kittens were skinny—some egg and turkey for the night might help them gain a little weight. If nothing else, they could buy some cat food or use the water-packed tuna he had in the cupboard until the kittens had a new home. The kittens had dug in like eating was a forgotten thing, and then Lewis had filled the kitchen sink with warm water and a little bit of people shampoo, and they'd given the creatures a flea bath. Finally, around three o'clock in the morning, Lewis and Killian had sunk exhaustedly onto Killian's extremely comfortable, extremely *durable* leather couch, each with a kitten wrapped in a towel, and let out a sigh.

"So," Killian muttered reluctantly, stupidly pleased by the black kitten's purring. "You'll find them homes tomorrow."

"Yeah," Lewis said, head moving like a bobble doll. His artfully shaggy hair was in stunning disarray, and he looked like he had fallen asleep an hour ago and his brain hadn't gotten the message yet. "No worries. Probably before you're awake. I promise."

Killian yawned. "Doesn't have to be too early," he murmured. "Here. Let me get you some sweats to wear to bed."

He'd set the kitten down on the couch then—he clearly remembered it. He came out with some extra blankets, a pillow, and a sheet, as well as some sweats and a T-shirt, because it was cold in the apartment, even with the cranky old heat register clicking away, and Lewis was wearing baggy jeans with lots of pockets and a dress shirt under his sweatshirt and denim jacket. None of it looked comfy, and sleeping on a stranger's couch sucked bad enough.

Lewis was standing by then, having taken his jacket and sweatshirt off, and he was in the process of unbuttoning his dress shirt. There was a T-shirt under that—Killian could see it clearly—but something about the moment, Lewis's hands on the buttons, the sudden quiet, maybe, made things unbearably intimate.

As though suddenly conscious of the moment, Lewis kept his head lowered but raised his eyes—enormous, almond-shaped brown eyes, rimmed with blond lashes and framed by artfully trimmed dark brown brows. The eyes, the bold nose, the lush mouth, all of it came together to create not only a stunning beauty, but also… *character*. Lewis was not just some random guy crashing on Killian's couch, those eyes seemed to say. He was *beautiful* and *sexy* and *special*.

Well, he must be special. Killian had never thought of having a cat in his home once in his entire life.

"Uhm," Killian rasped through a suddenly dry throat. "Uhm. Sweat. I mean sweats. Blankets. Uh, extra phone charger's there." He gestured with his chin to the computer desk in the corner. "There's milk and cereal in the fridge." He paused. "Lactose free," he admitted, feeling his cheeks stain.

"Awesome," Lewis said, nodding again. "That'll be more comfortable for *everybody*. Should I feed the cats in the morning if I wake up first?"

Killian swallowed, thinking about how domestic that sounded—thinking that Lewis was the first man (boy!) who had been in his apartment for more than pizza, beer, and a game in a long, long time.

"Yeah," he said. "There's leftover turkey in the fridge. I'd warm it about ten seconds to take the edge off."

"Awesome!" Lewis gave one of those guileless smiles, the kind that suggested they were just kids on a bus in high school, talking about a project or something. "I'm still running on Texas time, so, you know, I'll probably have the kittens out of your hair before you even wake up."

"That sounds painless," Killian mumbled, suddenly exhausted and wanting nothing more than his bed. "Let me know if you need anything—shower's yours if you want, extra toothbrushes are in the cupboard. See you in the morning."

And then he'd shaken off the moment and wandered to bed. As he'd crawled in, though, he'd flashed back to that... that shadow of intimacy, Lewis's head bent over his shirt, his bony fingers on the buttons, and Killian's sudden, powerful need to take over, to unbutton that shirt, to see what lay beneath. Smooth skin? Blond guys often had smooth chests, but sometimes one would surprise you with golden curly hair. Muscles? Killian liked the lean muscles that the boy's build suggested, although sometimes there would be a surprise tummy under the fly of the jeans, soft and a little squishy. Killian had seen the lean muscles in his shoulders and arms, the vulnerable pulse in Lewis's throat. Would he be rangy under those baggy jeans?

These were questions Killian would *desperately* love to get the answer to, but he knew better. Lewis was in town to find a job, find an apartment, to land. Killian had *landed*, and he'd grown roots, his toes curling into the Sacramento River mud like the willow trees along the banks.

Lewis was obviously still in flight. Killian had nothing to offer him but his small apartment and his contentment. With someone as bright, charming, and fun as Lewis Bernard, contentment wasn't enough.

As Killian closed his eyes resolutely against the wistfulness of his thoughts, he felt a slight depression on the bed. He opened his eyes to find two glowing green orbs regarding him indignantly from six inches away, seemingly floating independently against the matte black of his darkened room.

"Mew?"

Killian closed his eyes and opened them again, and the kitten was still there. This time the kitten reached out its little paw and batted unhappily at the covers Killian had pulled up to his chin.

"Mew!"

Oh hell. Killian yawned and lifted the covers just enough to let the kitten in. The last thing he remembered thinking as he closed his eyes in the dark was that he should have thought of having a cat much sooner, because that purr coming from its tiny throat really was all the contentment a man could need.

KILLIAN HAD awakened a little when Lewis had, remembered vaguely the pleasant sounds of another man in his bathroom and how he'd pretended that man was there for him before he'd closed his eyes again, the kitten sleeping in the crook of his neck at that point. He remembered the kitten getting lifted off the bed, mewling pitifully, probably as Lewis took it to go eat, and then, shortly after that, had felt *two* weights on the bed, and then the black kitten had curled up under his chin again, and the orange kitten had taken a turn making biscuits on his scalp.

"You're not gonna get what you want from that," he mumbled when the pinprickles and motorboat finally roused him from sleep enough to talk.

"Killian?"

Killian frowned at the shaggy blond kid with the brown eyes as he peered through the doorway into Killian's bedroom. "Timeizit?" he asked. "Whaddayouwant?"

The kid chuckled and ventured farther into the bedroom, glancing around appreciatively. "Nice," he said frankly. "Now scoot so I can sit and give you coffee and explain the sitch."

Killian scowled at him. "HowmIsposedtododat?" he growled, and the kid smiled and reached behind him to take the kitten out of his longish black hair.

"Not a morning person?" he asked kindly, and Killian managed to sit up, the other kitten sliding down his chest with claws extended.

"This isn't morning," he managed, proud of the actual words he was making. "This is night with the daystar present."

"Ah," Lewis said, stroking the orange kitten behind the ears. The kitten collapsed against the crook of his arm, and Lewis sighed softly. "This one's dumb," he said frankly. "I actually watched this cat run into the stove trying to get to his food."

"Why's that dumb?" Killian managed to catch a glimpse of his phone. Eight thirty? Was that all it was? Oh God.

"Because I put the cat food against the wall under the window. I have no idea what this guy thought he was going after, but food was not it."

Killian let out a huff of laughter. "Maybe he needed his coffee," he grumbled.

Lewis gave him a coy look from under black lashes. "Do *you* need your coffee?" he cajoled.

"Yes," Killian told him, not playing in the least. "I need my coffee. You woke me up at fuck-you in the morning, I need my coffee."

"Fair." Lewis handed him his cup, and Killian frowned at the kid again and realized he was wearing the sweats Killian had given him the night before, along with Killian's T-shirt under his sweatshirt-and-denim combo—and that he smelled cold and brisk.

"Where you been?" Killian asked.

Lewis let out a sigh. "Well, to get you cat food and a cat box and a cardboard carrier and some litter and stuff," he said. "There's a pet supply place about two blocks away."

"I know there is," Killian said, his eyes opened wide in alarm. "Why did you do that again?"

Lewis looked sheepish. "I'm sorry. The shelters are full—I called three of them, and the only ones open were the kill shelter and…." He sighed again. "I couldn't. I'm sorry, Killian. I'll get rid of them, I promise. I'll bring them to the bar—I can ask people there. I'll take them with me when I go job hunting."

Killian managed a chuckle. "What are you going to say? Hi, I'm a computer programmer. If you hire me I'll give you a kitten?"

Lewis laughed slightly. "Maybe not. But—"

Killian shrugged. "No worries. They're fine for now. We'll start hitting up friends, okay?" He lifted the kitten in his hand and pulled it up to his face, where it proceeded to bat his nose. "Maybe get it shots first," he said, remembering there were kitten diseases and stuff.

"Actually," Lewis said, some of his desperation dropping now that Killian had told him it was all okay, "I talked to the shelters about where to get that done, and they recommended a couple of clinics that will fix them and give them their shots for a reduced price, since they were rescues." He held out his phone. "I have locations and coupons if you like."

Killian took a hasty sip of coffee and stared at him. "You've got this all planned out, don't you?"

Lewis shrugged, and Killian would have believed he was all innocence, but he was starting to think innocence was one of the few things Lewis couldn't actually pull off.

"You do," Killian told him flatly, understanding dawning. "You've had this planned from the very beginning. You saw these kittens in the dark last night and thought, 'This, this is how I shall ruin Killian Thornton's life.'"

Lewis's grin was pure connivance. "Do you hear yourself say your name?" he asked, as though *this* explained everything. "You've got the name of a superhero. You can carry off the half ponytail. And you have your own apartment. I was simply doing the world a favor and hooking up kittens with a home."

The little black kitten started to attack his hand then, tiny sharp claws kicking madly against his wrist.

"Thanks," Killian said, keeping his inflection flat. "Thanks a lot."

And again that grin, but there was no sarcasm or connivance in it this time. Pure sunshine joy. "You're welcome," he said happily. He pulled the orange kitten up to his nose and got a gentle pat. "So cute, and so dumb."

Killian watched him rub noses with the purring furball and thought that could apply to more than one creature in this room—and *not* the one holding the orange cat.

Something told him Lewis had outthought Killian at every turn so far.

"I'll let you get dressed," Lewis said, taking the black kitten from him. He looked around again appreciatively. "This really is a great room. All the dark furniture and the pale bedspread. Even the picture frames are teakwood. Did you paint the walls yourself? Because Todd's apartment is all that crap white."

"I've lived here a while," Killian said with a shrug. "The landlord started letting me do a few upgrades."

"The tile in the kitchen and the bathroom?" Lewis asked, and Killian nodded. Like the walls, it wasn't the cheap stark white of most apartments, but more of a richer cream color with blue-and-green flecks.

"He takes some off the rent for every improvement. It's a system."

"You never wanted anything bigger?" Lewis asked, seemingly entranced by the intricate wrought iron pattern of leaves and birds that was stitched into his comforter.

"There was only me," Killian said, shrugging. "I guess if I need a bigger place, I'll move."

"Mm." Lewis nodded like he knew something Killian didn't.

"What?" God, there was not enough coffee in the world.

"Nothing." But the way his voice rose at the end told Killian it was something, but not something Lewis meant to share yet. "Go on. Get dressed. We've got things to do."

And then he left with the kittens, leaving Killian wondering what exactly had happened to his day, which he'd planned to spend decorating his apartment for Christmas, or his life, which he could have sworn he'd planned to be peaceful and solitary and quiet.

Two kittens and Lewis were definitely not quiet, but Killian couldn't figure out where he'd gone wrong.

LEWIS LIKED Killian's car. Killian had bought it used, but Subarus were well-made, and he took care of it, right down to getting it a new paint job in a sort of rusty red after he'd brought it home. Lewis was full of all sorts of questions, from warmed seats to horsepower, many of which Killian couldn't answer, if he could hear them at all over the mewling of the kittens, who were locked in their cardboard carrier in the back seat.

"Man, I don't know," he said after the hundredth *but what about this*? "You know what I do know?"

"What?" asked Lewis, big brown eyes alight with curiosity.

"When I get in the car with the keys in my pocket and push the little button, the car turns over. And you know what?"

Lewis smirked. "That's all you need to know."

"Right. On."

Killian let out a breath and piloted the car down J Street to Howe. While his apartment was in midtown, apparently the budget veterinarian was way down off of Folsom Blvd near Rancho Cordova. Dimly he registered that the tiny loud creatures that had taken over his life had perhaps gone to sleep in their nice warm cave, and he felt a little envious.

"Sorry," he said. "I've got sort of a headache. I don't know how you're so chipper, but I'm down a few hours of sleep."

Lewis yawned, because apparently underneath that gamine smile beat the heart of a sadistic bastard. "Yeah, I hear you. I'll probably nap around three o'clock if we're back at your place by then."

"I may have to do that too," Killian told him. "My shift starts at six. I can eat at work." He tried to avoid that because the food wasn't always healthy, but about once a week he caved. "Wait." Killian frowned. "Did you ever get hold of your brother?"

Lewis hitched up a shoulder. "Yeah, 'course. Told Todd where I was sleeping, that we were going to run some errands together." Even while driving, Killian could see the sort of affectionate smile Lewis gave for his rather clumsy, earnest brother. "Todd said he was glad I was making friends."

Aw. That was sweet. "You guys sound tight," he said, aware that his voice had a wistful quality he'd tried to squash for nearly the last ten years.

"You're not tight with your family?" Lewis asked, and Killian could feel the younger man's eyes searching his face.

"I, uh, got back from my second tour and came to visit a friend in Sacramento," he said. "I, uh, came out to my friend, which was great because, well, we'd been crushing on each other the whole time in Kabul. But he'd come out to *his* family, and the only problem he had was that suddenly everybody had a friend's cousin's bestie that they wanted to set him up with. So I came out to my family over the phone, hoping for the best."

Lewis's voice dropped softly. "Did you prepare for the worst?"

Killian's mouth twisted. "Well, I was already shacking up with Jaime, so sort of. Because in the end…." Everybody knew how this story ended.

"You couldn't go home."

"No, I could not," he confirmed and wondered if it was the same for anybody with that experience. If the "I couldn't go home" *always* masked the memory of a beloved parent's voice morphing, changing as though by a magic spell, into the hateful, shrill tones of an angry stranger, saying awful things because somebody who didn't *know* their child, hadn't *raised them* and *loved them* and promised to care for them, had told them this was bad.

It didn't seem to matter who heard the story. Even people who had come out into a land of sunshine and lollipops and rainbow-loving parents *knew* the story, because that story had been their biggest fear, had somehow lived with them since the first time they'd closed their eyes in the third grade and knew they wanted to marry Matt Dallas from *Kyle XY.*

Some people really did have a reason to fear.

Killian's luckiest break happened by accident because he'd come out from two-thousand miles away. His youngest sister, the only relative who still spoke to him, had called him up, terrified, the morning after his awful phone call with his mother and father, and told him not to come home. There had actually been a meeting at their church that night, and the universal opinion was that if Killian even showed his face in the state again, he'd be beaten and left on the road.

They'd been burning his possessions in the backyard as she'd called, in tears because she'd barely managed to save a picture of the two of them.

She'd since moved out of the house and to Chicago, and they still stayed in touch. The Christmas after he'd come out, Hildy had sent him a copy of the photo—a nice one, on photo paper—in a frame. She'd put on the card, "The original is mine, and I'm never giving it up."

He wouldn't change his sister for anything in the world, but he rather wished she'd found her freedom a little closer to his own new home.

"I'm sorry," Lewis said sincerely. "I… my parents were fine. Lots of 'Afterschool Very Special Gay Son' moments, which were embarrassing and cringey, but also… you know. They knew who I was and loved me and talked to me about other things *besides* being gay, and it wasn't a bad way to go."

"I'm glad," Killian replied. "I mean, it's nice when someone has a better story, you know?"

Lewis let out a little laugh. "In fact, I do," he said, and his tone of voice made Killian glance at him sideways.

Lewis had his *own* story there, he could tell, but at that moment his GPS gave another direction through the sound system, and for a moment Killian had to concentrate on a warren of buildings in an industrial complex.

The GPS finally said, "You have arrived," and Killian and Lewis exchanged dubious looks. The building was the same squat gray shoebox as the rest of the circa 1990 complex, but on the eaves, where usually a sign would be, was a banner that read Free Shot Clinic Saturdays, 7-10 a.m.

It was ten after ten, and with the exception of a few cars that probably belonged to employees, the parking lot was deserted.

"Well, they did say they were new," Lewis said uncertainly, and Killian shrugged. Only one way to find out.

"Go in and get in line or whatever," he said, opening the back-seat door to grab the cardboard box. The wind knifed through his old leather bomber jacket and he shivered, wondering why he always underestimated Sacramento winters. No, it wasn't Nebransas and definitely not Michesota, but forty degrees off the snowpack was forty degrees off the snowpack, and the leather jacket didn't always cut it.

Lewis had his hand on the front door of the office, and Killian was straightening out of the car with the cardboard carrier when they both heard the squealing of giant tires and a blown-out engine. A massive block of a truck came barreling off the main street into the parking lot, and as they watched, it loomed close enough to Killian's car for him to hoof it to the walkway under the eaves of the office building in alarm.

They both stared at the thing in disbelief, political flags, giant mufflers, and all, as it pulled a doughnut in the almost-empty lot. It was in full circle when the passenger door opened and a plastic box came tumbling out, landing far away from the truck as it roared back to the hellmouth from whence it came.

Killian glanced at the plastic box, remembered where they were, and got a *very* bad feeling about what was inside.

"Here," he said, thrusting his cardboard carrier into Lewis's arms, aware that the kittens had both awakened and were complaining vociferously about their change in venue. Prepared for the worst and wishing he'd gotten the goddamned license number of the truck, he jogged up to the pet carrier that had been dumped so rudely from the vehicle.

The indignant, angry "Mrowl!" from inside made him put his hand on his chest in relief.

He hoisted the battered thing up, thinking it probably didn't have much more mileage left on it since it had spent its life defending its precious cargo, and looked inside.

What he saw there made him rear back. "Mrowl!" the creature inside screamed, and while Killian couldn't blame the thing for being mad, he was more than surprised at the ginormous gray feline's apparent capacity for getting revenge.

"Is it a cat?" Lewis asked, drawing near.

"Mrowl!" it yelled again.

"Define cat," Killian said cautiously. He looked again. He'd never in his entire life seen a cat with a head that big—and a neck to match. The thing had battered ears, scars on his head, and… oh God. No eyes? Was it possible the poor thing was completely blind?

One more look as he held the carrier up confirmed the fur growing over sunken eye sockets, and the mountain lion (could not *possibly* be a cat—cats were *small*, and this thing must have weighed forty pounds!) let out a rather pathetic "Mrowl?"

Expecting to lose blood, Killian stuck his finger between the bars of the cat carrier and gently smoothed back a healthy placket of coarse, bold white whiskers.

The purr made the cat carrier vibrate hard enough to send a tingle up Killian's arm.

"Oh," Killian murmured as the mountain lion (still not a cat!) continued to rub his whiskers again and again on his finger. "He's sweet."

And as he made that observation, from the back of the carrier came a tiny, tentative "Mew?" and Lewis said, "I don't even believe this."

"So," THE vet tech told them as they stood at the counter, "you were late for the free shot clinic, so that's $200, but you're getting them fixed, and since that's $150 a kitten, we'll give you a discount. The whole thing comes to $400."

Killian made a little whistling sound in his throat, and Lewis murmured, "Killian, I'm so sorry."

"Fine," Killian muttered, trying not to think about his car payment and his rent and how he'd been thinking about taking a trip to Hawaii that February because he'd always wanted to go. "No worries."

With an effort he shook himself and addressed the perky technician. She had thick dark hair pulled back into a ponytail, olive skin, a pleasantly rounded body, and the whitest, biggest smile. All in all she seemed sweet, and she'd cooed all over the kittens as they'd delivered them, which somehow made him like her just because.

"What about the... uhm, drop-off cats?"

Her face fell, and she looked to the cat carrier unhappily. "Yeah. Boris and Natasha. That's sad. Their owner was the nicest woman— she used to walk Boris every morning. Can you believe that? She'd put him on a leash and take him around the neighborhood, and he'd sniff all the flowers like a dog. He's such a neat cat! But she passed away, and her son called us up this morning and asked us if we could take them in. We...." Her lower lip trembled. "He was so mean. And I was, like, 'We're not a shelter, but the shelters are awfully full. Can you keep them for a couple of weeks while we try to find a home for them and....'" That lip tremble again. "He told me to fuck off," she muttered. "And then, to just... just *dump them out* here?" Her eyes grew red-rimmed and shiny. "And the shelters really *are* full—I think somebody busted a kitten mill or something, and nobody's going to take them, and... and...."

"Oh no," Lewis said, sounding like he was in agony. "Killian, we...."

The look he sent, with big brown eyes and his own trembling lower lip, held two things.

One was a plea for mercy, and the other was this sort of faith, this bright and shining belief that Killian—*Killian* of all people—could fix anything.

Killian sighed. "Could you at least give us a discount on the shots?" he asked the vet tech.

Her face wreathed in smiles. "I'll put them under our free clinic hours," she said, dropping her voice confidentially. "It'll be fine." She worked her magic on the computer and said, "That'll be $300." Then she turned her own look of faith and pleading toward Killian. "So," she said, "how do you plan to find them a home?"

BORIS AND NATASHA

"So," Lewis said as Killian drove them back to the apartment, "what *are* your plans for finding them a home?"

"Fucked if I know," Killian muttered. "Could you look around the glove compartment? I think there's some aspirin in there."

Lewis did as he asked and sighed. "Nope," he said. "Tell you what. Pull up in front of the nearest grocery store and I'll go get you some, and some more cat food too."

Lewis had bought kitten kibble that morning, but the helpful vet tech had made it very clear that Boris and Natasha were middle-aged cats of four and six who needed wet food and adult kibble or bad things would happen to their digestive systems. Killian had asked rather sarcastically if they needed a leash too, and the tech had replied—completely without guile, "Oh no. If you look at the little compartment by the handle, that's where she keeps his harness and leash. It's fine."

And sure enough it was.

But that didn't stop Killian from looking... well, a little shell-shocked as they loaded the disintegrating plastic carrier with Boris and Natasha and the newly purchased cardboard carrier with the two cats Killian had started calling Moose and Squirrel into the back of the car.

"We don't need—"

"Please," Lewis said, feeling awful. "This was my fault in the first place."

Killian let out a snort and shook his head. "No, Lewis, it wasn't, because if it was your fault, you'd be the sort of asshole to pitch two housecats out of a moving vehicle, and then I'd absolutely have to beat your face into the ground. You're a nice kid who was trying to do a good thing. It's no big deal."

Lewis barely refrained from holding his hand to his heart and sighing, "My hero."

"It's a big deal to *me*" is what he did say. "Let me go pitch in on the expenses. I may not be able to do rent right now, but I can manage some ibuprofen and pet food. You stay in the car and hold down the fort."

"Yeah," Killian muttered, taking a turn into a shopping complex. "God forbid somebody break into my car and steal what we haven't been able to give away."

"Well, you want to be here anyway," Lewis said practically. "Moose and Squirrel are still loopy, and they may need reassurance."

"Loopy—is that another word for unconscious?" Killian asked sourly.

The veterinarian's office was apparently known for its quick turnaround—and Lewis got it. The people who caught strays and brought them in to be fixed and cared for and then released them back into the wild couldn't afford five-star treatment. Marly, their friendly neighborhood vet tech, had been happy to tell them that a lot of people would volunteer to clean cages and feed animals in exchange for medical services for the stray population. It was a nice idea, but it had still felt very mechanical when the kittens had been released into their care barely two hours after they'd gone back for their operation. Killian and Lewis had gone to get lunch during that time—and to find a local park so they could walk Boris and Natasha with the leads the vet tech had found for them in a compartment in the top of the cat carrier.

Natasha, a teeny calico who maybe weighed six pounds total, was apparently happy to curl up in a backpack, or in Lewis's case, the pocket of his hoodie. He liked the little animal—she was sweet and timid and docile and hard to *dis*like—but Moose and Squirrel had dug a gum wrapper out of Kilian's trash that morning and spent the half hour Lewis had used to freshen up and start coffee to bat the thing back and forth across the apartment. *Those* felines were *entertaining*, and Lewis had sustained hopes. Silly hopes, perhaps, but he had seen it all play out in his mind. Sure, he'd stay on Killian's couch for a little bit, but then… then maybe Killian would lose some of that quiet reserve that seemed so much a part of his character and kiss him.

Kiss him a *lot*.

And then maybe Lewis wouldn't have to sleep on the couch anymore.

And then he'd find his dream job, and he and Killian could keep living in that small, *interesting* apartment with their two cats and… and….

Live happily ever after?

God, Lewis knew better than that. He did. That's not how rational adult relationships worked, right?

But then, he acknowledged, they were silly hopes. He just didn't know how to kill them, and frankly, he didn't want to. Leaving his parents' house before Thanksgiving—although they'd begged him not to—because he'd managed to pull shame and scandal on the family name had been bad enough.

Oh, for sweet hell's sake, Lewis, I was the high school slut. If I didn't let these assholes drive me out of my hometown, I know you can take it!

His mother's voice telling that shocking lie rang in his ears.

You were not the high school slut, his father had replied mildly. *You were in the half of the class that didn't graduate pregnant. The fact that you weren't a virgin is my fault and immaterial.*

God, he loved them. He loved them so much, but he'd graduated in the spring and had such hopes for something—anything—different than to live and die in his parents' hometown.

Buying the cheapest possible flight to California had seemed like fate or something, just like Killian living in his brother's apartment house and being ready to walk him home.

And then the kittens… well, like little furry sorcerers, they'd managed to crystalize everything Lewis wanted in a future. One glimpse of Killian, half dozing on his own couch with a kitten in his arms, and Lewis had *known* what he wanted with his life.

That man. That man *there.* Being kind to the fuzzball and with wide eyes and perpetual bemusement, taking Lewis in to sleep on his couch because he could not seem to think of a way to leave him out in the cold.

Lewis wasn't stupid. In fact, he was sort of a genius with graphics cards and video software. Top of his class, had the only project in his advanced course to get an *A*. But all of the logic-based work he was so good at in his professional life had not rid him of a deep-seated belief in the whimsical power of fate.

For heaven's sake, he *played video games* for a living. The school system could disguise it with all the code and all the big words they wanted to, but at the end of the day, he'd prepared for his dream job by doing what he was good at and not choosing any classes after eleven o'clock.

If that didn't suggest that somebody was looking out for him, he had no idea what would.

Finding those kittens had been kismet—he was sure of it. The kittens would make Killian see Lewis as a good person, and then he'd fall in love, and it would all be cake!

Until Boris and Natasha, that is.

Because that happy cascade he'd seen with two adorable kittens seemed to have taken on a life of its own with Boris and Natasha. If Killian looked at Lewis and saw the feckless kid who had saddled him with four food-guzzling, time-sucking crap machines, the romance of the century Lewis had been envisioning had just died a tragic, cat-litter-scented death.

Which was why Lewis was currently buying the jumbo-sized ibuprofen, a *real* plastic cat carrier that was *not* hanging on by one lone bolt, the good cat food because Boris had… uhm… fertilized one of the plants at the park, and it did *not* smell healthy and… oh. That reminded him he was forgetting something. Something about plants and parks and—wait.

They needed the good adult cat food for Boris and Natasha. That was it.

And a pooper scooper because he'd forgotten one of those when he'd gotten the litter box earlier.

And a giant box of iced sugar cookies and Christmas-colored M&M's because Killian seemed to gravitate toward health food, and Lewis *really* needed sugar right now. And the sweet fake cream because Killian didn't even have any in his refrigerator, although he did have a Keurig and a ton of coffee pods.

And one of those fishy-on-a-stick cat toys for Moose and Squirrel, for fun.

And since he was at a drug store and they had *everything*, a package of T-shirts and one of underwear, because he'd had to catch that plane so fast he'd had to hide in absolute bare-bones economy. Everything he owned was in his backpack up in Todd's place, including his laptop and a spare pair of jeans. He was lucky Killian was tall and lean; the sweats were a little long at the ankles, but they fit fine at the hips.

And shit, a pair of cheap sweats as well.

By the time he hit the register, he had an armload of stuff, not including what he'd stuffed into the cat carrier because he hadn't thought he'd need a basket, and he sort of plopped it all on the counter in a panic.

It occurred to him that he'd said he'd be back in ten minutes, and at least twenty minutes had gone by since he'd disappeared into the store.

He had to fight not to do the pee-pee dance as the clerk was ringing shit up, wondering if Killian was spending the time stewing in the car, thinking of horrible things to say to Lewis when he got back.

It was how Lewis's last boyfriend worked, the guy who had broken up with Lewis before spring break, leaving him so vulnerable to Richie's dubious wiles. Kevin had been handsome, desirable, and popular, and God forbid you inconvenience *him* with a whim of kittens or M&M's and clean underwear.

Lewis could actually feel sweat slipping under his arms as he hauled his *three* bags and one cat carrier filled with cat food bags and cat toys out of the Rite Aid and into the parking lot. The apologies were pattering off his tongue like BBs off a tin roof when he arrived at the car and saw...

Killian, leaning back against the headrest, eyes closed, with Moose, the black kitten, folded up in his arms.

He was asleep.

Lewis's pee-pee dance receded, and he let out a sigh. He opened one of the doors to the back seat and set his purchases down on the floor since the seats were already taken. He checked on Boris and Natasha, who were curled around each other in their mauled carrier, and then on Squirrel, who was lying pitifully on his side, looking tremendously out of it.

Moose must have woken up, Lewis thought, and as he slid into the passenger's seat up front with Killian, he held out his hands to take the little guy, who didn't seem to want to leave Killian's arms.

Well, to be fair, if Lewis ever got to that same spot, he wouldn't want to leave either.

"C'mon, buddy," Lewis crooned, adjusting himself, the kitten, and the seat belt before nudging Killian on the arm.

"Killian? You okay?"

Killian's eyes fluttered open, and then he sat up with a start. "Moose?" he asked, panicked, and Lewis gave him a reassuring pat, trying hard not to go back and grope the muscle he'd just patted.

"Kitten's fine," he said, indicating Moose in his arms. "Back is filled with random crap. When you're good, we can go back to the apartment and get some lunch, and you can catch a nap."

Killian grunted and cast a glance behind him. "Good God. Did you buy out the store?"

Lewis lifted one shoulder. "I needed some stuff that I forgot from home."

"Like what?" Killian asked.

"Underwear," Lewis said with a sigh.

Killian frowned. "But…. Lewis, didn't you say your parents were great? Fine with you being gay? Wonderful people?"

"They are!" Lewis said, quick to defend them. "Mine and Todd's parents are sort of the greatest!"

"Then how did you end up in California a month before Christmas with no underwear?"

Lewis barely refrained from groaning. "I don't want to tell that story," he said decisively. "What do you have at your place for lunch?"

"Tuna sandwiches," Killian said. "But we just ate at the park."

"That is so weird," Lewis muttered to himself. "I usually forget to eat, and now that I'm here, I forgot I *ate*. Anyway—fair. Let's go home, erm, to your apartment, set up all the cats, and then you can go catch some sleep before your shift. How's that?"

Killian let out a yawn that seemed to inhale the entire Subaru before he was done making the yawning noise.

"How is this my life?" he asked, and Lewis gave a sigh, thinking about the entire neighborhood on his parents' lawn, screaming for his weenie ass on a pike.

"It's because you live downstairs from my brother," Lewis said. "That's the only possible explanation."

Killian let out a short bark of a laugh and then turned his radio, which was tuned in to Killian's alt-rock Spotify lists, up a little louder to get them home.

As many times as Lewis tried to say it for the sake of truth and reality, he was *not* convincing himself it was simply Killian's apartment anymore.

KILLIAN WAS not content to just let Lewis do his thing. He set out two saucers, one for Moose and Squirrel and one for Boris and Natasha, and pulled out a laminated place mat from Seattle to put under them. One of Lewis's *many* purchases had been a water dispenser for pets, and he set that up next to the food on *another* place mat. Then he'd taken Boris and Natasha's old pet carrier apart and set up the bottom half in a corner of the living room, filled with the same blanket they'd been wrapped in when the thing had been pitched out of the truck.

Killian had then hooked Boris up to the leash and walked him to the water and food and then back, and then to the sandbox in the bathroom and back. Lewis watched him in wonder.

"Do you think that will work?" he asked, awestruck. He never would have thought of that.

"I can hope—" Killian started to say. At that moment Boris, who'd been off leash and in the carrier, got out and started ambling vaguely toward the kitchen. Natasha—tiny though she was—got out of the carrier and started to bump him, a little at a time, guiding him to the food and water dishes.

Lewis and Killian watched, both of them with mouths open, completely impressed.

"Wow," Killian said on another yawn. "I swear, if she can do that to the litter box, we may survive this yet."

"I'll let you know," Lewis told him, *willing* him to go nap so Lewis's burden of guilt could lessen. "I swear, I'll take video on my phone."

For some reason that made Killian chuckle as he wandered to his bedroom. "Need my number first, kid," he called and then shut the bedroom door—but not enough to keep out Moose, who immediately started looking for his human.

HALF AN hour into Killian's nap, Lewis heard, of all things, Todd come home, blundering into the front door of the apartment building like the pile of exhaustion he probably was.

Lewis hurried to the front door of the apartment, waiting until the front door of the *building* had closed before he opened it and caught Todd trudging up the stairs.

"Todd? Oh shit."

At that moment, Squirrel chose his time to make a break for it, and Lewis had to stretch, keeping one foot in the doorway because he didn't have a key, to grab the little miscreant before he got completely away.

By the time he'd hauled the kitten back into his arms—and double-checked to make sure Boris and Natasha were still cuddling and Moose was still adoring a sleeping Killian, Todd had perked up and ambled back down the stairs.

"How you doin'?" he asked. Then, "And oh my God! Who's this?"

"Squirrel," Lewis said, grinning. "Killian and I found him and his brother when we were walking home last night." Squirrel, for all his rambunctiousness, was still a little sleepy, and he flopped to his back in the crook of Lewis's arm and stared into space as Lewis talked. "We...." He sighed. "Well, we sort of spent a lot of Killian's money this morning. The shelters were full, so we took them in to get them shots and fixed and stuff, and we had to buy food, and while we were there—" He felt a tremendous bump on the back of his calf, big enough to almost, *almost*, send him sprawling into the hall.

He twisted his body to see Boris thumping determinedly at him, probably thinking Lewis was blocking the way to the food, and that put him off balance enough for the door to swing shut, leaving Boris in the foyer with Lewis and Todd—and Squirrel.

The cat turned around abruptly, realized he couldn't get back to his buddy, and started singing the song of his people.

Todd and Lewis met horrified glances, and Lewis did an emergency handoff. "Hold Squirrel," he commanded before bending down to heft— *oolf!*—the screaming ex-tomcat into his arms.

"Boris. Buddy," Lewis soothed. "Man, hush. It's not that bad, I swear." He tried the door handle to be met with solid resistance.

"Dude," Todd muttered in commiseration. "Told you. Automatic lock."

"*Fuck*!" Lewis spat, absolutely mortified.

"No big deal," Todd said. "Killian's a good guy. He'll let you in." Completely without a clue, Todd started knocking on the door. "Killian! Dude, c'mon man! Your cat's out in the foyer waking the neighborhood."

"Meowl! Meowl! Meowl!"

"Todd, man, please, isn't there some other way we could do this?"

"Meowl! Meowl! Meowl!"

"But dude, he's a sweet guy. I swear!"

"Meowl! Meowl! Meowl!"

There was a sudden clatter from inside the apartment, followed by a "Goddammit! Natasha, I'm sorry, baby—no—no, don't go climb the—"

There was a louder clatter, followed by a thump, and Lewis winced, and then Killian howled in the way only a sleepy man who had stubbed his toe on the coffee table could howl, and then, "Oh—oh no—not the bookshelf—"

And another thump. The door shuddered as though under the weight of a whole human being and then opened inward.

Killian stood there, scratches down the side of his face, blood dripping from his little toe, and chaos behind him.

"I'm so sorry," Lewis mumbled, taking Squirrel from Todd and hefting Boris more securely as Killian hopped back and gestured him inside.

"I'll stop by later, little dude," Todd said as Killian shut the door in his face and then hobbled back into his bedroom, leaving Lewis to clean up the mess.

Neglecting a Civic Duty

"KILLIAN!" SUZANNE laughed, pulling pints of house draft. "Buddy, look alive there. You're getting behind!"

Killian shook himself and tried to keep up. It was hard. The scratches on his face from when he'd sat up in bed and Moose had slid down from his hair were still stinging in spite of the shower and the numbing antiseptic Lewis had made him sit for before he'd left for work. His little toe ached. Lewis had taped it to its nearest buddy, which probably helped, but it was going to hurt like a motherfucker before the night was out, and Killian already felt like he was hobbling.

And he was *exhausted.*

And he suddenly had four cats, and he was broke.

But Suzanne was right; Saturday was a big day for tips, and if he was going to keep those furry nuisances in kibble, he was going to have to step it up.

He'd left his spare key with Lewis, so he wasn't sure if the kid was still going to be on his couch when he got home, and part of him, remembering the clusterfuck of that afternoon, was thinking maybe that would be a good thing.

But most of him, the part, say, that remembered Lewis's look of absolute desolation when Killian opened the door to let him in? Or the part that'd awakened from what was left of his nap to a clean house and Lewis presenting him with a tuna melt so he could eat before work? Or that one part—the secret part that had caught the scent of Lewis's body, smelling like Killian's body wash as he'd leaned close, those amazing brown eyes melty and limpid and... and *open* to whatever Killian wanted—*that* part of him would be *really* disappointed to find Lewis had gone back up to Todd's tiny apartment to leave Killian up to his eyeballs in cats.

But somehow Killian trusted Lewis more than that. The kid had made some mistakes. He'd accidentally let the cat out, but that was bound to happen. Hadn't been his fault he'd been locked out of the apartment—no worries. And for all his apologies about Boris and Natasha, that had been *Killian's* doing, and Killian needed to own that. He'd been so… so *saddened* by the thought of these two friends just… *thrown away* like a crappy cat carrier. They were so devoted to each other. Natasha, for all her skittishness, was amazingly sweet. And Boris, for all he looked like a cat version of a no-neck bouncer, was, in fact, really *smart*. Those animals had been *loved*, and it was such a shameful way to pay them back for the companionship they could offer.

Killian wondered how long he'd lain awake planning the demise of the awful people in the stupid giant truck. He hadn't even seen their faces, but he hated them with the burning antipathy that angels reserved for the damned.

So it had been *his* idea to take home Boris and Natasha, and he couldn't possibly get mad at Lewis for that.

And let's face it, the kid had tried to do his share. From shopping to cleaning to doctoring Killian's ridiculous hurts, Lewis had been right on it with all the skill he possessed. Killian could well believe he was ready to move out and have a great career and land. Lewis had shown presence of mind in almost every circumstance.

Killian wondered how he'd gotten kicked out of Texas.

Lewis was adamant that it wasn't his parents' fault, but that left… what? How did a kid who rescued kittens and cleaned Killian's house and fixed tuna melts for dinner get kicked out of a whole state?

But then, Killian knew, it depended on the state. People had lost their minds in the last couple of years. What had seemed inconceivable when Marriage Equality had been passed had suddenly become a nightmarish reality for some people, and Killian wasn't deluded enough to think it couldn't happen to someone he knew.

It was just that Lewis was so… so… so *appealing*. A little bit manic, yes, but also practical and funny and very aware of absurdity.

And kind.

That's what had caught Killian's attention the night before. His kind insistence that they *could* save these kittens. They could do it *together*.

Suddenly Killian had believed they could. He'd believed he and this boy could do *anything*.

"Killian! Dude, what's happening?"

Killian was summoned from his working reverie to see a familiar face. "Joey!" he said, genuinely pleased to see the guy. "How're they hangin'?"

Joey had been one of Jaime's first friends in Sacramento. And, Killian had learned, one of his first lovers after he'd come out. When Killian and Jaime had broken up, Joey had jumped into the void, happy with his role as rebound lover, and while their thing hadn't lasted long— two weeks, tops—Killian had been grateful for the reminder that one failed love affair didn't equal a failed life.

Joey continued to haunt the Sacramento scene. Killian wasn't sure if there were many people he *hadn't* banged over the last ten years. But in spite of his haphazard sex life, Joey was actually a stand-up guy. He was the guy you could call out of the blue to help you move a refrigerator— and Killian should know because he had. Joey had shown up with a couple of guys from his housecleaning service, and they'd gotten the job done in no time.

He was the kind of guy you were always happy to see, and Killian reached across the bar for a handshake and a clasped fist to the chest in greeting.

"What can I get you?" Killian asked in the traditional bartender greeting.

"House draft. Two!" Joey pointed to a lion-like young blond. "One for me, one for Callum, my, uhm—"

"Date," Callum said dryly. "It's a date. We had a deal."

To Killian's utter shock, Joey blushed.

"Yeah. Sorry, Callum. I—you know. I told you. I don't do this often."

Callum rolled his green eyes. While not particularly remarkable in the looks department, just the fact that Callum wouldn't take any of Joey's shit already made him a gem.

"Well, we shall have to do it more often," Callum said dryly. He had an elfin face with enough baby fat around the chin to make Killian grimace.

"Uhm, ID?" he asked and was grateful Callum didn't take offense.

Instead he laughed softly and provided Killian with an ID that said that he was twenty-five, and Killian was forcibly reminded that Lewis was two years younger.

Oh Jesus—what was he doing?

"Dude," Joey said as Killian returned the ID. "What's on your mind? I mean, you were always the quiet, mysterious sort, but you just went positively dead-space."

Killian shook his head, not wanting to go into it. "You, uh, don't know anybody in the market for a cat, do you?"

"A cat? What sort of cat?"

Killian opened his mouth to say, "Any cat you want, that's what we've got," but then he closed it. He thought of giving away Moose *or* Squirrel, and couldn't, because he felt a sort of ownership for those two, and he *definitely* was not giving away Moose, and it seemed cruel to deprive him of his brother.

And Boris and Natasha, as entertaining and interesting as he and Lewis might have thought they were, did not have the sort of marketability of Moose and Squirrel.

Killian shook his head. "Never mind," he said. "The situation is still… uhm… fluctuating."

Joey snorted. "Yeah, as long as you're not Rivers. You remember Jackson?"

Killian frowned, remembering the rangy, rough-and-tumble young detective who used to troll the scene. "Haven't seen him around for a while. Where's he been?" He and Suzanne used to try to guess who Rivers was going to go home with on the nights he walked in. After a while they stopped laying down odds, because it didn't matter who either of them chose, he always went for someone they didn't expect. Was it going to be the free-spirited young thing with all the tattoos and the nose ring? Or the rugged fortysomething ex-cop with the scars? Or the thirtysomething businesshuman so buttoned down they looked etched in stone?

Nothing was locked in stone—not age, not appearance, not gender, not even *number*. Their joke was that if a wide-eyed alien had walked into Catches one night with a were-lemur, they *might* be able to predict that Rivers would go home with *them*.

Joey shook his head. "Would you believe he's engaged?"

"No!" Killian was floored. "To *what*?"

Joey's bemusement was palpable. "A stick-up-his-ass lawyer who drives a Lexus and…." Joey's voice dropped. "I'm not going to lie. Who takes care of him. Like, *cares* for him. Makes him take care of himself. Anyway, I clean for them now, and they've got two—count 'em—*two* three-legged cats. It's *amazing*. Those fuckin' animals are laying waste to this super nice house, and Rivers is, like, 'Oh my God, I'm so sorry,' and Cramer is like, 'But did the cat *hurt* itself as it did a triple gainer with a half twist off the mantle onto the coffee table and over the curtains?'"

Underneath the tiredness and the scratches and the dwindling savings account and the toe—oh my God the *toe*—Killian felt a chuckle well up. It started with his throbbing toe, worked its way past his wallet, picked up speed around his stomach, and burbled past the scratches on his neck. By the time it rolled out, it was a deep-throated, magnetic sound that punctuated the happy babble of the bar and upped the general merriment by about a thousand percent.

In that moment everybody was buying drinks again, and while Killian lost track of Joey and Callum, he was suddenly there, in the moment, smiling and efficient and on point with that casual friendliness that made people leave money in the tip jar and kept customers happy.

By the end of the night, his toe still hurt, he'd opened his scratches again, and he was *blind* tired—but the funny thing was, he didn't even care.

He hobbled home in that lovely, lonely dark of midtown, one of a surprising number of pedestrians who were doing the same thing now that the bar scene had faded, feeling the late November crispness of the air fill him with that sort of ebullient holiday peace.

He let himself into the apartment building and then the apartment carefully, very aware that one wrong move could send an animal unprepared for the outside world tumbling into chaos.

When he got inside, he found Lewis asleep on the couch in the center of a strange druidic ceremony.

Or at least that's what it looked like. All of the cats were gathered around him, Moose and Squirrel on the back of the couch, Natasha at the head, and Boris on the ground, faces turned toward him as he slept.

The effect was… well, fucking unnerving is what it was. It didn't get any less unnerving when to a one, even Boris, they all turned their faces toward Killian as he shut the door and then scattered, Boris bumping into the coffee table and the couch until Natasha got behind him and guided him to their sleeping box.

When Killian turned around, Moose was on Lewis's chest, and Squirrel was tucked up behind his neck, both of them curled up like they'd been there all along.

Killian let out a startled "Huh," before putting the takeout he'd brought home in the refrigerator, hanging his jacket up on the peg by the door, and putting his keys in the handmade wooden bowl his sister Hildy had sent him two years ago for his birthday.

Then he went back to the fridge. He had a series of stoneware magnets up there—antique-copper looking with magnets that could probably hold something up on the coils on the other side of the fridge—and there, on a piece of paper from his junk drawer, was a note with precise block printing:

Walk Boris To Poop Or Wake Me To Do It

Scanning the apartment again, Killian caught sight of the cleaner and a rag in the corner by the door, and his eyebrows went up.

Ah-ha. Lewis had told him about Boris's need to get out of the apartment, and Killian thought that perhaps he didn't need Natasha to guide him to the cat box if somebody could take him outside.

Another scan around the apartment and Killian could see Lewis's laptop on the small kitchen table, open to—oh yeah—job listings, and the apartment was cleaner and more dust free than it had been since Killian moved in.

Poor kid. He really was trying hard not to be a freeloader, and also apparently trying hard not to ruin Killian's life.

Killian sighed and snagged his jacket from the peg again, then his keys from the bowl, and then the lead from the compartment on top of the detached carrier.

Boris knew what Killian's hands were doing, and he arched his back to give better access to the loop on his harness. As Killian straightened, he gave the lead a little tug, and Boris strode out, confident as a boss, letting Killian's gentle pulls on the lead guide him.

BORIS APPARENTLY didn't just want to relieve himself—he wanted to wander the neighborhood, pick his way across the small complex's parking lot, and sniff around the retaining wall behind the restaurants on the corner of the block before doing his business. Killian grimaced as he did it, realizing he was being a *very* bad neighbor and promising himself he'd come back the next day and clean up really well to make up for this moment right here.

As he tugged Boris back toward the stairs, he heard muffled voices raised and glanced around the neighborhood, wondering if there was something to be concerned about. As he and Boris ambled up the stairs, he saw a woman across the street and a few buildings over wiping her eyes as she set a box outside her door. She glanced up and caught Killian's eyes, her astonishment showing as she realized it was just an average guy, walking his cat at oh-dark-thirty at night.

When he got back to the apartment, he walked Boris back to his box, and Natasha nuzzled her buddy carefully, exchanging sniffs to make sure some other blind cat hadn't gone for a walk and returned to a box sitting near Killian's heat register.

Killian sighed and did the key-and-jacket thing again, looking wistfully at his couch. He was exhausted but still a little wired from his shift and the second walk. Normally a night like this would warrant some stupid television before he fell asleep.

On the couch, Lewis rolled over and snuggled under the covers a little deeper, and Killian's eyes were drawn to him, his high cheekbones and bony jaw and fingers. It was funny how he seemed to project this air of flightiness when underneath the shaggy bangs and trouble-magnet demeanor, he was, in fact, built on strong lines. His jaw, the set of his mouth, his nose—these were not features without character. His body, while slender, held a rangy strength. More baseball player than football player, but still fit.

That voice that claimed Lewis was still in flight, searching for a place to land, quieted down enough for Killian to wonder at him again. He… he looked pretty solid. Pretty dependable. Could it be, Lewis *had* landed, and Killian just needed to give him some room to nest?

No, his brain said irritably. *You cannot and will not fall for a guy who cajoled his way onto your couch and keeps trying to ruin your life with kittens.*

Lewis's eyes, with their long brown lashes, fluttered open, and he gave Killian a muzzy smile. "'Sup?" he asked. "Izzit time for me to walk Boris?"

"I walked him," Killian said. "No worries." He yawned. "Honestly, I was hoping I could watch a little TV."

Lewis chuckled and gave his own yawn, pulling Squirrel tight to his chest. "Please," he murmured. "Don't mind me. I'll sleep."

His eyes fluttered closed again, and Killian took him at his word, keeping the volume low as he channel-surfed. He came across a comedy from twenty years ago, and Lewis said, surprisingly, "Love that one."

There were only forty-five minutes left. Perfect.

Killian pressed Play and leaned back in his chair, absurdly pleased when Lewis chuckled with him at the slapstick parts. Together they laughed their way through the silly movie, and Lewis yawned again. "Thanks. That was fun."

"It's Christmastime—they'll be playing all the Thin Man movies and the Katharine Hepburn/Cary Grant ones—"

"Oh, I love those," Lewis murmured. "Can we watch one tomorrow night? I'll wake up for that."

Killian found he was smiling, a sweet little glow building up around his chest. He didn't want to point out that Lewis should, by all accounts, move back up to his brother's pad sometime soon, or that after they got the cats settled, they wouldn't have anything else to talk about. He just… *really wanted* Lewis to be there the next morning, and then again the next evening when he got home from work. He didn't want to question it, he wanted it to *be*.

"What?" Lewis asked, starting to wake up a little in alarm.

"Nothing," Killian murmured. "It's a date. You and me, tomorrow night when I get home from work." His body was relaxed now, the long-assed day catching up to him. This time the yawn almost wiped him out, and he stood. Obeying an impulse he could have sworn he didn't have, he paused while crossing in front of the couch and smoothed Lewis's hair from his face, loving the feel of his skin, the satin coarseness of his hair.

Lewis was regarding him with wide eyes, and Killian bent down and placed a gentle kiss on his forehead before extricating Moose from behind his neck and cuddling *his* kitten to his chest. He turned off the lamp on his way to the bedroom and heard Lewis's satisfied voice calling, "Night, Killian. Pleasant dreams."

Killian smiled, happy in this moment as he could not remember being in some time.

"Night, Lewis. See you tomorrow."

He stripped down to his T-shirt and put on a pair of sweats before climbing into bed again, Moose cuddled against his chest. As he fell asleep so gently and seamlessly he couldn't feel the descent, he wondered how he'd ever, ever slept without a cat purring in his arms.

ONE LITTLE SLIP

LEWIS WAS grateful for the keys Killian had given him so trustingly the night before because it meant when Boris woke him up with a plaintive meow at around seven in the morning, he was ready for it. He was even more grateful for the shotgun style of the apartment. The living room fed into the kitchen, and the kitchen fed into a hallway. First door to the left was the bathroom, second door was the bedroom, and then the hallway led to a back door. Yes, you could literally fire a shotgun in the living room and—with a little magic and nonexistent cross breeze—the ordnance would sail out the back door unimpeded.

The good news here was that Lewis didn't have to brave the weird foyer/front door thing going on, where the front door opened into an echoing hallway with a stuck door that led outside. He'd used the front door the night before, and if Todd hadn't come home and seen him fiddling with it, he might have been parked on the front stoop when Killian got there, Boris purring on his lap.

He remembered to grab a bag and took Boris out for his morning amble, then put the waste neatly in a trash can and got back into the apartment in a whoosh of cold. Carefully, he peered into Killian's bedroom, smiling a little when he realized Killian was sleeping on his stomach, one hand flung over the side of the bed, with Moose curled up on top of the covers in the small of his back.

His dark hair had come out of its queue and was hanging in a messy curtain over his face, and as Lewis watched, he shivered a little, pulling his arm back under the comforter.

Lewis remembered that kiss on the forehead, the sweet little smile on Killian's face as he'd bent over to place it, and the smell of Killian's sweat and his exhaustion as he'd done it.

Killian Thornton was a fine-looking man—lean, with those dazzling blue-gray eyes surrounded by thick black lashes and the black rim around his iris. His cheekbones were high and almost delicate, and his jaw was strong in a narrow, appealing face. A man could get lost in the planes and angles of his face and the shadows they cast against each other.

All of that and Lewis wasn't snookered by the beauty, but he was leveled, taken out at the knees, destroyed, by the little smile, by the tenderness, by the playful hope of a good-night kiss on the forehead.

This was a man who, if he ever got naked with Lewis, ever held him and kissed him and brought him to climax, would *mean* it. The act would *mean* something with him, and Lewis knew that because a kiss on the forehead was such a deliberate, specific thing.

Lewis wouldn't be a throwaway boy or a one-and-done to Killian Thornton.

God, Lewis was ready for sex that was important. He was ready for a man who meant what he said and did, and who didn't play games or engage in cruelty or stupidity in any variation.

He would have flown across the country a long time ago if he'd known there was a Killian Thornton waiting on the other end of the flight.

Gently, he tucked the edge of the comforter under Killian's chin, then moved down the bed and covered his naked foot, careful of the taped and purple pinky toe. For some reason, the foot was… vulnerable like that, not to mention chilly. Lewis had noticed that Killian had set the thermostat timer to go off from five in the afternoon to eight in the morning. He'd given Lewis carte blanche to fiddle with it—and Lewis had—but the thought of Killian, alone in this place, trying to keep all his bare things safe and warm, made his heart hurt a little.

Yes, Killian seemed amazingly competent and self-contained, but *everybody* needed somebody to tuck them in, right? Even Lewis's perpetually exhausted, slightly goofy brother had made sure Lewis had been warm before leaving him to sleep in the recliner.

Killian gave a happy little grunt when his foot was covered, curling up into a tight ball on his side. Moose rolled with it, sliding into the hollow of Killian's body with only a little repositioning, and Killian *hmm*ed, moving his hands to protect the black kitten.

That relationship, at least, was true love, Lewis thought wryly. He'd never see a man take to a kitten so quickly.

Except for him and Squirrel, of course. If Lewis's parents called him up and told him he had to come home immediately, Lewis would leave all his clothes and take Squirrel, no questions asked. He and

Squirrel were ride or die—or in Squirrel's case, mostly die, because that kitten had come so close to destroying something irretrievable in this tidy little apartment that Lewis wondered if he already knew the Grim Reaper and was hoping for a reunion.

Carefully, Lewis tiptoed out of the room, figuring Killian had another four hours before he had to wake up and do something. In the meantime, Lewis was going to clean the cat box because dayum, that piled up fast, then feed everybody and start using his laptop to find a job.

It wasn't that he wanted to move out of Killian's, per se—he *liked* Killian's and thought that there might be room for him here on a permanent basis once Killian got past the kiss on the forehead stage and decided that Lewis needed a forever home.

But he *would* like to carry his own weight, and the only way to do that was to get a job. He'd done all the basic résumé things with the internet, sending his résumé off, shotgun style, to anybody who said they wanted a graphics engineer. He expected he was going to get a ton of hits—but mostly for crappy jobs. Well, not that he was a snob or anything, but he was *very*, *very* qualified in his field. He wasn't really a "start-up for coffee money" kind of engineer.

Fortunately there were a couple of big firms that had sent out nibbles, although he would need his own car to deal with those interviews—not to mention a suit, or at least slacks and a tie and a haircut—and he'd managed to politely say no to the least desirable jobs, but he hadn't spotted a true-romance situation yet. He knew from countless professors that the quickest way to foul up the work-well was to flit from job to job to job like a poisoned butterfly.

He needed to do more research before he made a decision, and quiet time with some coffee and oatmeal—Killian apparently lived on the stuff—so he could try to sort his work sitch out thoughtfully and responsibly.

He didn't get as much time as he'd hoped for.

HE'D ACTUALLY gotten a hit on his résumé profile that looked promising. It was for a talent co-op only a short bus ride away from Killian's building. Lewis, who had always liked the new and the shiny when it came to jobs, would get a chance to work short-term jobs as needed—a consultant or a highly paid, highly skilled temp. The description said specifically that if an employer asked to keep someone on permanently they could be released with no penalties, but in the meantime, if they were willing to put their skills toward the co-op—website upkeep, assistance to members, advertising, or whatever their specialty let them do—they were eligible for health and dental, and the company took a small cut of their checks until they found a permanent position.

It sounded *perfect* to Lewis—the perfect way to wet his toes in the work world, to start saving for an apartment of his own (as much as he hoped for, say, moving into this one after he moved into Killian's bed and very completely into his life), and to get a feel for what the job opportunities in the area really *were*. If nothing else it would connect him to an information pipeline or two, because that was *always* useful when trying to find a permanent position.

They already had his résumé, but they really wanted a face-to-face with him to see if he'd fit into their office space.

Lewis needed his good clothes.

He'd packed one outfit that *might* have been good for an interview, and it was currently up in Todd's pad and needed to be ironed. He sent Todd a text asking for his backpack and then scheduled his interview in three days. When he looked at the time, he hesitated. He... he was going to need a ride. He'd have to ask Killian for a ride to the office building, and God, hadn't Killian done enough for him already?

He checked out the address and thought that it looked like a complex. Maybe they could knock on some doors and... and what? Ask people if they wanted a blind cat and his seeing-eye girlfriend? Or maybe a twelve-or-so-week-old kitten that liked to bat around pieces of paper at five in the morning and was currently on Lewis's lap, making painful biscuits on his thigh.

Lewis rubbed a finger between Squirrel's ears and listened as the kitten upped the purring quotient by ten. He realized that he was pretty sure someone would have to pry this cat out of his cold dead hands in order to take possession of it, but in the meantime, he had no job, no car, and only a hope that someday Killian Thornton *might* want to kiss him.

He was in no position to own a cat, but that didn't stop the cat from owning him, did it.

With a quiet groan, he thunked his head into his palm, and that's when he experienced his first California earthquake.

"Killian, you disgusting motherfucker, get out here and clean up after your goddamned dog!"

Lewis was up out of the kitchen chair and trotting down the hallway toward the back door before his brain actually registered that it *wasn't* an earthquake. It was just that a giant or a troll or a leviathan or something was pounding on the back door.

A little part of him was thinking that *Jesus*, Killian wasn't going to get a decent day's sleep until Christmas, and most of him was trying to pull his D'n'D brain into the here and now because there was no way the angry voice on the other end of the hallway could belong to a giant or a troll or a—

"Whoa my God!" Lewis gasped as he yanked open the door.

"Who the fuck are you?" demanded the giant fucking troll on the other side.

"What are you doing banging on Killian's door like that?" Lewis blustered, not really wanting to answer the question. "Holy crap, do you hear yourself? It's early for *me*, and I'm on Texas time—he got in at fuck-you in the morning—"

"Oh, I know he did!" snarled the giant no-necked leviathan with biceps the size of Lewis's *head*. "I've got the tape to prove it!"

"What the hell do you think he did?" Lewis snapped, losing control of his voice. Vaguely, behind him, he heard Killian sounding muzzy and disoriented.

"Nicky, izzat you?"

"Yeah, Killian, you're goddamned right it's me! What the fucking hell, man! I thought we were friends."

"Friends don't try to shake down your apartment building at fuck-you in the morning!" Lewis said, wishing he had a stool to stand on. Dear God, the guy was *huge*. Six foot five if he was an inch, and no neck to speak of, with upper-body muscles so distortedly large Lewis wondered if he could wipe his own ass.

"And friends don't let their dogs crap behind their friend's restaurants!" Giant Leviathan Troll Nicky retorted, and for the first time a bit of humanity—of hurt—surfaced in the man's voice. "Jesus, Killian, why? I mean, I've been to your house. You live like a human being. Why would you just let your dog crap behind my patio like that! We had to fucking power-hose it before coffee drinkers got there!"

"He did not!" Lewis replied hotly, not even sure where this guy was coming from. "Killian is a good and decent human being. We both know he wouldn't do anything that—"

"Oh God," Killian said, and as Lewis turned toward him, he was covering his face with both hands. He was standing hip-cocked, and Lewis looked down to see him favoring his swollen foot. "Nicky, I'm so sorry. I totally forgot. I was so trashed when I got home last night. I planned to get that this morning. I'm *so* sorry."

Nicky grimaced, apparently taking in Killian's exhaustion and his injury and then glaring at Lewis as he snapped, "See?" in his face.

"Well then," Lewis said, not breaking his stride in the least, "*I* will buy him a poop bag!"

Killian chuckled weakly. "Seriously, Nicky, I didn't mean to do that. I—" A giant yawn racked him. "It's been a weird couple of days. I promise I won't let that happen again."

Nicky took a mean-spirited breath and then deflated, obviously unable to maintain his temper for long.

"Dude," he said, apparently helpless to deal with instant contrition. "What the hell? I mean… when did you even *get* a dog?"

Killian grunted and stepped back, gesturing Nicky into the apartment. "Would you believe it's a fucking cat? Seriously, Nick— weirdest fucking thing."

Killian limped down the hallway, and Lewis realized he'd been so out of it on the couch that he hadn't seen the limp from the night before. God. Poor Killian. Taking the cat out after a shift at work, too tired to think and too wired to sleep. Lewis really *was* ruining his life.

Nicky followed right behind Killian, and Lewis trailed them after closing the door, fighting a twinge of jealousy. Giant muscles and blond mullets had never been Lewis's thing, but they were *some* guys' thing, or all of that gym porn wouldn't do so well. This guy was a neighbor, obviously, but he'd been to Killian's apartment. He knew the place, and Killian obviously knew *him* well enough to invite Nicky right in.

"Oh wow," Nicky said as they came through the kitchen with the food and water setup and into the living room, where the cats were gathered. Squirrel and Moose were batting around a crumpled piece of paper, and Natasha was sitting on Boris's head, grooming his ears. "Dude, when did this—"

Killian gave an exhausted flop onto the couch, pulling the pillow Lewis had used the night before onto his lap. "Man, it's been wild. Lewis and I found the two young ones not far from your place when I was walking home and...." He yawned. "Boris and Natasha...." He yawned again, and Lewis took pity on him.

"We were driving up to the place to get the kittens their shots when someone threw a pet carrier out of their truck." He let out a dispirited sigh. "Some subhuman dickface, I should say."

"Oh *man*!" Nicky said, staring at Boris. "So, dude, you were... is that cat blind?"

"No eyes," Killian mumbled. "Sweet guy. No eyeballs. Natasha helps him find food, but—"

"But we have to take him walking because he can't find the cat box." Lewis gestured to the door where the lead hung. "He's a great cat. Loves being walked. The people at the free shot clinic knew both cats. I guess their person was elderly and passed away, but, you know...."

Nicky moved to the wall where the cat carrier sat and squatted to his heels, rubbing his finger along Boris's whiskers. The cat turned his face toward this new, friendly human and purred, and then Natasha did the same.

"God, they're sweet," Nicky murmured. "I mean...." Lewis heard the moment the thought hit him. "Who's gonna take care of them? I mean, the kittens everybody wants, but what about these guys?"

Killian let out a sigh. "I guess us, but I hope Kessler doesn't find out."

"Gah! Kessler's an asshole," Nicky muttered, and Lewis had gathered from his brother that Kessler was the landlord and all the tenants sort of hated him. "I mean, two cats, yeah, but four?"

"I don't know what—*oolf*—to do," Killian confessed as Moose leaped into his lap and headbutted him, asking for immediate affection.

Nicky looked over his shoulder and grinned. "Yeah, I can see that. Lookit your guy—he's in love."

Lewis startled, hoping neither of them had noticed the helpless way *he'd* been staring at Killian as he'd started chucking Moose under the chin and rubbing noses with the little doofus.

"And he's sort of bonded with Squirrel," Killian admitted. "But...." He looked over at Boris unhappily. "I can't cut them loose unless it's to someone who's gonna love them, you know? I mean... *look* at them."

Nicky nodded. "You know—look, wait. Hold on a sec. I gotta call my girlfriend."

"Nicky," Killian said, scowling. "I know your place doesn't take pets."

"Sadly no," Nicky said, rubbing Boris's whiskers some more. "But this is even better. Here, let me call Lia. I've got an idea."

With that he stepped into the kitchen, pulling his cell phone from his back pocket and putting the lie to Lewis's uncharitable suspicion that he had too many muscles to wipe his own ass.

"Lord," Killian mumbled, hiding his face in Moose's fur. "I'm so embarrassed. I can't believe I forgot to clean up last night."

"You were in *pain*!" Lewis protested. "Man, do you really have to work tonight?"

Killian let out a sigh. "I'm not taking a shift off because of a broken toe. It's Christmas season. I've got to make fudge for my friends, and apparently I have mouths to feed."

Moose mewled pitifully in his face, and he kept petting the kitten.

"Yes, you," Killian told it affectionately. "You. You starving, bottomless crap machine, I'm talking about you."

Moose did a kitten roll in his lap, exposing his tummy and stretching his paws, and Killian rolled his eyes. "You think I'm falling for that?"

He petted the cat's tummy anyway, wrestling it when the inevitable happened and Moose started clawing his wrist.

Lewis chuckled weakly, his heart still melty after that little speech about how they couldn't give Boris and Natasha away unless it was to a really good home. Could he maybe talk Killian into, say, not giving Lewis away either?

"I, uh, may have a line on a job, if that helps," he said into the silence. "I mean, you know, I can help pay for upkeep."

"A job?" Killian asked, sounding impressed. "So soon? What do you have lined up?"

Lewis felt heat sweeping his face as Killian turned those amazing eyes on him. "It's, well, it's sort of a co-op—they farm you out to companies that don't need you full-time, and you do stuff for them to get health and dental, and then if a company decides to, I dunno, adopt you, you can do that."

Killian started to chuckle. "So it's like a foster home for itinerant professionals?"

"Yeah," Lewis said, grinning. "Like you're a foster home for random pussycats!"

Moose let go of Killian's wrist and started licking the scratches.

"I, uh, have some news for you about this guy," Killian started to admit, but Nicky strode in, his footsteps shaking the floor.

"Dudes!" he said, sounding absolutely elated. "Dudes! Oh my God! I've got the best news. My girlfriend's father died."

Killian stared at him. "I'm... sorry?"

Nicky had the grace to look embarrassed. "No, man. I mean, it was awful. I liked the guy, and Lia was so sad. But that's the thing. Her *mom* has been so sad for a lot of months. And Lia and I have been really worried about her. But she loves cats—like *loves*—and she hasn't been able to have any for the last few years because her husband's lungs weren't so good and he was allergic. So, you know—she's super sad, and Lia's been working on her to maybe get some cats, and she *just* said yes, like, last night. I was checking with Lia because this was a project—we were both working on her. And... dude." His voice dropped tenderly. "Look at them. They'll be so good for her. She'll have to take him out to poop, and that'll make her leave the house. Both of the cats are sweethearts, and she *really* needs someone to take care of. She's been *so* lost—"

"But we can't just *leave* them with her," Killian said, his voice rising protectively.

Nicky held up both hands. "No worries. Lia's got a couple of days off—she was going to decorate her mom's place for Christmas, use her kitchen to bake cookies, that sort of thing. If it works out, great, but if it doesn't, man, I swear to you." He squatted in front of the cat carrier again, where both animals had settled into their post-grooming snooze. "If it doesn't work out, I'll bring them back and help you find someone. I like these guys." His voice dropped some more as he stroked his big, callused hand over tiny little Natasha's six-pound body. "They're...." He looked over his shoulder and gave a sheepish grin. "They're like Lia and me, you know? I'm a big bruiser and she's teeny. But she takes care of me, and I'd *die* for her, right? I swear, Killian, I'll make sure they're treated right. I just... I got a *real* good feeling about them. I think they need Lia's mom, and Trish needs them. It's...." He gave sort of a sunshiny smile. "Call it a Christmas miracle, right?"

Lewis stared down at the perfectly nice behemoth who had almost shaken down the apartment complex ten minutes before.

"Indeed," he said, sounding a little stunned.

"Lia's going to meet me in the front in about five," Nicky said. "She was so excited she put the morning manager in charge of the restaurant—I need to hustle so I can go back to work. What do I need?"

"I'll get it, Killian," Lewis said, glancing to where Killian hadn't moved on the couch. For his part, Killian's eyes were at half-mast, and Moose was curled up on his chest making that soporific purring sound.

"Mm...." Soundlessly, Killian slumped over, head resting on the pillow he'd been holding in his lap that now seemed sort of wedged underneath his head.

"Geez," Nicky said, eyes wide. "He's beat." He looked around the apartment at all the furry residents. "I guess I can see why he was so forgetful last night."

Lewis shrugged. "It's been sort of a weird couple of days."

Nicky frowned, looking at the blankets on the couch. "What's *your* deal?" he asked. "I mean, Killian's gone a while without a boyfriend. You and he—" He did that thing with his index finger from Killian to Lewis and back to Killian again. Lewis sighed, stood, and went to pull the blankets up to Killian's chin.

"It would be nice to have some time to find out," Lewis said, shaking his head. "Here—they came in this beat-up cat carrier, and we bought them a new one. We can lend you the new one, but, uhm...."

"You want it back," Nicky told him, nodding that he understood. Together, they packed up Boris and Natasha, and Lewis spent a moment rubbing the big guy's whiskers and soothing Natasha's suspicious hackles.

"You really do need to bring them back if they don't stick," he said apprehensively.

"Totally," Nicky said, doing the same thing to the two cats. "I have this hope, you know? That Lia's mom will... I don't know. She's so good at taking care of people. I think these guys are exactly the guys she needs."

Lewis nodded. "I should have known," he said, "that Killian would know good people." He stood and started rounding up stuff they might need while Nicky bundled the two cats with their old blanket into the new carrier.

"Killian?" Nicky let out a breath. "He's the best. He's one of our biggest customers for lunch. Couple of years ago, we got flooded out, and he showed up with a broom and gloves and helped us fix the place up again in his spare time. We go to each other's places for movies and basketball games—"

"Kings fans," Lewis said, nodding. "My brother told me they're sort of a religion here."

"Within walking distance of the arena? In Xander Karcek's name we pray, forever and ever amen!"

Lewis had to laugh, because even *he* had heard about the former center who had been pulled from the playoff lineup after admitting to having an affair with his fellow player. "Amen," he said soberly, and together they stood, Nicky's arms full of cat carrier and Lewis with a small bag with the lead and some cat food in it.

"Let me grab the keys," he murmured, "and I can help you out."

He made sure to close the front door before they opened the foyer door and then stood holding the foyer door open while Nicky ambled out. He waited until Nicky grabbed the bag of supplies and noticed a cardboard box sitting to the right of the foyer door.

Something was moving inside it.

"Oh no," he said, recognizing the sound almost immediately.

Nicky set down the carrier and bent to open the box. "It's got a note on it," he murmured, handing the note to Lewis.

Dear sir—we saw you walking your cat and thought you would be good people to give them to. The shelter is full and my husband threatened to drown them if I didn't get rid of them. I'm sorry but I don't know what else to do.

"Oh no," he said again, hearing the cascade of mews intensify as Nicky opened the lid.

"Oh, dude," Nicky said, peering inside. "Dude."

"What am I going to tell him?" Lewis mumbled as Nicky stood and hefted the box over.

Inside the box—which was sizable—was a skinny, exhausted tiger-striped cat who had apparently had a *very* good time with the local talent.

"Four?" Lewis asked, counting. "Four kittens?"

An orange one, a black one, a tiger-striped one, and a gray one.

"Dude," Nicky murmured, shaking his head. "Dude. What're you going to tell Killian?"

At that moment a small car pulled up in front of the apartment, and the door swung open. A tiny dark-haired woman stuck her head out and called, "Nicky, hurry up. My mom's so excited. She can't wait to meet them!"

Nicky looked at him apologetically as he stood in the doorway, not sure how they'd been about to get rid of two cats and had just gotten five more to replace them.

"Dude," Nicky said again. "I got nothin'. Thanks for everything. Tell me what he says—I'll be right over there later." He pointed over the retaining wall to the restaurant, and Lewis nodded weakly.

"I'll see you," he said numbly, looking inside the box again before he stepped back inside the apartment.

The kittens were all still nursing, although they looked old enough to be weaned. Lewis would have to see if they already ate soft food so they could feed the mother enough to gain a little weight.

As he looked, he saw—to his horror—three fleas simultaneously hop into the air and switch kittens.

The veterinarian's words about flea baths and how fleas could make kittens sick and dehydrated faster than anything else besides the runs rang in his ears.

Shit.

Shit shit shit shit—

And they were going to have to deal with that too.

Shit.

There's Something to be Said About Accepting Your Fate

KILLIAN YAWNED and stretched and realized he was on the couch and something had changed about the apartment. Next to the couch was a big cardboard box, as deep as it was wide and long, and he yawned again before he rolled over a little more to his side to see if he could look into it.

Moose grumbled from next to his chest, and Killian tried to orient himself. Had he just copped a two-hour nap on the couch? If so he had to try doing that some more—he hadn't felt so rested in… well, days.

Two days, to be specific. Two very exciting days with Lewis and cats that he'd never imagined he'd love so thoroughly but that he somehow did.

Moose started purring even louder, and Killian pushed his finger between the kitten's ears and smiled, feeling a sense of warmth, of peace and purpose, that he hadn't felt since Jaime had left.

He closed his eyes, letting that memory wash over him. They'd been such good friends, he mourned. Good friends but not great lovers. The sex had been fine—except when it was rote. The romance had been sweet—except when they forgot about it for weeks on end. The things Killian found he loved most about having someone in his life—the constant touching, the hugs, the long kisses without an endgame—were things they just forgot to do.

They were things he increasingly wanted to do with Lewis. There was something about the boy's smile, about the strength of his features, about the way he and Killian had jumped together straight into the "we have to save the kittens" pool; it felt as though a tender velvet rope was binding them tighter to each other with every minute that passed.

He stroked Moose's soft fur as the kitten snuggled against his chest, and then Squirrel's as he kneaded the flesh of Killian's hip through the blanket.

He didn't see Boris or Natasha anywhere, and he remembered, with relief and hope, that Nicky had been going to take them to his mother-in-law, and he thought that maybe, now that they were down to two kittens, he and Lewis might have a chance to—

"Mew."

Killian's eyes, which had gone to half-mast with sleepy musings, suddenly popped open.

"Mew?" he said, sitting up carefully. Squirrel and Moose were technically "kittens," but they were in the "mrewl" stage of new meowing. They were way beyond "mew." Where had that "mew" come from?

"Mew. Mew. Mew. Mew."

He set Moose and Squirrel on the couch and leaned forward to the large box between him and the coffee table, which now loomed larger, with a more sinister appearance.

"Mew. Mew. Mew. Mew. Mew."

Oh, for fuck's sake.

He read the note on top of the box, obviously written by somebody afraid of her husband and the fate of the mew, mew, mews coming from the box by his knees, and groaned. Vaguely he remembered the woman who had watched him walk Boris the night before. Oh Lord—she had no idea how much he did not know about what was in that box. Written on the bottom of the note, in what Killian was starting to recognize as Lewis's block printing, was another missive:

> *They've had a flea bath and are in with a heating*
> *pad. Made shot clinic appointments for next week. Had*
> *to run buy special kitten food for little ones.*
> *Seriously, Killian, I'm so sorry.*
> *Lewis*

Killian noticed the white cord running from the box to the outlet in the bottom of his lamp and laughed helplessly. The cardboard flaps made a rasping sound as he pulled them open and looked inside.

"Four," he muttered to himself. "Four and a mama cat. For sweet hell's sake—doesn't anybody keep kittens anymore?"

The little tiger-striped one looked up and opened its mouth. "Mew. Mew, mew, mew, mew."

The other three started in on the chorus, and he stroked the mama cat's sleek head. For her part, she gave him an exhausted look and started licking the kittens into submission, and Killian got it. She was thin and tired, and the kittens were big and more than ready to be weaned. It was seriously time for them to start eating soft food and kibble so they could give their mother a break.

"C'mon, mama cat," he crooned, reaching into the box and scooping her out. She lay on his arm limply, all maybe five pounds of her, and he rubbed her ears and massaged the back of her neck, trying to give her a spa day while her kittens protested vociferously. After a few moments of this she slithered out of his grasp and back into the box, and Killian sighed. Of course. It was warm in there. He could smell the wet food on her whiskers, so Lewis had obviously fed her, and she wanted the comfort of her family around her.

Wow.

The door opened, and Lewis bustled in. He grimaced when he saw Killian sitting up, peering into the box.

"Wow," he said, this time out loud.

"Can you fucking believe it?" Lewis asked on a faintly hysterical laugh. He shook his head. "Killian, I'm so, so very sorry—"

"Don't be," Killian said on a grimace. "I... I mean, seriously? She saw me walking Boris and decided that made me a good bet?" He let out a breath, remembering the argument that had raged behind her door. "Well, her husband sounds like a piece of work." He grimaced and stood, reaching out to take the bag from Lewis's hand. "Here, I'll set them up some food—"

Lewis pulled the bag back. "No," he said, looking miserable. "I don't want to give you any more work to do. I mean, you offer to walk me home and now we're running an animal shelter together? You didn't ask for any of this."

Lewis's cheeks were still hectic from the cold, and his eyes were bright and lively, and he smelled vaguely of Christmas trees and cookies. With a smile, Killian recognized that not all the bags in his hands were from the pet store—he'd brought more cookies.

"C'mere," Killian murmured, taking the bags and setting them on the coffee table.

Lewis's back straightened, as though he recognized Killian's mood, and he peered hopefully through his shaggy bangs.

"C'mere?" he prompted.

Killian reached out and grabbed his hand to pull him closer, close enough to feel the chill off his clothes, to feel the warmth radiating from underneath.

"Yeah," Killian whispered. "C'mere. I need to thank you."

"For what?" Lewis asked breathlessly.

Killian felt a smile pulling at the corners of his mouth. "For defending me from Nicky." He chuckled. "You'll buy me a poop bag?"

Lewis groaned softly in embarrassment and hid his eyes against Killian's shoulder. Killian didn't mind that. It only brought him closer, and every moment of Lewis closer made Killian want to get closer still.

"He was yelling at you," Lewis mumbled, and warmth swept up from the balls of Killian's bare feet to his nose.

"I've never had somebody defend my honor before," Killian teased, and then he remembered—oh Lordy—he'd just woken up. He swallowed, tasting his own morning breath, and grimaced.

He tried to take a step back, but Lewis wouldn't let him.

"Where you going?" Lewis demanded. "I thought we were having a moment."

"We were," Killian told him, pulling his hand up from where it had rested on Lewis's arm to cover his mouth. "But I haven't brushed my teeth."

Lewis stood straight and glared at him. "You interrupted that great moment because of morning breath?"

Killian swallowed again. "I... I've really wanted to kiss you since last night," he protested, feeling stupid. "I... I didn't want it to be icky because of—"

Lewis closed the distance between them and kissed him.

For a moment Killian was so surprised he simply stood there, but Lewis wrapped his arms around Killian's waist and pushed gently with his lips, and ah! He was so strong, so warm, so pretty, all at once. Killian melted a little, eyes closing, and opened his mouth enough to let Lewis decide if his morning breath was a deterrent.

Lewis's tongue swept inside his mouth without hesitation, and the last of Killian's reserve melted. He opened to the invasion and to the kiss, accepting and returning in the dance of intimacy that good kisses become.

And this wasn't just good—it was *great*. Killian's breath quickened, and he responded, pulling Lewis closer until Lewis raised one leg and hooked it over Killian's thigh in an effort to bring them closer still. Killian slid his hands into the back pockets of Lewis's jeans to find that tiny tight ass that he suspected was there so he could squeeze it… oooh… yes!

Lewis moaned softly into Killian's mouth, and he bucked up against Killian's groin until Killian moved his hands and cupped the back of Lewis's thighs. Lewis gave a little hop and was suddenly circling Killian's waist with his slender legs, and Killian kept holding him, not wanting him to move even enough to slide down his body.

Killian shifted his weight then, and his foot brushed the cardboard box, eliciting another round of "mew, mew, mew" from inside, and both of them froze.

Lewis slid carefully down his front, and with an awkward step and a hop, they both ended up sprawled on the couch, Lewis on top of Killian, but not in a good way.

"Mew, mew, mew…."

Moving almost completely in synch, they turned their heads to the new challenge in the cardboard box.

"Damn," Killian murmured.

"I know," Lewis said. "I… I mean, I've got no suggestions. They're sort of ours for the same reason the others were ours. I don't suppose you have any more ginormous friends who can drop down from heaven and take a box of kittens, do you?"

Killian grunted. "Nicky and I work out together at the Y—it's only a few blocks away. He's a good guy, but nope. No clones in this part of Sac that I can see."

"Would you have nailed one if you could have?" Lewis asked suspiciously, and Killian rolled his eyes because Lewis was transparent and it was flattering.

"No," he said softly. "Because Nicky's a friend. Also…?" He shrugged. "Giant muscles aren't my type." He chuckled a little and gave Lewis's ass a playful grope. "I prefer lean and strong."

Lewis's grin revealed one tooth in front that was slightly larger than the other—it was cute. "Lucky me," he said, and then he sobered. "I… I've wanted to kiss you since you walked me home the other night."

Killian felt his cheeks grow warm. "Really?" he asked, although he'd sensed that.

"You knew it too!" Lewis laughed. "Why... why didn't you?" His expression fell like he was expecting to hear something bad about himself.

Killian ran a thumb under Lewis's cheekbone. "I wanted to," he admitted softly. "It's just been a while. You... you get comfortable alone. Reaching outside that box is hard, especially when you know you can get hurt."

"Mm...." Lewis nodded, looking thoughtful. "You needed to know me for a couple of days. Maybe know I wasn't going anywhere anytime soon."

Killian grimaced and struggled to sit up, mindful that Lewis had been making himself comfortable on top of his chest and Killian had enjoyed having him there.

"Except you *are* going somewhere soon," he reminded him. "You're getting a job and an apartment—"

"Mm-hmm...." Lewis scrambled back onto his heels to let Killian up, but there was something in his voice that told Killian he was missing an obvious thing, but Killian couldn't see it.

"What?" he asked.

Lewis shook his head. "I like Sacramento, Killian. How do you know I won't stay right here?"

Killian loved the tilt to his brown eyes, loved how they made his face interesting and mischievous. For a moment he simply lost himself in them, half forgetting what they were talking about in the first place.

Lewis broke his concentration. "Why?" he asked softly.

Killian blinked. "Why what?"

"Why did you get so comfortable alone?"

Killian swallowed, not sure he could answer. "It's... relationships are hard," he said, his voice low. "It's hard opening yourself to someone. I'm... not good at it." He thought of his and Jaime's sad goodbye, both of them knowing it wasn't meant to be, neither of them knowing how to let go. Jaime had told him that Killian would know he was in love when he could risk something of his heart, anything small, with a lover he hadn't known forever.

Until he'd said that, Killian hadn't realized that he'd been the silent one, the cold one, the good boy who never asked for more.

He'd thought that Jaime hadn't loved him enough, that was all.

He'd had a few lovers since. He'd always treasure Joey, who had been in it for the fun of it, but he'd remembered Jaime's words about risking something of his heart. How much had he risked, really, in *this* relationship? Some time? Some effort? His apartment? His pinky toe?

But Lewis was looking at him with an exceptionally perceptive expression on his face.

"I get it," he said softly. "I came out, and I got the Afterschool Special treatment. If my heart gets broken, my parents will probably fly over here from Texas to pet me and make it all better. Who do you have, Killian?"

Killian swallowed and looked away. Gah! This kid was damned near clairvoyant. It wasn't fair! He watched Moose and Squirrel bat a crumpled piece of paper across the hardwood in front of the TV and said, "Well, thanks to you, now I have Moose."

Lewis's fingertips, stroking his temples, his jaw, his neck, seemed to make his skin flutter. In a moment he was going to flutter out of his skin, out of this room, out of this uncomfortable conversation, and he'd be someplace cool and remote—

And alone.

"Not Squirrel?" Lewis chided gently, and Killian found himself grounded in the here and now, where he and Lewis were still on the couch, and Lewis had moved closer, threatening to put Killian on his back again.

Killian found he wanted to go.

"We couldn't split them up," Killian mumbled, eyes closing. "Maybe he could visit."

"Sure," Lewis murmured, drawing closer still. Once again, Killian thought he was missing something. Lewis had a rather cloaked look of triumph in his expression, as though he knew something Killian didn't—and boy was Killian going to be excited when he was let in on the secret.

And then Lewis's lips were on his, and Lewis was bearing Killian back against the couch cushions, and for a few dreamy moments, making out was really the only thing either of them had to think about.

And who was doing that much thinking when they had a lean, muscular body in their arms?

Killian could have done that all afternoon—he could have done *more*—and he was tingly and aroused and *erect* when his watch went off on his wrist, which was attached to his hand, which was—oh my!—groping Lewis's ass through his jeans. Lewis, who was lying lengthwise on top of him, pulled away, looking around wildly, like a meerkat who'd been caught by his parents.

"What's that?" he panted, and Killian groaned, and not in the good, sexy way.

"That's my alarm. It's laundry day. I've got to get up or I'm not going to have anything to wear tomorrow."

This time he had no problem reading the expression on Lewis's face.

"Which doesn't mean I can hang around the house naked," he said dryly, laughing as Lewis's excitement dampened. "And if you throw yours in, I can do yours too. I've got quarters."

Lewis buried his face in Killian's shirt and arched his groin into Killian's erection as well, making them both whimper. "You're killing me," he wailed. "Dude, sex or clean laundry? It's like you're Satan!"

Killian let out a dry laugh and wriggled out from under Lewis, his rump falling awkwardly onto the floor while he kept one arm behind him. Lewis sat back on his heels and laughed at him, and Killian laughed back, scrambling upright and shaking his head.

"You know," he said, "I used to be a perfectly functional human being. Didn't stub my toe, fall off my own couch, piss off the neighbors. I swear, these last two days have been *highly* unusual for me!" After that half hour on the couch, Lewis warm and willing in his arms, their breaths mingling, his hands roaming Lewis's lithe body over his clothes, Killian suddenly felt the urge to not look like a schmuck.

But Lewis was gazing at him with that expression again—the one that said Lewis knew things Killian was completely blind to—and suddenly Killian wondered if he'd ever have dignity again.

He found himself gazing back, biting his lower lip, his face heating, remembering the weight of that body on top of his own, the sweet yielding of Lewis's lips against his, and he suddenly didn't care. What was dignity, really, but a way to stay cold and insulated against the world?

"What?" he demanded, that smile on Lewis's face growing really unnerving. "What is that look?"

"Has it been all bad?" Lewis asked with a coy little tilt of his head. "Be honest."

Killian swallowed, lost in Lewis's bright mischief. "No," he said helplessly. At that moment, Squirrel went running after the balled-up piece of paper, missed his mark, ran into Killian's ankle, and then climbed his pajama pants, with the aid of his claws hooking into Killian's flesh underneath.

"Ouch!" Killian reached for the kitten just as Moose ran under his foot. With a hop, he bounced against the cardboard box, setting off the finally-calm litter inside, and he found himself falling and twisting to land on the couch while Lewis scrambled out of his way.

Lewis succeeded, and Killian was once again flat on his back on the couch, but this time with Squirrel held triumphantly in his hand, surprised but unsquished, while Moose leaped onto his stomach from the floor.

Squirrel started batting at his wrist, and Killian sighed, pulling him and Moose to his chest.

"You guys are killing me," he said, trying to get their attention. "We're obviously not throwing you out into the cold. Would it kill you to make me look cool?"

Moose cuddled adoringly into the hollow under his chin, and Squirrel started to nurse on his earlobe.

"So that's a no?" he asked, and Lewis fell back against his arm of the couch and laughed until he couldn't breathe.

EVENTUALLY KILLIAN managed to get up and get moving while Lewis juggled kittens in his wake. Later, Lewis came with him, each of them bearing a giant hamper of laundry, as he made his way across the street to the small laundromat on the corner.

"Gotta admit," Lewis said as they hauled their baskets inside, "this could be worse."

Killian blew out a breath. "The laundromat across the street or the box of kittens on our doorstep?"

Lewis chuckled and shook his head. "My college dorm was the worst—four flights of stairs and the tiniest washing machines. They had a list you signed up for, and I was always, like, three in the morning, Wednesday morning, because I knew I'd be working on a paper anyway."

Killian grunted, busy dealing with the door to the laundromat, but ten minutes later, after they had four washing machines whirring away, he was able to think of something intelligent to say.

"You're lucky," he said. "College is a good thing. I mean, I know it's hard now because you're job hunting, and that always sucks, but it'll open doors."

"What was your major?" Lewis asked excitedly, and Killian hated to burst his bubble.

"Munitions and transport, Sergeant Class E-5," Killian responded dryly. "Don't be too impressed. It's about where everybody is after four years or two tours. I was good at driving and keeping track of shit. Go me."

Lewis tilted his head. "Why not college?"

Killian shrugged. "Too stupid," he said with a laugh, but Lewis didn't laugh back.

"Not according to your bookshelves," he replied with a vision Killian wasn't altogether comfortable with.

"Fiction," Killian mumbled, thinking of the spy thrillers, lawyer mysteries, histories, and romances in his bookcase.

Lewis snorted. "I took liberal studies classes, Killian, and one of their biggest pet peeves was that people underestimated how smart you have to be to read fiction. Seriously, why didn't you go to college?"

Ugh. Personal disclosure. The worst. "My parents had no money, but it was more than that." He shrugged and pulled up two of the foldable chairs to be closer to the back wall where the phone charging station was. "We were never really told college was an option. I assumed I'd get a factory job or a union job. The army came along, and it was a way to get the hell out of Indiana."

"Mmm," Lewis said thoughtfully, and once again Killian got the feeling there was something he was missing.

"What are you thinking right now?" Killian asked defensively.

"I'm thinking that I see why you like your cozy home, your framed artwork, and your teak bookshelves," Lewis said, regarding him with that sort of intensity that made Killian feel absolutely inadequate.

"Why is that?" Killian barely refrained from crossing his arms in front of his chest.

"Because it's yours. It's unique and interesting, and nobody in your life ever expected unique and interesting from you. So you keep it to yourself, and you please yourself, and most people invited over sleep on your couch. Am I right?"

Well, wasn't that what Jaime had said? "Yeah," he muttered. "That's me. Rethinking that half hour on the couch?"

"Definitely not," Lewis said, and his smile was quiet. "It's making me think that it was probably unusual for you, particularly since we haven't known each other long."

Killian scrubbed his face with his hand, feeling stubble, and listened to the *kachunk-kachunk* of the washing machines. Usually he brought a book and enjoyed his time here—including the time he spent listening to music while he was folding clothes—but he never dressed for the occasion. He'd showered but blown off the shave for another day, and now he felt like maybe he should have tried a little harder. Didn't Lewis deserve more than his "I've got to make sacrifices for laundry day," grooming?

"I've had relationships," he defended, but even he could hear the woundedness in his tone. How many men since Jaime had left? Four? Five if he counted Joey. That wasn't a lot in the last eight years, was it?

Lewis's hand on his thigh was warm—gentle even. "Hey, I get it," Lewis said quietly. "You had to be self-contained. It's hard for you to share your heart, your space with people. I understand." He gave one of those coy grins meant to make Killian want to know him better. They worked. "I just need to be more patient than usual, right?"

"What's, uhm, usual?" Killian asked, feeling stupid as his neck and cheeks heated.

That grin went from coy to downright naughty. "There's a happy medium in there somewhere," he said, waggling his eyebrows. "Somewhere between two months and two hours, but I'm not sure exactly where."

Killian laughed appreciatively. "I've seen enough of the two-hour variety at work—I'm not interested in where those end."

Lewis grimaced. "Well, yeah. Those are usually scratch-an-itch sorts of things. When you're a kid away from home for the first time, well, scratch away. By the time you get your MA, it's like, 'Oh please, I'm a grown-up now. I need dinner and conversation at the very least.'"

Killian gave a noncommittal shrug. "I've only had one of those itch-scratching things," he said. Then he smirked. "And I think that guy's finally met his match." He remembered his talk with Joey again. "In fact, the entire bar scene I knew when I started working at Catches has sort of grown up. It's a whole new scene now." He thought about hearing that Jackson Rivers had finally found somebody—and that man had demons. Anybody could see it. But apparently Jackson had found a demon-tamer. Maybe there was hope.

"So you're ready to move on?" Lewis asked with blatant purpose.

Killian gazed at him and sighed. It was like there was a thick clear fiberglass wall between them, impenetrable and invisible, and it was all in Killian's frightened little heart. "I want to," he said in a small voice. "I just, I'm sort of a cold fish, Lewis. You're… well, I get the feeling that's never been your problem."

Lewis snorted, shaking his head. "No it has not." The look he sent Killian was not without self-recrimination. "But that doesn't mean a little self-restraint on my part wouldn't have made my life easier."

And suddenly Killian was curious. "Which brings us to what *did* you do to get kicked out of Texas?"

Lewis squeezed his eyes tight and shook his head. "It's so dumb."

"Seriously—"

"No, really! It's so dumb, and it does *not* throw me in the best light."

"I unintentionally left cat poop next to my friend's alfresco eating porch," Killian told him bluntly. "I mean… that's *bad*."

Lewis shook his head. "The keyword there was 'unintentional,' Killian. And the guy loved you too much to stay mad. This was…. Look. My brother didn't tell me his best friend married his high school sweetheart while I was away at school."

Killian snorted and then clapped his hand over his mouth because he thought he might see where this was going. "And this was… bad?"

"Well, it was bad that the best friend didn't tell *me* when I was home over spring break, nursing a split with my cheating, douchey ex this last April. And it was *really* bad that the wife was off visiting her family and he came over and asked if I wanted to use his pool…."

"Oh no," Killian said, because this was opening itself up like a wide and beautiful road.

"Oh yes," Lewis retorted with a certain anger in his voice now. "And after we… well, after a couple of blowjobs between friends, I went into the bathroom to freshen up, and I saw their wedding picture, and—" He shook his head. "—I was out of there. I mean, that's so low. To me, definitely, but also to *her*. Anyway, I was thinking, 'Okay, that was a bad decision, but it's over,' but suddenly it's the week before Thanksgiving, and I'm sitting on my parents' couch trying to explain how I didn't have a job yet because suddenly nobody wants to hire the gay in Texas, and everybody in our area seemed to know me, when…." He sighed and shook his head.

"What?" Killian asked, absolutely riveted.

"Would you believe a mob showed up at my parents' door? My brother's friend's neighbor, who has the hots for the wife, apparently peep-showed the whole dumb blowjob thing through the fence. He thought that the best time to tell the guy's wife was at a pre-Thanksgiving neighborhood get-together, and suddenly I'm the star of the newest documentary episode of *Kill the Twinkie*." He shook his head and then grinned. "I went out to tell them to go to hell and… well, there were more than words exchanged."

Killian remembered the two yellowing bruises that had been under Lewis's eyes when he'd first shown up in the hallways of the apartment building and in the bar.

"Did you get some hits in?" he asked, suddenly furious that somebody had touched Lewis—*his* Lewis, who rescued kittens and defended him to giant muscled restaurant owners who apparently also rescued kittens. *His* Lewis, who had been running on a barrel over the last three days trying to stem the cascade of consequences that had come from picking two kittens up from a vacant lot in the dead of night.

His Lewis, who kept regarding him with that veiled excitement, that cheerful seduction, that made Killian want to fall into his obviously placed romantic snare.

"Oh yeah," Lewis said proudly, showing off the recently healed knuckles of his left hand. "Mine was not the only nose broken that day, my friend." He smiled fiercely with all his teeth, and Killian realized he'd fallen into another trap and didn't care.

He grasped Lewis's hand and rubbed his thumb gently along the roughened knuckle. "Good," he said. He glanced up and saw Lewis regarding him with a combination of hero worship and hunger and then dropped his gaze again. "You've got so much… passion. So much joy. Nobody tells you that you need to fight for these things."

Lewis threaded their fingers together. "What they need to tell you is that your own heart, your own passions, are worth the fight," he said. Without asking permission, he scooched his chair closer to Killian's until their thighs touched and then leaned his head on Killian's shoulder.

"I like this neighborhood," he said out of the blue, but Killian was already so stunned by the comforting weight on his shoulder that he didn't startle. "I've seen three different same-sex couples walk by in the time it's taken for our laundry to get halfway done. Lots of het couples too, but everyone was holding hands and smiling. This is a good place."

"I've always thought so," Killian murmured, sinking into Lewis's smell and his warmth as he gazed out into the gray day. Bare tree limbs thrust into their vision against the pewter sky like intruders. Sacramento's tree population had taken a hit the year before, but many of the old guard were still standing.

"How did you find this place?"

Killian rubbed his thumb along Lewis's wrist, liking how long and strong his hands were. Bony, because not everything about Lewis was comfortable, but strong. In spite of their age difference, Killian had increasing difficulty calling Lewis a "kid," even in his mind.

"A friend I met when we were deployed moved here. We'd kept in touch." He let out a strangled laugh. "Turned out we'd both been crushing. He… you know. Helped me come out. Was my first. We were together for about two years. It was… comfortable."

"Mmm." Lewis pulled their twined hands to his mouth and kissed Killian's knuckles. "Why'd you break up?"

"Too comfortable, I guess." Killian shrugged. "He… well, he almost cheated. Got caught up in some mad chemistry, came home, told me about it. I was hurt." He took a long, shuddery breath because even Jaime's painful honesty couldn't assuage the betrayal—not then. Now he recognized it for what it had been—a tortured admission that while there was love between them, it wasn't the kind of love either of them deserved in a life partner. It wasn't consuming or dedicated. It was friendship and kindness when they'd both needed it, but it wasn't forever.

"Bastard," Lewis defended staunchly, and Killian remembered *I will buy him poop bags*! and had to smile. No equivocation from Lewis, nosirree.

"No," Killian said now, meaning it. "We were friends. I don't want to say we shouldn't have been more, because for a little while it was exactly what we needed, but we'd outgrown it. It just didn't really hit us until that night. Anyway, I moved out, and he moved to Folsom. I kept my job at Catches, and he opened up the Cave Bar—which is the kind of thing he's wanted to run all his life. We still exchange Christmas cards, call each other on our birthday, get a drink together when he's nearby. I don't have so many friends that I want to turn my nose up at this guy because we weren't meant to be."

"God," Lewis said with a snort. "That's so mature. My last boyfriend was a douchey two-timing user, and I refuse to say anything nice about him. Is that bad?"

Killian chuckled. He couldn't help it. "Nope. Some guys *are* douchey two-timing users, and I think it's totally okay to call them out."

Lewis pulled back just enough to turn his head and go in for a kiss. It wasn't showy or urgent—they were still in the laundromat, and it turned out Lewis was more mature than he gave himself credit for. But it was kind and fun and a reminder that Killian hadn't died yet. He'd become more insular as time had gone by, but his heart could still beat fast, and he could still remember what it was like to be *really* attracted to someone and *really* attached at the same time.

Their washers started to beep, pulling both of them back in surprise, but they shared a smile before they got up and started to move things to the dryer. A kind smile, full of wryness and yearning, sexual and playful and genuinely happy.

As they stood up and started moving clothes, Killian could still hear his heartbeat, feel yearning thrumming through his veins as the part of him that allowed itself to love woke up and stretched, scenting the air for Lewis Bernard and the irrepressible passion and joy that had roused it.

Killian greeted it like a long-lost friend.

HELPLESSLY HOPING

LEWIS SHUT his laptop and sighed.

Three job interviews scheduled on Tuesday, with the most promising one still being the co-op—that was done.

More appointments with the shot clinic for Thursday while he and Killian weaned the kittens—that was done.

Several calls to local shelters, all of them once again confirming that *nobody* had space for kittens in December—depressing, but yes, that was done too.

Laundry—done.

Shopping—thanks to Killian that was also done, and Lewis had made some tasty BBQ mac and cheese that should keep him and Killian in leftovers for a couple of days, so shopping *and* cooking were both done.

Really, there was nothing for Lewis to do—

You know what you could *start looking for?*

Absolutely nothing for Lewis to do—

What would it hurt to pull up some listings?

Lewis couldn't think of a damned thing to do—

You can't sleep on his couch forever!

The only thing left for him to do was to go to Catches, play some darts, and wait for Killian to get off work.

Absolutely.

He couldn't think of a single other thing that should take precedence.

Nothing. Absolutely nothing.

At all.

SOMETHING ABOUT the brisk wind and the river dampness in the night air as Lewis slunk to the bar forced him to be honest with himself.

Of course he should start looking for an apartment. Jesus, if nothing else he and his brother could share rent on something slightly bigger so Todd could give up one of his jobs. Hell, Lewis's parents *had* start-up money for both of them for exactly such a contingency, but neither Lewis nor Todd had wanted to take them up on it until they had a good situation. Todd was still looking for a job that could pay the rent, and Lewis?

Lewis was looking for an idea of what he wanted to look for, mostly.

And whatever he wanted, wherever he wanted to end up, he wanted to be close enough to Killian to not give Killian the excuse to give up.

Lewis *had* been paying attention as Killian had spoken, and the one thing that had hit him the hardest was Killian's assertion that he was probably a cold fish.

Killian? Cold?

Lewis snorted at the thought. Quiet? Yes. Self-contained? Oh yeah—no question. But Lewis had seen the guy melt—just *melt*—over a blind cat and his seeing-eye-cat girlfriend. He'd watched Killian's friend go from absolute rage to *absolute* forgiveness when Killian had apologized, because, it had turned out, Killian had been a stand-up guy when it really mattered.

And it was not lost on Lewis that Moose and Squirrel, the two kittens that had seemed to start the kitten deluge, were probably not ever going to see the inside of a shelter—or anybody else's apartment—because Killian and Moose were soulmates, and Killian wasn't going to break up a couple.

No, Killian wasn't cold. His *kisses* weren't cold. In fact, they were gloriously, unapologetically hot. He kissed Lewis like Lewis was water and Killian was wandering the desert. The look in his eye, the hunger in his touch—no. None of those things were cold-fish qualities. In fact, everything about Killian spoke hot-blooded mammalian warmth, and Lewis wanted to snuggle into his orbit and *bask*.

And that was damned hard to do with an apartment and a job across town, or even in some place called Folsom, which appeared to be where Killian's ex had gone to start a business.

Lewis had been sorely tempted by the benefits and stability he'd seen in the Folsom job—but he had to be honest with himself.

He wanted to stay close to Killian.

Of course, he liked this part of the city too—although he suspected the rent in their area might be a little steeper than it would be farther away—but he couldn't lie. Killian was the driving force behind all of his decisions in Sacramento thus far, and he couldn't see how any of those had gone bad.

Boris and Natasha and the box full of kittens were absolutely positively not his fault; he knew he could make a case for that in court, dammit. He *could*.

He'd come to the part of his life where he thought he could find somebody real. Somebody *permanent*. He'd *learned* all his hard, expensive, stupid lessons during college. He didn't want a guy who drove a really cool car and would take any blowjob offered because "It's not like I can catch anything, dude." He didn't want a guy who would cheat on his wife because "Hey, what else were we doing?" And he *definitely* didn't want a guy who would sex him up on the same beanbag chairs they'd been gaming on and then refuse to wipe the chairs down because "It's not like it won't flake off, right?"

A guy who could open up his apartment to kittens because where else were they going to go?

Oh yeah. *That* guy was a keeper.

Lewis just needed a little more time, he thought, trying not to feel guilty about it. Just a *little more time* to get Killian see that he should keep *Lewis* in return.

It was ten o'clock on Sunday night, and Lewis could see why Killian had thought he'd be home a little early. Customers sat in patches, gathered around the tables and talking earnestly. A couple were shoulder-to-shoulder at the bar, staring worshipfully at the TV screen where the Kings were playing out of town. There was a winding-down feeling to the bar that night, and Lewis guessed that the tail end of Thanksgiving weekend really would be sort of a downer. He spotted Killian's boss at a corner table, facing the door, and waved, surprised when she nodded him over to sit by her.

"I didn't mean to interrupt your dinner," he told her. What was her name again? Oh yeah. Suzanne. In her early thirties, with blond hair swept up in a messy bun and an absolute strength and confidence of the sort that had always dazzled Lewis a little, Suzanne struck Lewis as the kind of woman who could eat with her own thoughts quite happily and not be even a tiny bit disturbed by the lack of company.

But she smiled at him and set her sandwich down to wipe her mouth as she swallowed. "Not at all," she said as he pulled out a seat. "Killian's been saying nice things about you all night."

Lewis felt his face heat. "Really? I thought I was ruining his life!"

She chuckled. "Kittens, right?"

He shrugged. "A box of them. I mean… an *entire box.*"

She made a happy little sound in her throat. "Yeah, I heard. Do you know he's already got names for them?"

Lewis felt his cheeks pucker as he grinned. "Really? I did not know that."

"Oh yeah. I mean, last night as we were closing I heard about Moose and Squirrel, but tonight he was talking about Lucky and Charming and Squid and Percy and… oh wait. He had a good one for the mama cat." She squeezed her eyes shut and opened them. "*Elinore!*" she said excitedly and sighed, hands at her heart. "I swear, his description of the mama cat and how tired she was, how ready for a break—it made *me* want to take that one home. I'm always afraid of kittens. My sister's cat spent his formative years leaping off staircases and onto her and her girlfriend's heads."

"Yikes!" Lewis laughed, partly because it was a chance to get a word in edgewise, and partly because, well, yikes!

"I know, right?" she said, shuddering. "That little fucker…." She paused and looked both ways. "I'm sorry, I meant that little *asshole* actually left a *gopher* on Shauna's porch. Bwah! What a terror. But a cat who could camp out on me when I'm in the mood to shotgun television on my day off? *That's* my kind of cat. If she's still totally chill after the kittens are weaned, let me know. I might take her off your hands."

Lewis smiled appreciatively, his cheeks stretching. "That's really awesome," he said, all sincerity. "I mean, poor Killian. We got rid of Boris and Natasha and—"

"Wait," she said, suddenly all interest. "Who's Boris and Natasha?"

Lewis cackled and launched into the story of Boris and Natasha and Killian's ginormous friend Nicky and his tiny girlfriend, Lia—whom Suzanne seemed to know—and how Boris and Natasha were exactly what they needed. Suzanne finished off her fries as she listened, her enormous green eyes alight with interest.

"Wow," she said, washing down her last bite with a gulp of soda. "Unbelievable. I'm so impressed!"

"With what?" Lewis asked, surprised.

"With Killian," she said, laughing. "I mean, don't get me wrong—Killian's *the best.* He holds a clothing drive every year. It'll start tomorrow, on his day off. New clothes for kids at the homeless shelter, toys and books too. He's the first person to help a neighbor. Last year when all the trees were blowing down, he formed a neighborhood crew to break the trees up and get them out of the roads before the power companies could get to them. He's like our go-to guy if we need anything. He has personally bailed me out of the shit six or seven times, from flat tires to shitty ex-boyfriends to"—her voice fell—"my father's funeral. God, that was the suck. He held on to my hand the entire time and kept me mildly buzzed during the reception. Got me home in one piece and stayed with me. Just… you know. Slept on the couch and made me breakfast until I could function. I *love* that man. He will never know how much. But you never see how *sweet* he can be unless you talk to him. You know, poke your way through that reserve bubble he's got going. I'm just impressed that he dropped his guard so quickly. A good guy? Yes. But I had no idea he could be so *ferocious* about something, you know?"

Lewis shrugged, remembering Killian's words about being a "cold fish" and how that didn't match the heat Lewis had felt coming off his body all morning. From his frowzy collapse into sleep on the couch to the heat of his mouth on Lewis's during their first kiss, Killian Thornton had been nothing but a warm-blooded, cave-dwelling mammal.

Lewis wanted so badly to curl up in his cave and warm himself by Killian's heart-fires.

"I think he's a lot more passionate than people give him credit for," Lewis said, trying not to titillate.

But Suzanne wasn't stupid, and apparently she and Killian had worked together for a while. "Yeah?" she prodded. "You and him?"

Lewis scowled. "If you scare him off by getting in his business, no cat for you. I'm not kidding. I'll drive to Texas and brave the mob of people out for my twinkie ass in my parents' neighborhood so I can give that cat to my mother instead."

"Ooh." Suzanne held up her hands, and while she was still smiling, she was also thoughtful. "I think *you* know how to be passionate and ferocious," she said, and Lewis knew he didn't have to tell her she'd scored a direct hit—the heat in his cheeks did it for her.

He swallowed and gave her an apologetic smile. "It's a failing," he admitted, thinking about the fight he'd had on his mother's lawn two days before Thanksgiving.

"I think you're *exactly* what Killian needs," she said quietly. "You keep working on it, kid. Killian is a *great* guy, but…." She sighed. "He could easily be laid-back and low-key and *lonely* for the rest of his life."

Lewis thought of all of the heat Killian had wrapped him up in all day—including a soft smiling kiss goodbye before he ran out the door, leaving Lewis to continue working on his computer.

So much promise of passion there, he thought dreamily. Lewis just had to have faith.

"I think there's a *lot* of fire in there," Lewis said with dignity. "He just… you know, needs to find the key."

She snorted. "I think *you're* the key." She looked around. "And I think my break is over. Killian's back doing inventory, but these last tables are looking ready to cash out. Hang in there, kiddo. I may let him go early tonight. I don't foresee a lot of folks wandering in the door in the next fifteen minutes, and he runs a pretty tight ship."

She stood and bussed her own table before taking the dishes to the back, where presumably they'd be washed. Lewis watched as a barback bussed glassware and fetched sodas for two of the tables hanging out and drinking soda. He'd never worked in a restaurant or bar, but he'd closed down his share. He recognized the pulse of the place, and this one was definitely slowing down. There was a rustle at the far end of the bar, near the door Suzanne had disappeared through, and Killian emerged, stripped off a sweatshirt, and hung it on a peg near the door—he must have been doing inventory in the walk-in fridge and freezer. Most restaurants had them. He clapped his hands together and blew on them and then caught sight of Lewis, still sitting in Suzanne's spot, and… oh God.

The smile that lit his face was *incendiary*.

Not laid-back. Not low-key. *Glorious. Hot. Dazzling.*

Lewis returned it, his heartbeat rumbling in his ears.

"'Sup?" Killian asked, drawing near, and although he stopped a few feet from the table, Lewis *knew* Killian wanted to kiss him.

Lewis gave him a "look," daring him to just stand there. Any other neighborhood and he would have understood—but not here.

Killian tried to contain his grin with a bitten lip and lowered brows, but Lewis tapped his cheek and raised his eyebrow.

The smile escaped again, and Killian closed the distance between them and kissed his cheek with a tenderness Lewis wasn't sure he'd *ever* deserved.

"What's up?" Killian asked again, but this time with his hand on Lewis's shoulder and a brief nuzzle of Lewis's temple before he stood up.

"Got bored," Lewis said, grinning. "Did work like a good boy, have some job interviews lined up, confirmed that no shelter's taking kittens, and, uhm, wanted some company." He batted his eyelashes. "Specific company."

Killian looked away, but above the sexy dark stubble on his face, Lewis could see his cheeks turn pink. "Fair," he said. He glanced around, probably confirming how many people were there and how close they were to cashing out. "Want me to get you some food before the kitchen closes?"

Lewis shook his head. "No thanks. I made some barbecue mac and cheese—it's waiting for us back at ho—erm, the apartment." Eek! Nope. Couldn't say that word too quickly. Abort! But Killian seemed focused on the first part of that sentence.

"I'm sorry, some what?"

Lewis blinked at him. "Some barbecue mac and cheese? You know, you had that roast, the instapot, and the Kraft blue box? Anyway, it's delicious. Wait until you try it."

Killian let out a bemused laugh. "You know, I've never even heard of that. I was going to make the roast with potatoes and carrots and onion soup."

Lewis spread his fingers over his eyes. "D'oh! I'm sorry. Did I ruin your whole budget and plans and stuff?"

Killian frowned—not like he was displeased but like he was thinking. "I guess it depends on how good the barbecue is. If it's delicious—"

"Oh, it *is*. And there's *lots*. We'll have leftovers for days!"

Killian laughed. "I look forward to it. Now let me get busy, and we can be gone in half an hour."

Lewis smiled at him, suddenly ridiculously happy to be here in a bar at closing time on a Sunday. "Can I get a draft first?"

"Yeah."

LEWIS THOUGHT about going to the dartboard again, but like two nights ago, watching Killian proved far more entertaining. Not because he was funny or clumsy—quite the opposite. He moved smoothly and efficiently, but there was a rhythm to his movements, almost like he was dancing to the soundtrack being played overhead. Every now and then, Lewis would watch his lips move, as though he was giving himself instructions or having a conversation in his own head.

Maybe he was talking to Lewis.

Maybe he was saying, *I think we should make love tonight*.

Maybe he was saying, *You don't have to leave, ever*.

Or maybe he was trying to figure out a way to get four people who were well-meaning, responsible, and not psychopaths in giant, stupid, noisy trucks to take a kitten home.

At one point, after the last customer had cashed out and while he was sweeping the floor, waiting for Suzanne to come grab his drawer, he looked up in midconversation, caught Lewis's eyes on him, and ducked his head in obvious embarrassment.

"What?" he asked defensively.

"Just wondering who you were talking to," Lewis told him frankly.

Killian rolled his eyes. "Honestly? I was adding scenes to my favorite Marvel movie."

"Didn't like the ending?" Lewis asked, fascinated. Sometimes he rewrote the code of the apps he was using when he found a glitch that drove him batshit. This was even better.

"Oh no," Killian said earnestly. "*Loved* the ending. Just, you know. Wanted more."

"And thus, fanfic was born."

Imagine his joy when Killian said, "Fan-what?"

Lewis stared at him. "You… you know. Fanfiction? Fanfic? Where people write imaginary scenes from movies or TV shows? They put the characters together that *they* thought should have ended up together, like—"

"Tony Stark and Steve Rogers," Killian said promptly.

"Absolutely not," Lewis retorted. "Bucky and Steve—"

"Bucky was an asshole," Killian said, and his shy smile told Lewis everything he ever wanted to know about how Killian had kept this part of himself separate. "And Pepper was a beard."

Lewis sputtered. "What a terrible thing to say about a female character! Pepper was her own superhero in the comic book series."

Killian looked sheepish. "I only watch the movies," he apologized. "Sorry."

"No worries. Most of the fanfic written is about the cinematic universe."

"Written?" Killian asked, and Lewis remembered all the books on his shelf. Action, adventure, romance....

"Whoo boy," Lewis told him, waving a wistful goodbye to his hopes for ending up in Killian's bed that night. "Let's get back to our computers. I have a big, beautiful world to introduce you to."

For a moment, Killian looked *really* excited about this, but then he seemed to remember himself. "We had plans tonight," he said. "I was going to eat some of your—what did you call it?"

"Barbecue mac and cheese," Lewis said happily.

"And we were going to watch a movie," Killian told him.

"Will we kiss some more?" Lewis goaded, not sure what he was hoping for.

"Perhaps," Killian said, but he bit his lip, and suddenly Lewis got it.

"But only kiss," he murmured. Killian had been an island too long to suddenly spring up a land bridge to another being. "It will be the highlight of my night," he reassured.

"Mine too." Killian winked at him and then went back to sweeping the bar, and Lewis resumed watching him.

He wanted to tell Killian a thousand things. He wanted to say that Lewis was pretty easy, and Killian didn't have to work this hard. He wanted to say that, hey, Lewis wasn't going anywhere—they might as well sleep in the same bed, right? *Or maybe I should mention that I'm completely in love with him already and having sex or not having sex isn't going to change much?*

He squashed down that last thing because he figured that might send Killian screaming in the other direction like his hair was on fire.

Because as he watched Killian resume his work—and resume talking to himself, once he forgot Lewis was watching—he realized that the reason Killian was taking this slow was because it was *important*. Lewis may have given lots of blowjobs, but Killian obviously hadn't. If Lewis wanted more than kisses—and at this point, after three days, Lewis would have married the guy if that had been on the table—then he had to let Killian set the pace.

Killian wanted more than kisses too, but if things went south, who wanted a hostile stranger stuck on his couch with a roomful of kittens they didn't ask for?

No, Killian wasn't a cold fish, but he did have a cooler, wiser head, and Lewis needed to abide by that.

But that didn't stop him from writing his *own* scenarios as he watched that lithe, rangy body practically dance around the room in rhythm to dialog from a movie that had never been seen.

FINALLY THEY walked Suzanne out to her car in the parking lot behind the bar and then walked home. After a couple of strides, Lewis snaked his hand into Killian's before they could both put their hands in their pockets, shivering against the cold, and Killian took it, giving Lewis another one of those devastating smiles.

"How come nobody wears, you know, hats, gloves, scarves around here?" Lewis asked.

Killian shrugged. "Dunno. I think because there's no snow. It still gets chilly. I mean, I've got hats and gloves and scarves, but it's like we tell ourselves if there's no snow, why do we need to dress for winter?"

Lewis laughed out loud at that, the sound ringing off the streets and the buildings along the block until he clapped his free hand over his mouth. "Maybe because our fingers are cold, you think?" he asked, when he'd gotten himself under control.

"Would you like to go through my winter gear?" Killian asked, still smiling.

"Yes. Yes. Thank you very much, that would be awesome." Lewis blew out a breath. "And while we're at it, I should maybe offer to buy Todd some hats and stuff. It doesn't get that cold in Houston."

Killian gave half a laugh. "He should have his Christmas present from last year," he said. "Remind him of it—I got him a scarf and a hat. I know the dude is tired, man, but he's going to catch his death."

Lewis remembered what Suzanne had said about how Killian was a really good guy, and he wanted to sob on the guy's chest and *then* take him to bed and put the lie to that cold-fish idea forever. Forget kissing him—forget *sleeping* with him. Even moving in seemed too passé at this moment. Lewis was going to *marry* this guy, just for taking care of Lewis's clueless brother.

But first things first.

Tonight was like a date.

Lewis had broken up with his faithless douchey college boyfriend right before spring break; hence the hookup with Todd's worthless, faithless douchey high school bestie. Fact was, he hadn't *had* a date in a lot of months, but this quiet moment in the darkness, Killian's warmth by his side, their breath steaming in the cold, the smells of woodsmoke and river in the air—this was almost the most romantic moment in Lewis's life.

"I have job interviews lined up," he told Killian. "If, you know, you could drive me, that would be…." He sighed.

"What?" Killian asked. "I'd be happy to drive you."

"Yeah, but it's pretty presumptuous of me, right? Hey, can I sleep on your couch? Let's take home kittens! Wait, how 'bout I ruin your life! Now give me a ride!"

Killian guffawed, but he didn't let go of Lewis's hand. "It *is* a rather unique approach to a new relationship," he conceded. "But so far my life is not ruined. Now tell me about the job offerings. I want to see how the other half lives."

Lewis frowned. "What other half?"

"You know, the half with the college degree."

"Well, apparently we make barbecue mac and cheese instead of pot roast with onion soup and potatoes. So far that's the only difference."

"I'm serious!" Killian told him, and oh my God, wasn't *that* a difference. Lewis remembered trying to explain to his ex how all his job searching in Houston was falling flat, only to have Richard tell him, "Well, dude—play it straight!" like that was a thing people could do.

Of course, it *was* a thing people could do. It had kept people alive for a very long time, but Lewis wasn't going to commit himself to not putting up a picture of his boyfriend or wearing rainbows in June for the rest of his life for health and dental. To save his life, yes. But his parents would obviously have him leave the state as opposed to *not* be Lewis, and he was going to keep interviewing in hope until he got hungry enough or his optimism died. He wasn't sure which would happen first.

But the point was Killian wanted to know. About Lewis. And suddenly Lewis was telling him *all* about it. He told him about the start-up company that could offer an amazing salary—but no bennies. He told him about the co-op that could offer bennies *and* salary, and possibly a window into the job of his dreams. And he told him about the holy-grail job from Folsom, the one with the *perfect* salary, bennies, stock options, promotional tiers, the works! And felt his heart stutter as Killian's expression went from *really* excited to perfectly blank.

"Oh," Killian murmured. "You'd have to find someplace in Folsom to live. That's a helluva commute."

"A lot of it is from home," Lewis told him. "In fact, I'd only have to go in one day a week, but I'm not locked into it. I, uh, looked at your calendar on the fridge—Monday and Tuesday are your days off, so I scheduled the interviews on Tuesday. I figured you could take me around, maybe. And we could, you know, hit a place to eat or something. It could be fun!"

Killian nodded slowly. "Yeah," he said, and suddenly his eyes got dreamy. "Granite Bay in the winter has these paths.... I mean, there's bike riders, and they're awfully pushy assholes who don't pay any entrance fees, but if you bring a change of clothes, there's some good walking paths out there." He paused and looked guilty. "Sorry. You'll be all excited about the jobs. We'll save the hiking plan for later."

Later? They could have a later? Then Killian groaned.

"Except for the kittens. How long can we leave everybody, you know, bouncing around the house?"

Lewis frowned. "Well, I think Moose and Squirrel are good as long as there's food and water. I think maybe we should... I don't know. Get a playpen for the younger kittens? I have no idea where—"

"No worries," Killian said. "The people across the hall have one. Michelle kept it for watching her niece, but her niece is way too big for it now. Yeah. That's a good idea. We leave mama in there, use the box as a bed—tilt it on its side, right?"

"Yeah!" Lewis said, excited. "We'll have to leave the heat on—"

"Not a problem," Killian agreed.

"But yeah," Lewis said. "Let's do the eating-out thing when I'm all dressed nice and shit but, uhm, I'll be around, you know?" He gave Killian a hopeful smile, and Killian laughed softly.

"I guess you will be," he said. "I'm looking forward to it."

Well, it wasn't an invitation to move in and get married, but it wasn't a boot in the ass, either. Lewis would take it!

LEWIS FED Killian barbecue mac and cheese as they watched *Love Actually* and discussed how Killian's usual Christmas décor might have to get a makeover because of the *many* furry bodies currently milling around on the floor in front of them.

Killian ate a little of the dish, and when Lewis asked anxiously if he liked it, Killian managed to look embarrassed. "Cheese gives me, uhm...." He grimaced, and Lewis got it. He'd just come from a dorm situation with a gazillion other guys—including Lewis. Everybody knew what cheese did to the unlucky ones.

"D'oh!" he said. "Here, let me put some barbecue in a sandwich. It'll be much better."

"No, Lewis. It's fine!"

But Lewis shook his head. "No, it's not. I ruined your perfectly good pork roast. Let me feed you something that won't gas us out of the house."

Killian let him, and after the sandwich was done, when Lewis would have bustled around and washed the plate, Killian stopped him.

"I'm tired," he said around a yawn. "I know you took a nap after I left, but... come here. Sit down next to me. Please? A date doesn't mean a clean house afterward. It, uhm, means cuddling."

Lewis stopped his frenetic activity, his "Let's prove to Killian that I'm useful *and* adorable," and took a breath.

"Yeah?" he asked softly. "Cuddling?"

"Please."

And, like a date, Lewis hadn't had cuddling in too long a time. Killian was a champion cuddler. He drew Lewis back against his chest, wrapped his arm around his waist, and allowed himself to sink into the couch while Lewis sank into him. For a moment there was just warmth, the strength of that arm wrapped around him, and that joyous, heartbreaking movie reminding them that it was Christmas, and if you couldn't say what you meant at Christmas, when could you?

Lewis felt the tension leave his body, the need to prove to Killian that he was worth it, worth all the activity, worth the aggravation, and for the moment there was just Killian, who was *definitely* worth the effort.

As the credits wound down, Killian nuzzled his temple, and Lewis turned in his arms to accept the kiss.

For a few breaths, it was sweetness, tenderness, their lips moving together in the dark, their hands moving over each other's bodies, exploring.

Lewis wanted to write poetry about the silk of Killian's skin under his palms, the corrugation of his ribs, the soft exhalation he made when Lewis's thumb brushed a nipple.

The gentle gasp he made when Lewis took it into his mouth.

Killian's arms tightened around his shoulders, and his hips bucked upward, grinding into Lewis's stomach as he slid down Killian's body on the couch.

"Lewis…," Killian breathed, and Lewis wasn't sure if he meant to slow him down or urge him on, but suddenly Lewis wanted Killian in a way that defied prudence—defied *logic*.

He wanted Killian inside him, wanted Killian's mark somewhere on his body so everybody would know that Lewis had come and staked his claim. Here was a perfectly great man, just *living his life*, and nobody had snapped that up? Made him think he was cold and imperfect when he was spreading his feet on the couch and lifting his hips as Lewis stripped off his jeans, his need blazing from every line of his body?

Lewis wanted him. Lewis wanted him *for good*. Lewis placed taunting kisses on the inside of Killian's thighs, nibbling to hear him whimper. He sucked in the soft skin of Killian's ridged abdomen, knowing he was leaving a mark on the pale oasis but not caring—this was *his*, dammit, and marking it made it so. Then he made his way to Killian's cock, wishing he could gush about it because it did *not* disappoint.

He *did* make a hum of hunger in his throat as he licked it, base to tip, and listened to Killian's sounds as he came undone. Killian dragged his fingers through Lewis's hair, tightening his grip as Lewis, using skills learned from all those encounters that didn't matter on this one person who did, sucked Killian into his mouth and proceeded to drive Killian wild.

Long, glorious minutes passed in which Lewis used his fist around the base and his mouth around the head, teasing with his tongue, edging ever so gently with his teeth, and using his stomach and neck muscles to bob rhythmically until he heard the sounds of the man underneath him trying not to cry out in ecstasy.

Lewis drove his head down until Killian filled the back of his throat, and then he swallowed, milking the tip with the motion.

Killian's cry of release, the way his fingers massaged Lewis's scalp, the way his body arched up into Lewis's mouth without self-consciousness, without fear—all of it plunged Lewis right over the edge of a precipice he hadn't known had been at his feet. With a groan he swallowed Killian's come, welcoming the bitterness even as his own hips spasmed and he—dammit—got one of two pairs of jeans dirty when it should have had another three days before it needed to be washed.

The streaming service had bumped the film to *The Holiday,* starring Jack Black and Cameron Diaz, in the background while Lewis rested his head against Killian's naked thigh and tried to pull the scrambled pieces of his mind back between his ears.

"Sorry," Killian gasped.

"Don't you dare," Lewis mumbled. "Don't you dare apologize for that." He lifted his head to see Killian's expression, wiping his mouth with the back of his hand as he did so. "Do you know how long it's been since I came in my pants?"

Killian looked horrified. "I'm so sorry!" he said, scrambling to sit up.

"The hell you say!" Lewis laughed, throwing himself into Killian's arms before he could run away in embarrassment. "Oh my God. *Killian.* That was *amazing.* I... I *loved* doing that. I can't wait to do it again." He chuckled to himself, resting his head on Killian's chest. "I have *never* enjoyed giving a blowjob like that. I was always, 'Okay, gotta look at that one-eyed bastard and do the thing, 'cause that's what you do with sex.' But not with you. I *loved* that."

Killian gave a weak chuckle of his own, palming Lewis's head against his chest. "I, uhm, obviously loved it too," he said. "Just... you know. I enjoy doing that too."

Lewis grinned up at him. "Really?"

"Yes, really! My God, Lewis, who did you hook up with in school? Were they all bastards?"

Lewis shook his head. "I don't remember. None of them were you."

Killian laughed softly and dropped a kiss on the crown of his head. Languidly, like he was suddenly too tired to move, he reached out for the remote and turned the television off.

"We should go to bed," he mumbled.

Lewis lifted his head. "Are you going to make me sleep on the couch?" he asked suspiciously.

"No," Killian whispered, and in the soft lamplight of the room, his eyes seemed to glint. "I'm weak. I'd love to wake up next to you."

"Awesome." Lewis preened for a moment before he sighed. "But first, I've gotta go…." He made a vague gesture to his body below the waist.

"C'mon." Killian slid out from under him and stood, carefully avoiding Moose and Squirrel, who had fallen asleep around them on the couch. "Let's get cleaned up for bed."

LIKE IT WAS NORMAL

KILLIAN WOKE up slowly, aware of the lean body backed into his and the slow, even breath sounds that had lulled him to sleep the night before. The sun came in, slivered by the blinds and diluted by the curtains, but still illuminating dust motes into fairy dazzle as it crisscrossed the room.

A single beam landed on Lewis's cheek, barely touching his blond eyelashes and cheerfully shaggy hair.

Moose was perched in the small of Killian's back, and Squirrel was behind his knees, and for a moment, Killian wondered how he'd get out of bed to pee, when Lewis spoke up, his chest rising and falling under Killian's arm.

"One lousy time you get to sleep in, and you're watching me as I sleep?"

If it hadn't been for the full bladder, Killian would have clenched him so tightly to his chest, neither of them could breathe.

But first things first. "Must pee," he squeaked, and Lewis chuckled.

"Kittens at your back?"

"I'm so afraid I'm going to squish them," Killian confessed.

"I'll get up to let you out, but on one condition."

Killian shifted his hips uncomfortably. He didn't want to whine, but, well, things were getting dire. "Name it."

"You have to climb back in with me and sleep for another hour," Lewis mumbled, rolling out of bed quickly. "Remember, you promised."

Killian ran to the toilet. Behind him, he could hear Lewis admonishing the cats. "Look, you furry freeloaders, you're taking up half the bed—and you're taking advantage of him. Move. Yes, you. Over…. Over… okay. Good. Now *I'll* sleep in the middle. Assholes. Good."

By the time Killian had washed his hands and brushed his teeth, Lewis *had* rolled to the middle, with his back facing toward Killian in a blatant invitation to spoon him some more. Killian practically danced back under the covers, knowing the thermostat would turn on at nine and perfectly content to let Lewis have his way until then. He clutched Lewis to his chest, so pleased when Lewis snuggled back he almost giggled. Feeling possessive and needy, he slid his hand under Lewis's shirt so he could stroke the soft skin of Lewis's stomach as he fell asleep.

Lewis laced their fingers together. "That had better be a promise," he mumbled. "But later. When we're awake. I want more."

A smile stretched Killian's cheeks even as his eyes fluttered closed. "Me too," he mumbled. He would dream of Lewis's smooth skin under his palms and of all the things they could do together in the sunlight.

LEWIS'S STOMACH gurgling under his palm woke him up next, and he sighed.

"What?" Lewis asked, sounding like he'd been awake for a little while. "What was that sigh?"

"You're hungry," Killian rumbled, nuzzling the back of his neck. "I should feed you before I ravish you."

"But there *will* be ravishing?" Lewis asked anxiously. With some effort—probably not to squash the kittens, he rolled over in Killian's arms. "I am *dying* to be ravished, but yeah, you're right." His stomach gurgled again. "There's an order to things." He gave an abashed smile. "My, uh, digestion is still working on Texas time, and in Texas, I, uh, have certain duties to perform...."

Killian laughed and—thanking his foresight with the toothbrush the last time he'd gotten up—kissed Lewis soundly.

Lewis kissed him back, and Killian fell into the kiss happily, only ending it when Lewis's stomach growled again.

Killian got out of bed and let Lewis head for the bathroom. As soon as Lewis was gone, he pulled the comforter up to the pillows, much to the dismay of Moose and Squirrel, who thought that was something *they* should have a say about.

What followed was a rather wonderful breathless round of kitten pinball wherein one of them would rush to attack his hand, and he'd push him back, and then he'd run to the edge of the bed to plan his next attack while the other kitten took advantage of the pause to take his turn to rush.

By the time Lewis came out of the bathroom, both of the kittens had flounced off, winded, to curl up on the edge of the bed and lick their paws, feigning indifference.

Lewis wrapped his arms around Killian's waist and dug his pointed chin into Killian's shoulder. "So," he murmured. "Your day off. I managed to fill tomorrow up, but what were your plans for today?"

Killian turned to take his mouth, noting with a smile that Lewis had brushed his teeth too. Oh, this felt good. Lewis was so easy to kiss, easy to touch, easy to pull into his arms. Killian could live with walking across the apartment just to kiss him.

They pulled back, and Killian thought longingly of the plan to ravish him all day but realized they had some other things to do first.

"Well, I'd love to do more of this," he murmured, rubbing noses, pleased when Lewis seemed to get it counted as a kiss but still let Killian talk. "But I've got a few things I was going to do today, including decorate the apartment." He frowned. "I think, uhm, given all of the…." In the pause they could both hear the boxed kittens mewing. "New company," he said diplomatically, "I should probably, uhm, not get a tree. I usually get a little one and put it up on a card table, but…."

"Moose and Squirrel would see that as a challenge," Lewis said seriously.

"The possible devastation numbs the mind," Killian confirmed. "I was thinking maybe stopping at a tree place and getting some boughs—maybe making a wreath and putting it up on the wall." He glanced around his apartment. "In a place nowhere near a television or, uhm, tchotchkes or, you know, accessible by human beings or animals."

Lewis's entire body vibrated with his chuckle, and Killian shivered deliciously. He got to hold all that joy. How awesome was *that*.

"So is that first?" Lewis asked, as excited as a kid.

Killian shook his head. "No. Actually I need to start the warm clothing drive. First I check with the local charities to see what they need most, and then I set up donation boxes at the local businesses. I need to make signs and drop off the boxes and stuff. I, uh…." He gave a hopeful smile. "I, uhm, was thinking you'd want to help?"

"Hell yeah!" Lewis told him. "I think that's the coolest thing ever!"

Killian ducked his head. "Seriously?"

"Yes, seriously!" Lewis tilted his head back far enough to hit him with a megawatt grin. "That's, like, hero shit. I mean, I know I'm freeloading on your… uhm—" He gave Killian a sly look. "—couch," he said, "but I still know how lucky I am."

Killian nuzzled his ear. "It's not my couch anymore," he murmured.

"Thank God," Lewis said passionately, and then he took Killian's mouth in a kiss that left Killian's stomach quivering and started a low burn in the place underneath.

Finally they pulled away, and Lewis placed one last kiss on his cheek. "You shower, I'll make breakfast."

Killian shook his head. "Nope. I figured we'd eat at Nicky and Lia's bistro. You shower first, and I'll knock on Michelle's place next door to see if we can get that porta crib." The mew, mew, mew from the cardboard box had reached a new decibel level. "Those guys really need more room."

Lewis laughed a little. "You know, my family has had cats and dogs my entire life, and you say you're a newbie."

"I am!" Killian protested, surprised. It had never occurred to him that he'd enjoy a kitten or want a kitten or love… a kitten. "It's just, you know. Living things. They need space and sunshine and clean water and food."

"And love," Lewis said gently, nodding.

Killian nodded back, feeling like he was signing a contract, though he wasn't sure for what. "Yeah," he said, but Lewis got that look on his face, the one that said he knew and eventually Killian would too.

"You're good at it," Lewis said gently. "You should keep doing it."

Killian chuckled. "Moose and Squirrel aren't going anywhere soon," he said, and Lewis kissed his cheek again.

"Neither am I," he said. "I mean, except for the bathroom. Let's move it. I'm starving!"

MICHELLE WAS one of the tiniest women Killian had ever met. She stood four feet, ten inches in her stocking feet, and she often threatened to tease her natural hair into a halo to add another six inches to her height. Michelle's boyfriend, who was five feet, seven inches of good-humored ginger, asked her politely not to because he was pretty sure he'd have hair tickling his nose every time they hugged, and she obliged, usually settling for a scrunchie to keep it out of her way.

She worked as a special education teacher in one of the nearby middle schools and had sworn devoutly that she was never having children of her own. Since Kevin adored her—and also taught English at a neighboring high school—he was fine with that.

Both of them were *delighted* to get rid of the playpen.

"But what do you want it for?" Michelle asked, watching as Kevin got it out of the top of their closet. He was on a step stool—she never would have reached it.

Killian found himself looking over his shoulder, afraid that their super would appear like a magician in a puff of smoke. "Kittens," he whispered. "Somebody dumped an *entire box* of kittens on our doorstep, and we're going to get them shots and find them homes, but in the meantime…."

"It would be nice not to step on the little carpet fleas," Michelle said with a solid nod. "Understood. Wait." Her amazing brown eyes sharpened in her fine-boned face. "Our? Who is the we in our? Kevin, did you know Killian is dating again? Did Killian start dating again and not tell us?"

Killian scrubbed at his beard stubble, sort of wishing he'd gotten his shower and shave before he'd gone across the hallway to knock on their door.

"He, uhm…."

"No, babe." Kevin stepped down from the stool, gripping the folded-up playpen by the handles. "In fact, the only new person in the complex that I know of is…." His eyebrows lifted. "Todd's little brother? Dude, are you hooking up with Todd's little brother?"

Killian tried to take the fancy pop-up porta crib/playpen thing from Kevin, but he held it back.

"No, dude," Kevin said seriously. "You're gonna need some help with this."

"Absolutely," Michelle said. "We need to set this up."

"You said that with a straight face," Killian accused, surprised by their blatant nosiness. "Don't you guys have… you know. Work to go to? Kids? That sort of thing?"

"It's a district-wide in-service day," Kevin said, wrinkling his nose. "In December. Our admin is so dumb, they deserve for us all to show up late, with our best coffee and doughnuts."

Michelle's expression got dreamy. "Doughnuts," she said on a sigh. "Can we stop for some on the way, Kev?"

"Yeah, babe." Kevin kissed the top of her head, which was set in tiny braids. "But first—"

"Let's go meet Todd's little brother." Michelle gave Killian a brilliant smile. "The man who apparently warmed the cockles of Killian's cockles."

"*That*," Killian sputtered, "is a little bit personal!"

"Well yeah, Killian," Michelle retorted. "But that's because you don't give us a whole lot of personal to work with. Now come on. We have to set this monster up and then go get doughnuts."

Lewis was, thank God, dressed and shaved when Killian let Kevin and Michelle into the front room.

He grinned at both of them, showing them the place behind the couch that they'd cleared, making the tiny living room even tinier but still giving Killian access to his computer area. "Will it fit?" he asked anxiously, picking up the box of kittens. "I've got an extra litter box ready. I hope you're okay with, you know, never using this thing for people again."

"Oh yeah, dude," Kevin said. "I understand the entire baby merchandise *gig* is built on a two-year cycle. So two years after you get a crib or a car seat or whatever, they come up with a better one, and the one you thought was space-age is suddenly passe. Or worse, they discovered something horrible about it, and they've all been recalled. So yeah, if Michelle's sister has another ankle-biter, we're getting another porta-pen-play-crib or whatever. But this one's a trip. Wanna see how it's assembled?"

With that Kevin unwrapped what looked like a nylon-coated board that had been acting as a case from around a metal framework that was connected by nylon panels, with an extra one sewn in as the floor. He handed the case to Killian and set the framework on the ground, tugging each of the corners out until it formed a four-sided box with a tent in the middle where the framework hadn't popped into place, making all the nylon taut so the structure had sides and a floor. Then he lifted his tiny girlfriend up by the waist, and she swung her legs forward and pushed one foot down in the center.

With an audible *whop*, the thing was set up, and Kevin swung Michelle back out, set her on the floor, and then took the "case" from

Killian and spread it out on the bottom the playpen, making sure the Velcro tabs on the bottom aligned so it would stay put.

Killian and Lewis stared at them, wide-eyed.

"Yeah," Lewis said, "but if we have to put it together again, where are we going to get another tiny Black woman to make the center thing do that?"

Michelle grinned at him. "I'm a special feature," she told him proudly. "But you or Killian are tall enough to reach over the side. Kev and I developed this method after I fell in once. Embarrassing, trust me."

"I was going to leave her in there," Kevin said, his lips twitching. Michelle socked him gently in the arm.

"Now put the kittens in!" Michelle said. "I want to see them!"

"Here," Lewis told her. "You go ahead and put them in the playpen, and I'll go get the stuff." He frowned. "Where are Moose and Squirrel?"

"Check the bedroom," Killian told him. "They were asleep on the bed when I left."

"Wait," Michelle said, picking out the ginger kitten and cooing at it. "Look, Kev—a soulless ginger. Just like you."

"And just like that, you fell in love," Kevin said proudly, reaching over her shoulder to stroke its little head. "Who else do we have in there?"

"Well, mama got busy," she murmured, giving him the ginger kitten and setting the box down to pull out the black kitten and the tiger-striped. The black kitten leaned his head on her shoulder and started patting her neck with his little paw, and she gave Kevin a limpid look. "Okay, now. This one is really ingratiating. I like that in a minion."

Kevin laughed softly and took the tiger-stripe from her hand. Tiger-stripe yawned and fell asleep again, legs dangling limply from his palm.

"You are no fun at all," Kevin accused, and since the ginger was trying to tunnel into his hoodie pocket, Killian had to agree. Kevin put both his kittens into the playpen and then reached out for the little black one and lifted her up to his face to nuzzle.

The black kitten bit his nose, and before he could yelp, she started to lick it.

"This is our kitten," he said, enchanted.

"I don't know," Michelle murmured. "See this gray one? He's judging me. He's terminally cool."

"Yeah, but honey, this one bit me. I gotta admit, the masochistic side of me is just really impressed."

"We are *not* going black and ginger," she said, flat eyed, and he grinned.

"But think of the jokes we could make at parties," he told her, nodding manically.

"But look at him!" She held up the gray one. "Terminally cool." The little gray kitten held out a magnanimous paw, and Kevin shook it soberly.

"I think we'll have to kitten-sit," he told Killian. "Or at least visit for movie night and play with all of them. You know. To see."

While they'd been talking, Lewis had bustled in and out, first with a towel, which he put in the bottom of the pen in the corner with the two puzzled kittens, who wanted to go back to sleep apparently, and then with a small water dispenser. The bowl was shallow, and the little tank let water out as the bowl emptied. Killian had thought it was an odd expense when Lewis bought it, but now, thinking about the kittens in the playpen and now much damage they could do to a full bowl of water while nobody was there to supervise, he highly approved.

Then he brought in a food bowl with a fresh cake of pâté in it, and then a small cardboard litter box, which he put in the corner farthest away from the food. He paused for a moment when he came back and picked up the box the kittens had come in. With a soft little murmur, he pulled out the exhausted mama cat and put her in the corner with her babies, on top of the old towels. The room itself was warm and welcoming, and the mother cat started looking around, her first real attempt at exploration besides her few trips to the litter box and the food bowls. Lewis spent a tender moment stroking the poor thing's whiskers and telling her she was a great mother and she'd get a chance to rest soon before looking up at Kevin and Michelle.

"They're not weaned yet," he said apologetically. "But I'd love to have a movie night this week. Killian and I have no idea how we're going to find homes for all five of them. Feel free to call dibs."

Michelle blinked and set the gray kitten down reluctantly. Killian was putting money down on Michelle getting her way and going home with that one. "You and Killian?" she asked, batting those big brown eyes at him.

Lewis grinned, absolutely unapologetic. "Yup," he said. "Killian let me sleep on his couch."

Michelle cast Killian an unfriendly look. "Couch?" she asked, arching her eyebrow.

Killian could feel his face heat. "I, uhm…." He smiled apologetically. "You know, I need to shower. I promised Lewis I'd take him to the café for coffee and breakfast and—"

Kevin sighed and set his kitten in the pen. "And we need to leave if we're stopping for doughnuts," he said regretfully. He turned his attention back to Killian. "But don't think we're not coming back tomorrow night on your day off."

"Lewis is job hunting all tomorrow," Killian said, thinking about the date he'd planned.

"Then tomorrow night it is," Michelle told him. "Six o'clock. We'll bring pizza. You call Nicky and Lia, and feel free to invite Todd and your boss, if she's off. There are Christmas movies we need to see and kittens we need to place, and I know you're starting the mitten drive today, so I need to tell you what my kids need so you can put a bug in people's ears. And you and me need to have a discussion about—" She scowled at Lewis. "—the couch."

Twin flags of color appeared in Lewis's cheeks. "I, uh, didn't sleep on the couch last night," he supplied. "If that, uh, helps."

"I'll tell you tomorrow," Michelle said, as though Lewis's blush—and disclosure—meant she had more investigation to do. "What do you like on your pizza?"

Lewis smiled dreamily. "Everything," he told them.

"Good man," Kevin said. "Killian and I get feta and spinach so we don't have to share. See you tomorrow."

And with that, the two of them let themselves out, leaving Killian feeling like he'd gotten smacked by a truck.

"Wow," Lewis said into the sudden silence.

"I had plans," Killian mumbled, wondering how that date he'd envisioned could have gone so wrong. "We were going to be dressed up. I was going to take you to a nice place to eat—"

Lewis grinned. "That's okay," he said. "I take it you guys do movie nights a lot?"

"About once a month," Killian said. "She's right—we're due. I haven't done my Christmas shopping yet, and I need to find out what everyone needs."

Lewis snorted. "I think it's perfectly obvious that everyone's getting a kitten!"

Killian gave a weak chuckle. "Well, that's fortunate. It seems we have kittens to spare." His own stomach gave a rumble. "Now let's get a move on. You're not the only one who's starving."

LIA WAITED on them first, bringing hot chocolate and omelets and absolutely decadent spiced potatoes with sausage while keeping up a nonstop monologue about Boris and Natasha and how the two cats were fitting right in with her mother. When she finally paused for breath, she said, "Yeah, you guys really are lifesavers." She had sturdy features— almond-shaped brown eyes in a pale-skinned face, sloped cheekbones, a fearless spate of freckles, as well as wavy brown hair that she kept back in a loose ponytail as she worked—and her earnestness was a nice foil for Nicky's rather sudden jumps to judgment. "It's too bad you got a whole other box of kittens after you got rid of Boris and Natasha. What are you going to do?"

"Apparently have a movie night with Michelle and Kevin tomorrow," Killian said, sounding as bemused as he felt. "Like, I don't know how it happened, but Michelle loaned me her playpen and suddenly—"

"We're having a movie and kitten night," Lia agreed, like it made perfect sense. "Who's bringing what?"

"They're bringing pizza," Lewis said.

"Then we'll bring a big Greek salad," she said delightedly. "Perfect! Is Suzanne coming?"

"I was going to invite her when I dropped off the mitten box," Killian admitted. It was a good thing he'd mapped his progress through the neighborhood a week ago, or he'd be too scattered to do either thing—plan for the kittens or plan for the mittens—with any efficacy.

"Good. Make her bring dessert. You bring drinks—soda, wine, you know the drill."

Killian felt as though he had no choice. He saluted. "Will do."

She left, and Lewis shook his head.

"What?" Killian asked, digging into the dreamy, cheesy, mushroomy, oniony feta omelet. "What is that look?"

"You have a lot of friends," Lewis said.

"Isn't that a good thing?" Killian asked, because Lewis had made it sound like it wasn't.

"Why no boyfriends?"

Killian concentrated on his potatoes. "I told you. I'm... uhm... reserved."

"Afraid," Lewis said softly.

"I lack passion," Killian said, popping a potato into his mouth and avoiding Lewis's eyes.

Lewis's low, filthy chuckle almost made him cough it out. "Not from last night's standpoint."

Killian took a hasty sip of water and then went to work on his omelet. Lewis waited until he was done with his bite before saying, "Killian, look at me."

Killian met his eyes, feeling like a child who was afraid of punishment. "What?" he asked.

"You *really* are a great guy," Lewis said softly. "I just want you to know that. I have *zero* intention of going back to the couch."

Killian gave him a small smile. "Good," he said, his stomach warming.

"We're going to have a good day," Lewis said with confidence. "Trust me. You'll never want to run errands without me after this. I'll grow on you, like fungus."

Killian laughed like he was supposed to, because it was way too early to tell Lewis that his job was done. Killian was already attached. He was looking forward to the next two days like he'd been looking forward to that Hawaiian vacation he hadn't been able to save for.

Instead he forked a mushroom, dripping with feta and butter, off his plate and popped it into his mouth. "So happens," he said mildly, "I like fungus."

Lewis's grin had a certain catlike cant to it, and Killian wondered for the millionth time how he'd never known he liked cats.

AS THE KITTEN GROWS

LEWIS LEANED back against Killian's lean body on the couch as Killian indulged in his apparent love of dramadies on television.

"Oh look," Lewis murmured. "Another show that makes me laugh, cry, and learn something about myself."

Killian chuckled in his ear. "Why? Do you have the urge to watch something blow up?"

Lewis arched his back lazily, knowing exactly where he was in the frame of Killian's thighs and what that movement would do to him.

"Nope," he purred.

Killian gasped—if he hadn't been nuzzling Lewis's temple, Lewis wouldn't have heard it—and Lewis smiled. Message delivered.

Killian slid his hand under Lewis's T-shirt and hoodie, stroking Lewis's flat tummy and his happy trail.

Which made everything in Lewis's body *very* happy.

"Are you trying to tell me something?" Killian asked, sounding suspicious.

"God, I hope so," Lewis said softly. Communication was important in long-term relationships, and Lewis had decided that's what he was aiming for pretty much the moment Killian had picked up his first kitten.

Killian's hand moved up, spanning Lewis's chest, his fingers lightly teasing a nipple.

Lewis sucked in his breath as the nipple peaked, a nerve-center lightning rod for all his pent-up desire.

"Aren't you sleepy?" Killian asked, and at first Lewis thought he was teasing, and then he realized the hand had stopped, and he was being absolutely serious.

Well, it was a fair question. Their day had been *incredibly* busy. They'd driven to the grocery store to collect boxes that one of Killian's customers had saved for him and then driven to FedEx to pick up colorful posters that Killian had apparently ordered the week before.

What followed after that was a walking tour of the ten-block radius surrounding Killian's apartment, hitting business after business that either Killian frequented or that had an employee who frequented Catches. Killian and Lewis pinned, duct taped, or clipped the signs proclaiming a coat and outerwear drive for the local homeless shelter, children's clothes in especially high demand, and Killian set a decorated peanut butter jar on the counter. He'd been keeping the jars—all of them plastic and well cleaned—in his trunk. He'd had Michelle's students decorate labels for the front and had put a computer-generated label with the cause and the sponsor on the other side, explaining what monetary donations would go toward and giving a phone number to contact for more information. Each destination got one of these too, and Lewis's admiration for Killian grew and grew and grew.

How was it this man had evaded capture, containment, and domestication?

As Lewis watched Killian smile at his various business contacts, remembering the names of boyfriends, girlfriends, children, and parents, his chest grew warmer and warmer and warmer. Had Killian called himself a cold fish? Really? Who had told him he was cold?

No, seriously. Lewis wanted to know. He wasn't afraid of a little bloodshed, and he needed to take somebody out.

But first he wanted to take all of that warmth, all of that *incendiary heat*, for himself.

When they'd finally gotten back to the apartment, Killian busied himself with kitten care while Lewis busied himself with dinner. It wasn't that he didn't *like* Killian's cooking, but there were things like hot sauce, garlic, and curry that he thought Killian might need educating about. For his part, Killian didn't seem to object to anything Lewis plated up for him—as long as it didn't have cheese.

Fair trade, Lewis thought, adding some Sriracha he'd bought at the local bodega to fried potatoes and onions. He could live without cheese if Killian let Lewis train his taste buds up to acceptable levels.

By the time Lewis had two bowls of crispy potatoes with a little bit of leftover barbecue on the side, Killian was sitting on the couch, holding Moose to his chest and scratching Squirrel under his chin as the cat perched on the back of the couch and regarded him with interest.

"Kitchen or living room?"

Killian had yawned, and living room it had been.

They'd talked through dinner, and apparently revived by the need for multiple glasses of water and finally one of lactose-free milk, Killian had cleaned the kitchen while Lewis found something on TV.

Which was fine.

TV, a few cookies for dessert, some more TV, and now Lewis wanted his *real* dessert.

The one he'd been craving all day, every time he'd seen Killian's eyes crinkle or that lean smile on his lips or that sweet incline to his head when he was listening to somebody tell him about their life.

It was like being a bartender was a *calling*. He took that kindness, that ability to listen, that firmness about facing your limitations, and applied it to everybody he met. But Lewis had never seen him take his turn. He wanted dessert—so very, very much, yes he did—but more than that.

He wanted the aftermath, the talking time, that moment when they were skin-to-skin and deeply embedded in each other's souls and telling their secrets.

Lewis wanted Killian to talk to *him*.

He wanted to hear about *Killian's* day, *Killian's* troubles.

Killian's heart.

But first… ooh, first, he needed. He'd spent all day helping Killian achieve good works, and Lewis wanted his reward.

With a happy little sigh, Lewis rippled his body against Killian's again, shivering when he felt the unmistakable reaction through Killian's worn-soft jeans.

"I," he said, taking Killian's hand and sliding it down his stomach toward the waistband of his own jeans, "am *not* tired."

Killian tilted his head sideways and nuzzled his neck. "Good," he murmured, pushing the placket of his jeans against Lewis's backside. "Any requests?"

Lewis bucked against him again. "Do suggestions count?"

Killian's low rumble made him, if anything, needier. "They do tend to speed up the process," he said, sliding his fingertips lower, teasing the waistband of Lewis's briefs now. "But I think I could have guessed."

"Good." Lewis arched up, trying to get contact between his burgeoning erection and Killian's bare skin. "I *am* a type."

Killian's laughter tickled Lewis's ear, but only in the barest, most erotic way. Lewis let out a tortured breath and did a slow, careful roll so he and Killian were face-to-face.

Lewis captured his mouth, open and carnal and unapologetic, and Killian answered, his hands cruising Lewis's back and backside under his clothes. Lewis pulled back and looked Killian in the eyes.

"If we go to the bedroom and do this deliberately, are you going to get weird?"

Killian's slow smile was the best reward for his boldness he could have asked for. "I don't have accidental sex," he murmured. "Is that a thing that's happened to you? You wake up with someone and say, 'Oops! Sorry! I thought this was the cloakroom'?"

Lewis didn't laugh. "No. But I have woken up with people and thought, 'That was neither pleasant nor emotionally useful.' I want to wake up with you and think, 'I rocked his world, and I was important to him.'"

He heard Killian's gulp. "You've already rocked my world," Killian confessed. "You *are* important to me."

Lewis smiled, but even *he* knew his eyes were heavy-lidded, and the expression was sultry. "We're gonna be fine."

With that he slid off of Killian's lap and the couch and made his way to the bedroom, perfectly okay with Killian lingering to shut off the lights and check the door. By the time Killian looked in on the kittens and made sure Moose and Squirrel were fast asleep on the couch, Lewis had brushed his teeth, undressed, rinsed all his important places with a washcloth, and slid under the blankets.

Killian arched his eyebrows at Lewis's prepared, naked self, but Lewis had been listening. He knew Killian would be minty fresh and sparkly clean when he undressed, because that was the beauty of deliberate sex. You took the time to do nice things to your body for the person who was going to get *really close* to it and hopefully to make them feel good when you did it.

To Lewis's amusement, Killian turned off the lights before undressing, but there was ambient light coming through the blinds from the soda lamp at the back of the complex.

"I can see you," Lewis murmured, turning to his side and resting his head on his hand.

Killian ducked his head, obviously embarrassed. "We could have just given each other hand jobs on the couch and slunk off to our corners," he threatened.

"Not on your life." Lewis was deadly serious about this. "I know you think you get it, but you don't. Killian, I saw you walking in the hallway last week and thought, 'Please, God, let him be gay… and single… but please. *Pretty please.*' And hallelujah, pass the potatoes, you *were*. And then you *liked me*. Only an idiot burns a wagyu steak and then slathers it with ketchup. I'm gonna *savor* you, dammit!"

While Lewis talked, he watched as Killian's pale skin was revealed. Chest first, defined and wider than it seemed under his customary black T-shirt, with the long abdominal muscles of someone who *worked* more than worked out. He had a patch of curly black hair between his nipples, and a bold happy trail that Lewis had noticed the night before. Then the slim hips and wiry legs of a very active man, and if Lewis hadn't been trying to coax that fineness into bed with him, he would have whistled in appreciation.

He still might, when he could catch his breath.

Then Killian slid in next to him, and suddenly he thought he might *never* catch his breath.

"I, uh, turned the heat up a degree or two," Killian promised. "So, uh…." Gently he tugged the blanket down, his face lighting up when he could see *Lewis*, naked and vulnerable, open to Killian's perusal.

Killian started by kissing his shoulder, and then moved down to his chest, and Lewis caught his breath. "That's it?" he breathed, his fingers threading through Killian's loose silky hair. "You're going to take me over and—ahh…."

Killian's mouth on his nipple was absolutely everything Lewis had been led to believe. He shuddered, his entire body unfurling as he spread his legs and gave himself over to Killian's hands, his mouth taking over Lewis's body.

He could not have chosen a better pilot.

Killian paid the same exquisite attention to detail while making love that he paid while cleaning the brass in Catches or running the clothing drive for the homeless shelter. He didn't just suckle Lewis's nipple, he also ran his hand across Lewis's stomach, over his thighs, down the insides of Lewis's knees.

The stimulation coupled with the teasing turned Lewis into a shameless, greedy, slutty bottom, and he wasn't proud of the whimpers he made as he arched his hips in invitation, but he wasn't going to silence them either.

Killian moved to his other nipple, but not before murmuring, "You wanted something?" just loud enough for Lewis to hear.

"Ple—ease!" Lewis begged, reaching down to clasp Killian's hand.

Killian laced their fingers together, and then—oh Lord—started fondling Lewis's cock with their laced hands.

The combination of his own fingers and Killian's traveling his flesh blew his mind.

"Ah! God!" He tried to tighten his grip, but Killian wouldn't let him. Instead they stroked, they skittered, they danced around his shaft, sometimes stroking his head, sometimes gently skating around his balls. "Killian," he sobbed, his entire body shuddering. "Please!"

"Please what?" Killian murmured, releasing his nipple, which tingled from the attention, begging for more.

"Please suck my cock," Lewis begged. "Please—oh God—oh—*yes*!"

Killian's mouth, sweeping down his shaft, was everything heaven promised but life seldom delivered.

He tightened his lips at the base and then sucked hard, pulling his head back as Lewis saw stars in an effort not to come.

Then Killian did it again… and again… and then, using a little bit of spit, he snuck his finger into Lewis's cleft and grazed it—just grazed it, his finger slipping into the indentation if not actually penetrating, and that was it. Lewis's vision exploded into stars, and his body shot light from his fingertips as he launched into orgasm, pouring into Killian's mouth.

Lewis sank into the mattress, fingers moving restlessly in Killian's silky hair, his body shaking in comedown and grateful for the contact.

Killian cleaned his cock off with that sinful mouth, but more… he was doing more. He was kissing Lewis's thighs, fingering his cleft again, gently massaging his balls. Lewis's legs fell open as his arousal began to permeate his postorgasmic haze.

"Not yet," he mumbled, tugging on Killian's head. Killian looked up, traces of ejaculate tracking from the corners of his mouth, and Lewis shuddered. "Never mind," he said clearly. "Carry on."

God, if there was ever a vision of debauchery in Lewis's fantasies, it was Killian's face between his legs, mouth dripping come. Killian's slickened finger penetrated him, and he took a breath, stomach muscles fluttering, as he began to tremble all over again.

"Whoa-my-God," he managed. "Oh wow—Killian—what—"

Two fingers and he would have come off the bed, but he was grabbing his knees instead, arching his hips, making his body accessible, begging.

Killian pulled away, and Lewis must have lost time because he hadn't seen where the lubricant had come from, and the condom was a surprise too. Lewis would have objected—he knew *he* was negative, and he was pretty sure Killian was too—but Killian had smoothed on the lubricant and placed himself at Lewis's entrance before he could even form the words.

And then he breached Lewis's entrance, and words were not a thing.

Lewis had always loved to bottom—he loved letting go of himself and riding a lover's thrusts to oblivion—but this was a whole different level. He had never been *so* aware of who was inside him, who was pleasuring him, who was thrusting into him while kissing Lewis's forehead, his chin, his mouth.

Lewis wrapped his legs around Killian's hips so he could dig his fingers into those muscled shoulders and hold on—oh please, hold on—stay on this earth, feel every kiss, every drop of sweat, every millimeter.

But nobody could hold on forever. Killian kept pounding, driving Lewis higher, higher all over again, every burst of pleasure so acute it hurt, so necessary Lewis found himself chanting, "Please, please, please, please...." Needing what was coming, needing his body to explode, needing the world to shift until—oh God!

Killian cried out, his head thrown back, the cords in his neck pulsing as he lost himself, climaxing so hard Lewis followed him, body throwing him off the precipice of desire until he flew.

Killian stayed inside him, hips stuttering, for a long time, and Lewis was still not ready to let him roll away, to leave.

"Shh...." Killian nuzzled his ear. "Baby, you gotta let me move sometime."

"No condom," Lewis panted. "Next time."

Killian chuffed out a breath, and Lewis finally let him go. He rolled to the side and got rid of the condom in the waste bin before rolling back and snuggling under the covers. He may have left the thermostat on, but sixty-eight degrees still needed a blanket if you weren't working up a sweat.

Lewis pretty much rolled into his arms as soon as he settled, wrapping his outer leg and outer arm around Killian's lean, slightly damp body in an act of sheer possessiveness.

Lewis kissed Killian's throat, enjoying the aftershock that started as Killian's body rippled. Then he licked the sweat there, snuggling even tighter when Killian chuckled because it probably tickled.

"Stop wiggling," Killian murmured. "I'm here. Let me hold you."

And Lewis finally, *finally*, settled down. "You're amazing," he mumbled. "*That* was amazing." *I love you. Let me live here forever. Please let me stay. It's all I ever wanted, but I didn't know you so I didn't know how to ask.* "But I'm serious. I'm negative. I've tested once a month since spring break."

"Why?" Killian asked, puzzled.

"Douchey two-timing ex who wouldn't know how to put a condom on a banana if the banana did all the work for him," Lewis all but spat. "Don't make me talk about him. My taste has definitely improved. But you?"

Killian laughed a little. "Also negative. I just... you know. We didn't have the discussion, so it seemed prudent."

"Oh no—I get it. In fact, it's one of the reasons I was pretty sure you weren't pos." Lewis wondered how close they could actually get without wearing the same skin.

"How?" Killian pulled his head back to look Lewis in the eyes.

"Stop that," Lewis admonished, and buried his face against Killian's chest. "Snuggling. Now."

"Okay, okay, I'm snuggling. But the question?"

"Oh. Easy," Lewis murmured. "Because you're careful. Because of the way you take care of the kittens, take care of your neighborhood—you're careful. You take care of things. It's good."

Killian's rumbly chest would rock him to sleep in a moment or two. Lewis couldn't remember the last time he'd been so content.

"I loved this," Killian murmured. "I want to do more of it, if that's okay."

"God yes," Lewis responded fervently, and he wanted to say more. He wanted to say that he'd stay, thank you very much, you're welcome, and that he was just like Moose and Squirrel. It had only taken one night, one touch, one kiss, and he'd found his forever home.

But unlike Moose and Squirrel—who had made their way to the bed now that the humans weren't making so much noise and were currently finding safe spots to plant their bodies so that the humans had to contort around them—Lewis's species didn't usually *find* their forever home after a couple of meals and some copulating. Lewis and Killian's species had to complicate things with dating and compatibility and courtship and blah blah blah blah who cared, when Lewis knew for certain—had known from the moment he'd seen Killian waving quietly to Todd from down the hallway—that Lewis could curl up in this man's house like any mammal in its den, having found himself a mate and a home he would never want to leave.

Now all that remained was for Lewis to convince Killian of that before Killian started talking about Lewis leaving. Not that Lewis suspected Killian *wanted* him to leave, but because Lewis was pretty sure Killian thought Lewis finding his own apartment would be the "right thing to do."

Lewis had news for him.

The "right thing to do" was to date the same guy for a while, grow to trust him, grow to love him, and then invite him to be a part of your life. Lewis had tried that with stupid cheating Richie, and he'd ended up alone and embarrassed and humiliated. And the only reason he *hadn't* ended up with an STD was that Lewis had never quite trusted Richie enough to go without condoms. Richie had bitched about it—almost constantly— but he'd also refused to go get tested, saying that he wouldn't need to because Lewis was the only one he'd been with all year.

Lewis's sixth sense or guardian angel must have been working overtime, because right before his trip home—the one with the blowjob with Todd's best friend—he'd gotten a call from one of Richie's *many* side pieces telling him that he had a chlamydia infection and was waiting on his HIV status and that Lewis might want to get himself tested.

Lewis had—because not even condoms were 100 percent—and then he'd broken the relationship off, gone home, and gotten a blowjob that had gotten him kicked out right before Thanksgiving.

And Lewis was actually grateful to all those people—the cheating ex, the side piece, Todd's ex-best friend, the best friend's wife, even the guy who had a crush on the wife and who had outed everybody for her approval—because that entire whackadoodle, tragicomic, college-hijinks chain of events had ended up with Lewis *here*, curled up in the arms of a man he trusted implicitly, and Lewis would be damned if he had to leave.

The hard part was convincing Killian that instant love and living together, forever, common sense to the contrary, was the only acceptable course of action.

Lewis snuggled even deeper, lulled by Killian's even breathing as he fell asleep, and tried to devise a plan to make it so.

KITTENS AND THEIR DAGGER-LIKE CLAWS

"YO, LITTLE bro," Todd said as Lewis opened the door for him. "Long time, no see."

Lewis huffed out a breath. "We've been busy," he said.

"Love what you've done with the place," Todd joked, and Killian could hear Lewis wince.

Killian was in the kitchen, making sure the sodas were iced and the paper- and plasticware were set out, but he could imagine Todd looking around his front room incredulously.

The blinds were dented because Moose and Squirrel had apparently been running in and out of them every time Lewis and Killian left the apartment. Lewis had rehung the drapes after Killian's unfortunate run-in with them when Lewis had locked himself out of the apartment, but there was still plaster dust on the desk behind the couch, and the drapes looked more and more ragged every time Killian checked, telling them that yes, shit was going down when the humans' backs were turned. And hey, there was a playpen back there now, filled with mewling kittens and a blessedly clean cat box. The playpen's mesh sides were fraying. There weren't any gaps yet, but there was a definite halo.

And Killian's soft leather couch now sported long score marks on the sides. He and Lewis had noticed this when they'd gotten back from Lewis's job hunt that afternoon, and Lewis had said something about needing to buy a scratching post.

Of course they did.

Hawaii was really not happening in February.

But on the plus side, the night before had been some of the best sex of Killian's life.

Should he have made more of that? Should he have told Lewis that his mind was blown and that he'd needed Lewis to keep still in the aftermath so Killian could hold him close and just *feel*, know that Lewis, spectacular, bold, sparkly, irrepressible *Lewis*, had let Killian inside his body, inside his trust, maybe even inside his heart?

Killian had wanted to—so badly. He'd startled awake at least three times the night before, beset by the urgent need to *do something important*, only to realize that the important thing he'd forgotten to do had been to tell Lewis that Killian's heart was fully engaged. *Don't leave. Don't move out. Being with you is the single most passionate thing I've ever done. Please stay with me until you can't stand me anymore. Please.*

Moving inside the haven of Lewis's body been a revelation. Oh! *This* is what all the shouting had been about! *This* was why sex was everybody's favorite thing. Killian could do this a *lot* if it was always with Lewis. Always bone deep. Always this resonance inside Killian's chest, his stomach, his balls. His heart.

Why hadn't he said that? Why *couldn't* he say that? What was wrong with him?

In the living room, Todd was picking out a kitten to hold while he sprawled on the couch. Killian watched him, using an absurdly delicate touch for such a big, doofy guy. When he'd pulled up the little tiger-stripe, he'd grinned at Lewis, who was out of Killian's line of sight, and said, "So, dude, how goeth the job hunt? Saw you leaving this morning in your interview duds. What's the good word?"

Killian's stomach froze. Oh. Yeah. *This* was why he'd kept his thoughts to himself. Because Lewis may have shown up in Sacramento with his hat in his hand, but it was a pretty damned decent hat! Apparently the kid was a superstar in his field—a thing Killian had suspected because he just *vibrated* that sort of competence and good thinking (except, maybe, in his personal life, but that could be excused by youth).

"Dude!" Lewis said delightedly. "It's looking *good*. I mean, *great*. As in, two of the jobs had rainbow flags at the desks as I walked by, and the one I like the most? The one that will let me, you know, taste the jobs in the area as a contractor while pooling some income for bennies? That one is run by two guys—a couple. The entire contractor pool is *so* diverse. I'm, like, *super* excited about it."

Todd frowned. "Yeah, but how did Folsom go?"

"Mmm...."

Lewis held back, and Killian's heart fell.

Around Sacramento, Intel was *the* shit. Stock options, opportunities for professional growth, benefits—everybody knew about it. But as Killian had piloted them down Hwy 50 toward the Folsom campus, Lewis had balked. "Gees, this is a bit of a drive. And the freeways here are the worst. Are they always this congested? Isn't this by the free-kitten-shot vet? I mean, they're nice people and all, but that industrial complex sort of sucked. You know, that one place with the two guys was only blocks from your apartment. I *liked* that place!"

Even as they pulled off onto Iron Point Road, and the nearly deserted campus loomed in front of them, Lewis was not impressed. "Yeah, this place was probably bustling pre-virus, but it is looking big and haunted now."

"Didn't you say most of your work would be from home?" Killian asked.

Lewis wrinkled his nose. "So're most jobs in my field now. I mean, if I have to come to this place once a week…."

Killian had always liked Folsom. He glanced around and said, "Too bad we already ate before we left Sacramento. I'd show you Old Folsom. You'd like it."

"Yeah, well, I could like coming up here for a good dinner or to explore," Lewis said, "but right now I'm sort of attracted to Sacramento." He shrugged. "Sorry, dude—can't help what the heart wants."

He'd left it at that and had gone into the interview and gotten a date for a second, but Killian had the sinking feeling that Lewis wasn't giving it a fair shake, which, yeah, was Lewis's choice, but he wasn't doing that because of Killian, right?

Right?

And Killian had no idea how to have that conversation on the way home. How do you say, "Hey, man, I know we had mind-blowing, world-changing sex last night, but, you know, don't give up your future for *me*. You just met me. We can work it out."

Except he couldn't say that last part, because you couldn't always. Sometimes two people who really cared about each other couldn't work it out, and what if Lewis decided Killian was a bad idea next year, and in the meantime, he'd thrown away a great opportunity?

Lewis's future was so bright—Killian had never had a chance at that kind of future. Killian didn't want to ruin it for him.

But he didn't want Lewis to take a job he didn't want for Killian either.

It was something he'd resolved to talk about—or be awkweird about, because that was fun too—but Lewis had been super excited about every interview, and he'd spent the entire trip home, er, back to the apartment, from Folsom talking about the pluses and minuses of each job, emphasizing the contractor pool the most heavily, which thrilled Killian and terrified him at the same time.

And then they'd been getting ready to have people over.

Todd had shown up first, and Killian had let out a deep breath that he seemed okay with Lewis crashing at Killian's place, even if the living sitch *was* sort of amorphous. But Killian's gut was still sending up signal flares. Before Killian could obsess *too* badly, Kevin and Michelle showed up with three enormous pizzas, which had freaked Killian out the first time they'd done this, but then he'd counted, and there had been seven people crammed into his tiny apartment, eight now with Lewis, and the pizzas did tend to disappear. If nothing else, he knew that sometimes Todd's only meal for the rest of the week was pizza, and there was a general, unspoken rule to send the guy home with as much as they could manage.

Killian and Michelle were setting up food when Suzanne arrived, arms full of a pastry box that Killian was *really* looking forward to because Suzanne had great taste in desserts, and she had just started her tentative courtship with the mama cat when there was a knock on the door again and Nick and Lia arrived, a giant salad bowl in hand.

For a moment, the noise in the apartment was at a dull roar, and Killian had a sudden guilty thought for all of the frightened fuzzballs in the playpen when there was a sudden hush and then Lewis, Todd, and Kevin came trooping back through the kitchen and toward the bedroom, each of them bearing either a cat carrier, the original cardboard box, or the water and towels from the playpen.

"Too loud," Lewis said on his way through. "We're setting them up in the bedroom, but I'm not sure how—"

"Dump out the laundry," Killian called. "Use the big square hamper. I don't think they can crawl out."

"Good thinking!" The little procession disappeared, and Killian took a deep breath.

"What?" Suzanne asked, coming in and rooting through the refrigerator until she came up with the two bottles of chardonnay Killian had bought especially for her on the way home. "Why do you look so relieved?"

"Because everybody's as careful of the little buggers as we are," Killian admitted. "I heard it takes a village to raise a child, but I had no idea that carried over to furry crap machines too."

"Live and learn," Suzanne told him with a grin. "Michelle, you want some?"

"God, please." The building was outfitted with the super-high Victorian cupboards that a lot of places in Sacramento sported, so Killian kept a step stool under his table. Michelle pulled the thing out and got down the wineglasses, calling, "Nicky? Lia? You want?"

"Definitely," Lia said, coming in with Nicky on her heels. "Killian, where's the two original kittens? Moose and Squirrel? Enquiring minds want to know."

"Last check, they were in my closet," Killian told her. "Todd knocked, and I went to lock them in the bedroom, and they heard the strange voice, and that's where they ended up. I think putting the tiny babies in the bedroom is a good idea too, but damn. Stuff you don't think about when you see the little fuzzballs, right?"

"Yeah—it's a trip. But it's good you're keeping them out of all the noise. They get freaked out." He grinned. "We can take visiting trips into your bedroom, which is fine 'cause I can envy that comforter again."

Killian laughed and opened a beer for Nicky and a soda for himself. "Internet find, my friend. It went with the shelves."

"So," Lia said, taking a grateful sip of wine. "About the bed. And the bedroom. And the drawers Lewis told us you'd given him…."

Killian stared at her. He'd had a couple empty drawers that he told Lewis he could use because, he figured, even if Lewis only stayed a week—and it looked like longer than that, truth be told—the drawers made things neater.

And even if Lewis fled before Christmas, Killian could pretend, right?

"It was easier," he said truthfully. "Between the cats and the cat stuff, we kept tripping over his backpack."

Every woman in the kitchen tilted her head and ogled him as though he had turned green and grown another head. Nicky nodded earnestly in complete understanding.

"What?" he asked, feeling sweat in the crack of his ass.

Nicky—alerted by Killian's tone of voice—glanced around at the women and adjusted his expression.

"That's… you moved him in so you wouldn't trip over his backpack?" Suzanne asked, sounding stunned and sort of disapproving.

"He, uh, needed a place to stay?" Killian said in a small voice.

"On the couch," Michelle clarified, looking as though she didn't believe that detail at all.

"In the beginning," Killian muttered, because after the night before, Lewis wasn't ever going back to the couch if Killian had anything to say about it.

"Dude!" Nicky said happily, breaking ranks and raising his fist to bump. Lia elbowed him in the side, and he dropped his fist, glancing around wildly as though trying to figure out how to get out of this trap.

"What are you doing here, Killian?" Michelle asked, arms folded. "I like the kid, but Kev and I were here when you moved in after Jaime, and we don't want a repeat of that."

Killian scowled. "I was fine," he said. He'd gotten drunk a couple of times, listened to a lot of Boxer Rebellion, and worked out until he got nosebleeds. And since he'd just moved into the apartment, he'd done a *lot* of home improvement.

"Mmm…," Suzanne said. "We were tending bar together then, remember? You passed up the management position—"

"I hate management," Killian muttered.

"You'd be great at it," Suzanne retorted. "But your confidence was shot—anyone could see it."

Killian scrubbed at his face. "Guys, that was six years ago."

"Yeah," Nicky said, suddenly catching on. "But your dating life since then has been…. Lia, what's the word?"

"Sparse," she said, her face stony.

"Yeah. Sparse. Like, spotty." Nicky nodded. "This is a little far a little fast, isn't it, bro?"

Killian took a breath. "I'm not locking him in the apartment," he said, hurt. "You guys—I'm finally seeing someone. After all your nagging, I thought you'd be happy!"

"Yo! You're seeing someone?" Todd practically yelled as he ambled down the hall. "That's great! Who is it?"

"Me, moron," Lewis snapped, and then, bless him, he hip-checked his brother into the bathroom and strode into the kitchen and into Killian's arms.

He grinned up into Killian's face, and Killian smiled gently back.

"How're the furry crap machines?" Killian asked, tucking some of the shaggy hair behind Lewis's ear.

"Crapping and furring," Lewis confirmed cheerfully. "How's the friendly interrogation?"

Killian looked out at his friends hopefully, and while he saw some painfully closed eyes, Suzanne broke first.

"Over," she said. "We're moving on to how to help you guys find homes for all the little dudes before Christmas."

"Not all," Killian said hurriedly. "Moose and Squirrel stay."

Suzanne regarded him with a neutral expression. "Sure. The mythical kittens that I haven't seen can stay, Killian. That's fine."

Ugh. Killian remembered his older sisters—not the younger one, who stuck by him, but the two older ones who would torment him and then throw him under the bus of their parents' churchgoing wrath. "Have I ever told you about my sisters Jill and MaryJo?" he asked suspiciously.

"Yes, and fuck you very much," Suzanne retorted, cracking a smile. "All right. I'll believe you have kept two kittens for yourself. But what are we going to do with the other five?"

"You're taking one, right?" Lewis asked, and Suzanne's begrudging acceptance turned sheepish.

"Yes, yes I am. As soon as the kittens are weaned, I'll take the mama cat. Poor thing needs lots of days on the couch, painting her toenails, no kids in sight, and I am *down* with that."

"So there's one," Killian said. "Kev? Michelle?"

"The gray one," they said in tandem, and Killian had to laugh.

"Ah, compromise," he said, and they grinned at him, because he'd seen how they'd gone from getting the black one to getting the ginger to getting the one that was nothing like either of them and creating an entirely new family. He was pretty sure they'd be having kids someday, Michelle's objections to the contrary. They had all the makings of fantastic parents.

"That leaves three," Lewis said. "Nicky, you and Lia are off the hook because you placed Boris and Natasha—"

"Best Christmas present my mom's ever gotten," Lia confirmed, a gentle smile on her face. "But we'll still keep an eye out for people who want kittens."

"We could post a flier at the bar," Suzanne said, "and have it say Ask Management so we can vet out the creepers or the people who'd leave the kitten homeless after Christmas or the people who can't afford their own alcohol."

"Good idea," Lewis enthused. "That way we can meet the person at the bar with the kitten and we don't have to give them Killian's address." He glanced at Killian apologetically. "I mean, the only creepy stalker-slash-freeloader you can afford right now is me."

Killian sent him a droll look. "And all the furry crap machines."

"Without saying," Lewis agreed.

"When should it go up?" Michelle asked. "I've got a couple of people with ten-year-olds who've been talking about getting a pet. Normally I eschew the whole 'giving a pet for Christmas' thing, but they've been researching and talking about pet adoption for months. This isn't a spur-of-the-moment thing, it's more of a good-timing thing. Should I ask them? They'd probably reimburse you for shots and spaying and neutering, since you seem to have a line on that."

"They're not little kids?" Killian asked anxiously. "Because, you know. Little kids—"

"Are a nightmare," Michelle said and laughed. "Yeah, I get it. It's always a balance. But no—these are people with kids old enough to be kind and responsible. I wouldn't send your babies into a health hazard, Killian." She shook her head. "So worried. You must have been fun as a little kid. 'Hey, Killian, you want to go on the roller coaster?' 'I don't know, Mom, are they indemnified?'"

Lewis sputtered into his T-shirt, and Killian squeezed him a little closer.

"Only the ones that sprang up around shopping malls," he said, and everybody in the kitchen laughed.

"I'm starving," Kevin said. "Let's eat and plan and dish and then eat whatever Suzanne brought in the bakery box and then fall asleep during whatever movie we decide on. Believe it or not, this is the most exciting thing we do all month. Let's get to it."

IT WAS one of the best pizza movie nights Killian could remember. They ended up watching some *really bad* Christmas horror movie, and snarking through it had them laughing until their stomachs hurt. They settled it down with *Klaus*, which Lewis and Todd had never seen before, and it had them riveted. They finished up with *While You Were Sleeping*, a movie so comfortable and soft that pretty much everybody had to wake up and yawn and stretch before leaving for home. Suzanne had driven, and Nicky and Lia lived two blocks away, so after making sure they made it out okay, Michelle and Kevin went back across the hallway to get some sleep before their alarms went off at an ungodly hour.

They'd spent the quieter pert of the evening bonding with the little gray kitten, and Michelle promised him they'd be back to visit some more before he came to live with them. Watching her fawn over the tiny creature made Killian smile, but it also made him *really happy* about what he and Lewis had been doing. He'd had no idea he had a Moose-shaped hole in his life, but now he didn't, and he was giving that to his friend as well.

Finally everybody was out the door, the tiny kittens had been returned to the playpen, and the extra pizza that hadn't been divvied up and sent home now sat in Killian's fridge, along with the three extra eclairs that Suzanne had brought that nobody had eaten and everybody had refused to take home because they were already feeling fat enough, thank you, and what? Was Killian trying to fatten them up before he ate them?

Lewis and Killian fell into bed, limp with exhaustion because the day had been big and busy and they were only human. But even as they fell, Lewis, wearing a T-shirt and briefs, rolled into Killian's arms and sighed.

"No T-shirt," he said happily.

"Got a big glob of custard on it," Killian mumbled. Besides, Lewis was there, warming their space under the comforter and smoothing his hands over Killian's bare chest.

"Liar," Lewis teased.

"It's the truth," Killian said mildly. "Not the *whole* truth, but...."

Lewis chuckled, his breath dusting Killian's skin, and Killian thought wistfully that he didn't see himself not wanting Lewis's company anytime soon.

"Killian?"

"Mmm?"

"I don't want to work in Folsom."

Killian let out a soft breath. "Your education, Lewis. Your job. Ultimately your life—"

"Yeah. But I don't want that job. You can stop worrying now. The two down here are fine, and the one over on F Street is, like, a bus ride or a bike ride away. I like that one best."

Under the cover of darkness, Killian felt the smile, Grinch-like, stretch his cheeks.

"Yeah?" he asked, unable to keep himself from being happy about it.

"Yeah, Killian. Is that okay?"

Killian's eyelids were heavy, but his heart was a thousand pounds lighter. "Yeah," he murmured. "That's awesome."

"Good."

Stay here. Live here. Buy furniture. Make decisions. Own kittens. Make love. Don't go.

All those things pressing on Killian's heart that he really wanted to say, but he fell asleep instead.

ANOTHER BOX

"HEY, LEWIS," Derek Huston said. "You got a minute?"

"Sure." Lewis saved the work at his computer and looked up, smiling. Derek Huston—midsized, sandy-haired, with a boyish face and a smattering of freckles—was worth smiling at because Lewis wasn't *dead*, and unless the toddler Derek and his husband had adopted was teething, he was usually in a good mood, and that helped too. "What do you need?"

Derek shrugged. "It depends. How are you doing on your current job?"

The start-up boutique for trans-male and trans-female clothing had needed a sales and inventory program, as well as help building a website. The owner was tech-savvy enough to run things after Lewis had installed and built them but too busy to muddle through herself. The work was pretty easy for someone with Lewis's credentials, but Lewis had enjoyed working with Beatrice. She'd patiently explained to him how women's clothes in larger sizes and men's clothes tailored to fit specific bodies could really give her community a sense of joy and support and pride that it didn't always get in the mainstream places, and Lewis had felt good about the job, even if it would be finished the week before Christmas.

"Pretty good," he said. "I should be able to turn Beatrice over to Sandy next week." Sandy specialized in website upkeep and updating, and while she could probably run her own business just fine, Derek's co-op had bigger servers for better internet connection *and* health and dental.

And people to talk to on the daily, if she chose to come in, or the flexibility to stay home, so she'd stayed with Huston and Gonsalves-Macias even when she could have left.

Lewis had noted that more than one of the people in the co-op office had a similar story, and he thought he couldn't have landed in a better spot. Killian didn't use his computer space that often, so he'd set Lewis up there for the days he preferred to work at home, and since Killian could walk to work, most of the time Lewis took Killian's car on the days he needed to go in. Lewis thought that maybe a small fuel-efficient coupe would be his first major purchase, now that he was making grown-up money, but he had to remind himself that *first* he had to cement his situation with Killian.

But it was hard.

They'd made love almost every night for the past three weeks—and it had been *brilliant*. Every time they touched, even if it was a simple good morning kiss or a hug or a pat on the hip as they passed each other in the hall, Lewis felt like he had been missing the thing that made his body complete until *that moment*.

The kittens had grown more and more independent, with the older cats executing acrobatics through the living room that had made *Lewis* start calculating the cost of fixing the damage, while the younger, tinier ones were climbing out of the playpen when they thought nobody was watching. As long as one of them was home, somebody was *always* watching, because Lewis had locked himself out of the apartment four times diving for the door to keep them from escaping. They'd started to keep the spare key on a chain by the door frame so whoever was answering the knock or getting the mail or kissing the other goodbye—which happened a lot—could snag it as the little goobers made a break for freedom.

Moose and Squirrel had gotten their second round of shots, and the babies and mama had gotten their first. The new kittens had been too young for the spay/neuter phase of their upkeep, but since they were now considered "partners in rescue" at the vet's office, they got coupons to give out when somebody adopted one. The night before, two families had visited, both of them friends of Michelle and Kevin, and each family—fourth grader in tow—had left with a new family member. Killian's lower lip had trembled, although he'd tried to hide it from Lewis, and Lewis had been feeling pretty wobbly himself. After about ten minutes of *that* bullshit, Lewis had thrown himself into Killian's arms and had himself a good cry.

Killian had stood there, holding him, an absolute rock of comfort and warmth. It hadn't been until Lewis had looked up that he'd seen the red-rimmed eyes and damp cheeks.

"It's stupid," Lewis muttered thickly.

"So dumb," Killian agreed.

"Nobody can keep five hundred cats," Lewis told him.

"Two is the perfect number," Killian said.

"They promised to text pictures."

Killian nodded, then sniffed with finality, and then wiped the tears from under Lewis's eyes with his thumbs. He dropped his head and kissed Lewis, a gentle briny benediction. He'd been leaving for work in half an hour, so the kiss couldn't get too heated, but when he pulled back, Lewis realized he felt infinitely better.

"Moose and Squirrel are never leaving," he told Lewis soberly. "They're ours."

Lewis had given him a watery smile then and hugged him for a minute more before letting Killian go to get ready for work. As Killian headed for the bedroom, Lewis wondered if he'd *ever* had a boyfriend who would have held him while he got sad over giving two foster kittens away to good homes without laughing over what a waterpot he was.

For the umpteenth time, he wondered how Killian could, even for a minute, believe that cold-fish thing.

There was such a well of passion, of caring, inside that man, and it wasn't just in bed—although Lewis had *zero* complaints and *no* notes. How anybody could think Killian wasn't a banked fire waiting to blaze was beyond Lewis.

God, Lewis wanted to camp out at his hearth for a while. For a lifetime. Forever.

But how did you ask for that when you were technically a freeloader who had never gone home after a night on the couch?

How did you convince the guy with the couch that that night had been his first night at the threshold, and all the nights following in Killian's bed had been coming home?

Lewis had caught Killian making plans for the future and then catching himself, looking sideways, embarrassed, as though he'd spoken a bad word.

"Yeah, after Christmas maybe we can…. Never mind."

And Lewis hadn't wanted to make him finish that sentence because what if the end was, "…find you an apartment to get you out of my hair."

Lewis was pretty sure it was something like "After Christmas we can go do that hike in Folsom like I mentioned," or "After Christmas we can see about getting you a car." Maybe it was, "After Christmas we can get more of your clothes from your parents," or "After Christmas we can shop for a whole new wardrobe," or "After Christmas I can get you enrolled at the Y so we can work out together." There were a whole lot of "after Christmas" promises that Killian could be invested in making that Lewis was desperate for, but every time Killian said it, he stopped and looked like he was going to cry, and Lewis was too much of a chicken to make him commit.

After Christmas maybe Lewis could press him for what they'd be doing after Christmas.

But right now it was five days *before* Christmas, and Lewis's new boss was asking him for a favor.

"Excellent," Derek said. "You know the lawyers' suite in the corner of the second floor?"

Did Lewis *ever*. The sign said Ellery Cramer and Galen Henderson, Attorneys at Law, and sometimes Lewis saw the men, both in their early thirties wearing suits almost as natty as Derek's but not as trendy. He knew their paralegal, Jade, by sight, and she was hard to miss because she was a stunningly pretty, curvy Black woman who liked to dye her hair magenta and dress to match. He knew their timid tech guy, AJ, who was often sent out for coffee and sometimes came to Derek's office to see who wanted extra because the two PIs he'd gone out for had suddenly bolted out of the office and—in his words—the grown-ups in suits would convulse and die with that much sugar and caffeine.

And he knew the two PIs, Jackson and Henry, who frequently ran down the stairs to the company's ugly brown minivan looking excited and fierce and then dragged their battered, bloody, bedraggled asses back up the stairs almost incandescent with triumph.

It was like working next to a television show, the one where the *B* cast was frequently either killed or injured or kidnapped, and Lewis was both excited to be on the show, even peripherally, and a little bit worried that he'd get his own episode, which was never good for the people on TV.

"Yeah," Lewis said, hiding his excitement. "What do they need? I mean, they've got their own tech guy, right?"

"Yeah, but I gather they want to write a program to help them track down certain victim criteria—you know, if their guy is charged with something he didn't do and they can prove it because a crime committed by somebody else was going on when they had a solid alibi."

Lewis sucked in a breath. "That's... that's *beautiful*," he said. "That's next level!" Already he could see how the code would start and finish in his brain. "I *want* to do this!"

"Awesome," Derek said, smiling. "They can only offer you a flat fee, and they don't have a deadline. They want you free to work on other projects while you're doing it. It was just, you know, Jackson brought me and Rico sandwiches, asked how the kid was doing, said his firm and some guys he knew were looking for someone who could do this...."

"And he worked you over like a prizefighter," Lewis said, seeing it clearly.

Derek nodded. "And he worked me over like a prizefighter," he agreed. "But a nice one, who's willing to pay for a product one of my people can design. I mean, you've got one of the best resumes I've ever seen, kid. You ready to put up or shut up?"

Lewis all but cackled. "Oh, I am so there. *So* there. So you want me to go over now?"

Derek shrugged. "You'll be done with the thing for Beatrice tomorrow, and we take a week and a half off. December twenty-third is our last official day until January third. This way, you can get a head start on this before you get another assignment, okay?"

"Groovy!" Lewis saved his work and closed his laptop, disconnecting it so he could take it along for notes. "I'll tell them you said hi!"

"Tell them those were some kickass sandwiches," Derek said, laughing, and Lewis gave him a happy wave as he darted out of the office.

The lawyers' office was not what Lewis had expected. Derek and Rico were great about letting people work from home at their own hours, so day care had never really come up as a need, but the first thing Lewis noticed as he walked into Cramer and Henderson was that part of the lobby was a play area, with big stationary toys and a basket full of smaller ones, as well as a couple of tablets in colorful rubber cases that were attached to the furniture by spiral cords and were probably damned near indestructible.

It had never occurred to Lewis that the people who needed lawyers might also need babysitters, but the area looked clean and well-used.

It also looked full of... uhm... very suspiciously shaped crates. Crates with sides that joined together to create a handle. Crates with air-holes. Crates with a *very* familiar sound.

"Hi," he said. "Uhm, I'm Lewis, from Derek and Rico's co-op—"

The curvy woman with the magenta hair glanced up from notes she was making on a pad of paper as she spoke on the phone, and waved him over, holding a finger up to indicate she'd be with him as soon as the phone call was over.

"Look, I know you all hate us," she was saying, "but it's not our fault. Our client got busted for stealing cats, that's all. It turned out he was stealing them from a kitten mill because the animals were being mistreated, the humane department shut them down, and you guys got the outflow. All I'm asking—*all* I'm asking—is if you have any vacancies. Any. Any at all."

She grimaced and held the receiver away from her ear. When the yelling died down, she spoke again. "Thank you so much for your time. You will never hear from us again."

Lewis half expected her to slam the phone down in a fit of pique, but she didn't. Instead she gently lowered it into the cradle and let out a sigh.

"Any luck?" called a voice from across the hall.

"No, Galen, I did *not* have any luck. Did you think I'd have any luck? We literally ground the entire kitten placement industry to a screeching halt. Did you *think* any of the shelters were going to talk to us again?"

"That was not our intention," said a man with a low southern drawl. He emerged from his office, a slender man in an outstanding wide-lapeled suit, leaning heavily on a cane. He had curly dark hair and a dark goatee, both of which mostly disguised the scars from a long-ago accident, and Lewis wondered if he wasn't in pain.

He wasn't the only one.

"Galen, sit down," said the woman behind the desk. Her placard read Jade Cameron, and Lewis was glad to be able to put her full name to the face.

"Here," Jade continued, taking Galen's elbow gently and guiding him to the stool she'd been sitting on as Lewis came in.

"Thank you, Jade," Galen said humbly. "I forget sometimes how the cold gets into the bones."

"Henry should be here in a few minutes," said a voice coming down the hall, presumably from the office in the back. "He should take you home early so you can have John work some magic with heating pads and massage."

Galen grimaced. "As nice as that would be, I think he's working overtime. As is Henry. Doesn't he have one more…?" Galen waved his hands in the general direction of the mewing crates at the other end of the reception area.

"Yeah," Jade said. "I may just have Mike come get them. The guys next door at the halfway house have been really good at taking care of them, cleaning the crates, getting everybody fed—"

"Keeping a few kittens off the top," a new voice said dryly.

"Four's the limit," Jade told the man who'd walked from the back—the other guy in the suit that Lewis had seen prior. If the first guy was Galen Henderson, this must be Ellery Cramer. He wore a sharply creased olive-colored suit and had crisply gelled black hair and sharp brown eyes over a prominent nose and a rather bony jaw. He *could* be handsome, Lewis decided critically, but he seemed to care more about being precise.

"Sure," said Ellery, staring at her in horror.

"Not that we're telling Jackson that," she said hurriedly, before glancing around like they weren't the only people in the office. "We're not, right? Not telling Jackson that?"

Ellery and Galen both shook their heads vehemently. "The two we own are breaking my house," Ellery said, his voice tinged with a little bit of desperation.

"And Ellery is my friend," Galen pronounced, "and I do believe I have an obligation to back him up on things like not letting his boyfriend—erm, fiancé—bring home another mouth to feed."

"I think it's in the handbook," Lewis confirmed, glancing warily at the boxes. He was almost afraid to look in them, given his and Killian's luck in the last month.

"Hey, wait a minute…." Jade was staring at him with a predatory gleam in her eyes, and Lewis held up both hands.

"Nope," he said, absolutely firm on this. "Been there, done that, have the scratch marks on my boyfriend's couch to prove it. I'm only here because Derek and Rico said you had some code for me to write?"

"Oh!" Ellery said, looking at Lewis as though he'd just now seen him. "Yes! Yes, Jackson told me he was going to look for someone to do that."

"His dream program?" Jade asked, sounding dubious. "The one that could help rule out suspects by looking for crimes with the same indicators in other locations?"

"That's the one," Ellery said. "I, uh…." He gave Lewis a bland smile. "I do believe Jackson got some, uhm, backing to get the program written."

Lewis frowned. "This isn't black-hat CIA shit?" he asked. "Because I'm not up for any of that."

Ellery shook his head. "No, don't worry. I, uhm… don't worry. You'll be fine." He gave a sharklike smile then, and Lewis very nearly ran out of the room.

"Ellery, you are scaring him," Jade said. Then she turned to Lewis. "Don't worry. We have the money, and the program is legal. Jackson cleared it with his backers in the military, that's all. Anyway—are you still up for writing it?"

"Yeah," Lewis said. "Do you have a list of criteria?"

"Do you have an email?" Jade asked, and Lewis grinned and handed her one of the cards that Derek had printed for all his co-op employees. Sometimes letterhead and documentation really *were* all they were cracked up to be. "Excellent." She set the card next to her laptop and, leaning in front of Galen so she could access the keyboard, set about sending documents to Lewis.

"Do you want me to take notes now?" Lewis asked, indicating his computer.

The other three people grimaced.

"Sadly," Galen said, apparently speaking for them, "all of the grown-up things we were planning to do in this firm were put on hold when we ended up responsible for all of this." He gave a frustrated wave at the crates of kittens, each one seeming to have the resonance and frequency of a banshee in a cathedral bell.

"Dear God," Lewis muttered. "What kind of cats do you have in there anyway?"

"Look at your own peril," Jade told him, and at that moment the door burst open.

A stocky man in his late twenties stood there, wearing cargo shorts and a hooded sweatshirt, with another cardboard cat crate in his arms.

"Is Jackson here?" he asked hurriedly. "I didn't see the minivan. Is he here?"

"No," Jade snapped. "And close the door, Henry. You're letting out all the warm air."

"Oh, thank God," Henry muttered. He looked despairingly at the cardboard crates, and Lewis thought he might even have seen his lower lip wobble. "Because these things are his kryptonite. I hadn't even realized it when I was picking kittens to take to the Walnut Creek shelter, but you guys! Look!"

Ellery and Jade gathered around him, both of them looking concerned, and Ellery, after melting for a moment—because apparently even Mr. Precision wasn't immune to kittens—suddenly backed up in a seeming panic.

"Oh dear God," he said, glaring at Henry. "How could you!"

"They wouldn't take them!" Henry said. "I mean, they would, but Ellery—they said they'd only take them to euthanize them and…." His voice wobbled, and Lewis peered around Ellery to see what the problem was.

"Aww," he muttered, reaching into the box. "You guys!"

Lewis put his hands into the box and came out with the three kittens, all of them friendly and purring—and very, very… odd.

"They're Cornish Rexes," Henry said. "And it was a kitten mill—there was lots of inbreeding. And this entire litter came out…."

Well, odd. The kittens themselves had giant, almost alien-sized eyes and *enormous* sail-like ears, but that was apparently a feature. One was black, one was calico, and one was an almost pearlescent white, and in addition to crimped fur—another feature—they had… glitches. All of the kittens had the distinctive, almost emaciated figures of the standard Cornish Rex, but one of them had a spine that was *too* long. The black kitten was permanently bent over, folded, with a giant lump in its back, and Lewis held him up, rubbing his whiskers.

"He doesn't seem to be in pain," he said, glancing at Henry.

"He's not," Henry said. "I watched him move—he can scamper with the others, but he gets tired quickly. I think because he has to work harder on his back legs."

"Well, he's sweet," Lewis said decisively. "I mean, someone's gotta want him." The little calico mewed and bit his finger in greeting. "And you—oh." On closer examination he could see that both of her feet were deformed, folding outward at the joint instead of back. "Oh, princess. That's a challenge." He set her down in the box, where she proceeded to sit on her hindquarters and bat awkwardly at his hand. Then she *leaped*, forcing him to try to catch her while he juggled the other two kittens.

"Okay," he said, setting the black one into the box with the calico and picking up the white one with the bright blue eyes. "I hear you, you can deal. And you, young lady, appear to be perfect. What seems to be your glitch?"

"She's deaf," Henry said with a sigh. "You have to be really careful with her—she doesn't hear anybody coming."

"Aw," Lewis murmured, and set the white one down in the box. "You guys, I know it's a challenge, but my boyfriend and I ended up with a cat—a bruiser, like, six years old—who was blind. I think congenitally. He had a buddy cat who helped him find food and stuff, and we thought we'd never place them, but, like, the perfect home dropped out of the sky and into our laps, and Boris and Natasha are seriously living their best lives now. I really think with a little work you can...." He noticed everybody was staring at him with the light of mania in their eyes, and he stammered to a stop. Oh God, he hoped he wasn't taking liberties. He'd called Killian his boyfriend *twice* in this conversation, but explaining to these people seemed like an unnecessary complication! And they seemed to be nice, and they were listening to what he was saying, and he was just commiserating because it looked like they had a big job, and one he was familiar with.

Oh.

Oh no.

He looked up into the faces of his new employers.

"Absolutely not," he said.

"You have to," Henry all but begged. "Dude, you do not understand. Ellery's boyfriend—"

"Fiancé," Jade and Galen corrected, but it sounded automatic.

"Ellery's fiancé has two of the most destructive animals I've ever *seen*. They're three-legged monsters—"

"Wait—three-legged?" Oh, Lewis was beginning to spot a theme here.

"You are starting to see the problem," Ellery said, his voice probably sharper than he intended, but, well, Lewis could understand where the panic came from.

"We absolutely…," Jade began.

"Positively…," Galen added.

"Cannot let Jackson see these animals," Ellery finished.

From outside came the distinct sound of a car backfiring.

"Oh shit," Henry said. "He's here. Kid, we'll pay you double."

"Henry, he's making our profit margin *now*!" Jade squawked.

"Then Constance and Burton will pay him double," Ellery snapped decisively. "They're the ones backing this project. They'll understand. Kid, we'll pay you double, but you have to leave this office *now*."

As Lewis was staring at them, Henry shoved the box into his arms while Jade shoved a business card into his jeans pocket, and together they turned him toward the door. He had no idea how it happened, but he was entering Derek and Rico's office suite even as he heard the thump of the elusive and legendary Jackson Rivers's tennis shoes on the concrete stairs to the second floor.

He found himself in the open office of the firm, holding a box of kittens, staring at his bemused coworkers in absolute shock.

"Oh God," he said, looking into the box. "Killian's going to murder me."

In Which Killian Kills Nobody

KILLIAN WAS elbows deep in cookies when there was a knock at the back door. His phone buzzed almost simultaneously, and Killian's eyes widened.

"On my way!" he called, hurrying from the kitchen down the hallway. He was careful, of course, scooping up the tiger-striped kitten on his way down the hall. Moose and Squirrel had stopped trying to make a break for it over the last week. As rambunctious as they became *inside* the apartment, it was starting to dawn on them that they *liked* it there. What wasn't to like? Three hots, a cot, and a squat, not to mention two ridiculous humans who catered to their every whim— it was sort of a cat's dream gig, Killian was sure. And since the tiger-striped kitten was the only one left of the now-infamous "box o' kittens," if Killian knew where *he* was, opening the door was generally safe. After all, locking Lewis and Killian out of the apartment was only fun when they forgot their keys, and neither of them were going to do *that* again anytime soon.

He opened the door, knowing his smile was slightly harried but genuine just the same.

Jaime looked good. His raven's-wing black hair was cut short enough to tame some of the curl, his dark gold skin glowed with health, and his nearly-black eyes glinted with their usual mischief. He'd always been handsome—his features in perfect balance. Between a bold nose, a square jaw, and a kind, lean-lipped mouth, he'd attracted more than his share of attention when they'd been dating.

"Is that a kitten in your arms, or are you just happy to see me?" Jaime deadpanned, and Killian felt some of his tension drain away. Killian usually enjoyed Jaime's unexpected visits, but in this case Lewis was due home soon, and Killian had to leave for work not long after that, and Killian wanted that twenty minutes for hugging and the rubbing of backs under T-shirts and playing with kittens and general discussing of their days. Lewis was often asleep when Killian got home, and while he invariably woke up so they could go to bed together—and *then* go to sleep—Killian liked their talking time. He knew Lewis took advantage of his working from home option, so they'd been able to take "weekends" on Monday and Tuesday, but that spending time thing was so important—and so joyful—that he'd come to treasure that twenty minutes of passing time to simply connect.

But then… gah! Jaime had shown up an hour before Lewis was due.

"Both, mostly," Killian confessed. He backed up and gestured Jaime inside. "Come in! Sit down! But you've got about half an hour before my boyfriend gets home and you have to piss off." He used the word "boyfriend," which was, well, sort of a misnomer, wasn't it? But explaining the uncertainty he and Lewis had been living under, the lack of clarity, that was a little personal. Killian and Jaime had been broken up for a long time—he was a friend, but Killian wasn't sure they were still in the realm of being personal.

Jaime snorted, oblivious to Killian's inner waffling. "Boyfriend? Does *he* have your car? I almost didn't knock, you know, because I didn't see that thing in the driveway."

"Yeah. He works just far enough away for it to be a pain in the ass, so he gets the Subaru. Which, like I said…." Killian had to be firm about this. He and Jaime could definitely spend their time bullshitting.

But Jaime got it. "I hear you. *My* boyfriend's picking me up for dinner and Christmas shopping in less than an hour, so I'll get out of your hair."

Oh, that was welcome news. "Christmas shopping. Sounds domestic!" Killian said, laughing, although given the giant counter of sugar cookies he was currently packaging, thanks to *his* boyfriend, he was one to talk. Lewis had talked him out of fudge, which was his usual thing—probably because Lewis liked to *eat* the cookies as much as he liked to decorate.

"You have no idea how domestic," Jaime said, walking down the hall and looking around. "Nice bedspread. Where'd you get it?"

"Taking notes?" Killian asked smugly. That had always been his talent—finding that one thing that could bring a room together. Jaime was good at concept. Killian had never been to his bar, but he felt like he knew the place because Jaime had been planning it for so long. But Killian could do both concept and detail. Jaime used to get so mad that he never had any ambition to take that further than his own nest.

Killian's own nest had been such a luxury, he'd never felt the need.

"Yes, actually," Jaime muttered. "I'm trying to find the perfect gift—the one that says I still love you even if you tell me you don't feel like getting married yet."

Oh wow! "Married? That's amazing! Congratulations!"

Jaime rolled his eyes as Killian brought him to the kitchen. "We'll see if he says yes," he muttered.

"Are you kidding? It's you. It's a lock." Killian nodded to the kitchen chair. "Sit down." He thrust the tiger-striped into Jaime's arms. "Hold a kitten. I'm packaging Christmas cookies here. Talk to me while I finish."

So Jaime did. While Killian filled him in on the saga of Lewis and the kittens, Jaime told him about how he'd almost lost the bar because, of all his talents, bookkeeping was not among them. He'd gotten help with it, though, and Killian felt nothing but happiness for his old friend—and amusement at his stories. Apparently he was indebted to a group of "random rogue accountants" who'd taken pity on him and helped him organize his business, and partly to a sort of superstar bartender, a world traveler who, in Jaime's words, "Oozes charisma. If you don't want to fuck him, you want to be him, and it doesn't matter that he's taken. That only seems to make people love him more."

Killian snorted and watched, bemused, as Jaime fawned over the quiet kitten. The kitten, true to his personality, gave a tiny mew and curled up in the crook of Jaime's arm for a snooze. "You sound jealous," he observed, and Jaime gave a sheepish shrug.

"I was, at first. Particularly because the guy I was crushing on was helplessly in love with him."

"What happened?" Killian asked, curious.

"They got married this summer," Jaime said with a grin. "But *his* best friend turned out to be the love of my life."

Killian chuckled. "And I take it the bartender stayed."

Jaime let out a low whistle. "The guy is a moneymaking *machine*. But he also really helps set the tone of the bar—and he and Crispin like to go out and explore the area and the local attractions and stuff, along with their buddies, the, you know, rogue philanthropic accountants—"

Killian laughed some more, because Jaime had that gift.

"Seriously, they come in with adventure stories and photos for the wall, and it really does liven up the place. Encourages other people to come and do the same. It's…." Jaime gave him a small smile. "I want you to come work there."

Killian sobered quickly. They'd had this discussion before. "But Jaime—"

"Yeah, I know you love Sacramento. I know you love Catches even. But Killian, this place—*my* place—it's got character. And I'm in love with someone else, you're in love with someone else—"

Killian's cheeks grew hot. "I never said—"

"Because the minute I walked in, it was nothing but 'Lewis and I planned to do this,' and 'Lewis and I need to do that.' Don't you understand? When it was you and me, we didn't have any plans for the future. We didn't have any excitement about… about kittens, or trips to go hiking, or… or our next date. That's *all* I'm getting from you right now. You're practically radiating 'Lewis and I,' You're a we!"

Killian gaped at him, stunned. He'd always wanted to be that guy—the guy who was so passionate about something, about someone, that people could see it in his eyes, hear it in his voice, know who he was by knowing how he felt about a thing or a pet… or a person.

"We are new," he said, feeling unbearably private about this. "He sort of accidentally moved in, and I don't want to pressure him, you know? Because what feels like, you know, a thing for me—what if I'm only a stop for him? That's not fair."

Jaime held up his hand. "Killian," he said, looking Killian in the eyes. "What makes you think you'll just be a stop for this guy? Nothing about you screams 'just a stop.' You're the most grounded man I know."

Killian must have been raw, because he said the thing he'd never said, because he'd wanted Jaime's friendship more than he'd ever wanted revenge. "Yeah, but *you* didn't want to stay, did you?"

Jaime sucked in a breath and, unconsciously, drew the kitten closer to his chest in self-defense.

"I'm sorry," Killian muttered, standing up. "That was stupid. We're both obviously better off now, and I never meant to—"

"Don't be sorry," Jaime said, his voice a low rumble, but not an angry one. "I deserved that. But don't you see? You… you never tried to hurt me, not even when we broke up. What made you send that out now?"

"Do you want a beer? A soda? Lewis made a thousand cookies—"

"No thank you," Jaime said. "Cam's picking me up in ten." He glanced down at the kitten in his arms. "Apparently with a friend."

That managed to snap Killian out of his fluster. "Seriously?"

"I… it's *weird*. Crispin and Luka—the bartender—they've got a cat. Our other friend Nick has a cat. The whole time, I thought, 'Huh—nice idea, but why?'" The kitten's purring amped up a little. "Now I know."

Killian laughed, and Jaime focused on him standing uncertainly by the refrigerator. For a moment Killian wondered if he should bolt out the door, or at least go hide in his bedroom, so he could get far, far away from the perceptiveness in Jaime's eyes.

"And now that you're in love," Jaime said softly, "so do you. Know why." He wasn't talking about the kitten. He was talking about *them*. It was as much as either of them had spoken about it after that terrible, painful night they'd broken up, with the resolution to still be friends.

Killian swallowed and looked away. "I knew why then," he admitted. "It was just… a hard dream to let go of."

"You have different dreams now," Jaime said. It was a statement, not a question.

"I do, but like I said, he just sort of moved in accidentally—"

Jaime's laugh had a provocative edge to it. "So did you, Killian. Remember? Just gonna stay for a week? Come to Sacramento, we said. Look around. See what the left coast is thinking, nudge nudge wink wink. And then you found out what it was thinking, and it was a lot of fun, but it took you two years to leave!"

"And look how well that worked out," Killian muttered.

"Well, it wasn't forever," Jaime agreed, and his voice softened. "But Killian, it wasn't bad either."

Killian caught his breath because he knew the answer to this one too. "But it wasn't forever."

"And aren't we glad it wasn't?"

Killian took a breath to think that over, think about his time with Jaime, roll it around in his heart with the time he'd spent with Lewis. Lewis's time was brighter, with more vibrant colors. The shadows had more depth, and a little light at the end so he could understand the darkness. The lights didn't just illuminate, they *twinkled*—because now he knew what would happen if they went away completely. The person he'd been when he'd been with Jaime was not the person who could understand what a wonder it was to be with Lewis, because maybe that's what growing up, both the wonderful and the painful, could give a person.

It could give him Lewis.

"But not sorry it happened," Killian said, his heart finally free and clear of this shadow. "You're right. I could be so much happier now. But for my first, we did okay."

Jaime gave him a quick grin. "You weren't my first, baby, but it was still better than okay."

Killian laughed. "Good to know. Are you sure you don't want a cookie?"

Jaime got up and peered at the big batches of iced sugar cookies on the counter. Killian and Lewis had let them sit out long enough for the icing to set, and Killian had already portioned out small batches in aluminum foil, with ribbons around it so they could give the packets to their friends. *Their* friends—Lewis had decorated at least one "specific" cookie for each person in their orbit. His brother, for example, had a snowman with tiny bags under his eyes. Nicky had one with an exaggerated muscular chest. Lia had had a reindeer with a beanie like she wore at the restaurant. And so on. Killian was careful to put the special cookie on top and label each packet accordingly, hopeful that it would still be identifiable when the package was opened.

But Jaime was only interested in quantity. "One? That's all you're going to give me? One cookie? Did you not hear me say I'm taking a kitten off your hands? I have a boyfriend? My friend, I have *responsibilities*!"

Killian laughed and told him, "Take one now, and I'll put together a package for you. But I really do need to get ready for work, so I'm going to need you to—"

"I know, I know," Jaime said with a laugh. "I'll piss off when I get my cookies."

And he did, hopping up when his phone buzzed with the text that his boyfriend was back. Killian let him out the front door, carrying the tiger-striped kitten and some supplies in the little cardboard crate they'd been using to take the kittens to the vet in one hand, and the package of cookies in the other. As Jaime was walking toward the SUV waiting in one of the visitor's spots in front of the building, Killian's own car pulled into the apartment lot, and Killian stayed at the foyer door to let Lewis in.

Lewis walked up the steps in short order, a suspicious-looking box held behind his back.

"Who was that?" he asked, watching as Jaime leaned over to kiss the driver of the SUV before he belted up. "And why is he carrying the kitten crate?"

"That was Jaime," Killian said, peering unsuccessfully around Lewis's body as he angled himself to hide the box in his hand. "He wanted to tell me he's getting married and ask me to work for him."

"What did you say?" Lewis demanded, practically dancing in a circle.

"I said congratulations, and probably no on the job, and I gave him the last kitten. Lewis, what's in your hand?"

Lewis stopped moving, twisting again, the box behind his back. "You said no on the job?" he asked, the hope in his eyes painful to see.

Killian brushed a knuckle along his cheek. "Everything I want is in Sacramento. Seems to like the place, even," he said tenderly. Then he got down to business. "Lewis, I can hear them—how in God's name did you manage to bring home more kittens?"

Lewis sighed and pulled the cardboard crate up to his chest. "Here," he said in absolute utter defeat. "Look at them, Killian. They… well, it's a story."

Killian let out a helpless laugh and guided Lewis in through the foyer before opening the front door—carefully, because Moose and Squirrel.

"Well, you've got about twenty minutes to tell it to me," he said. "You'd better make it count."

"Do I get a kiss?" Lewis asked pitifully, and Killian pulled him into the apartment to do just that. Kissing Lewis, feeling his mouth open, his breath quicken, his flesh warm and yield to Killian's touch—that went a long way toward softening the blow that, no, they couldn't put the playpen away yet, because yes, they were still ankle-deep in kittens.

The Boiling Fury of a Cold Fish

KILLIAN HADN'T *seemed* that mad.

Lewis sat on the couch, his knees pulled up to his chest, and watched as Moose and Squirrel moved in on the calico kitten with the twisted feet. They weren't sadists, weren't trying to hurt her, more like trying to *test* her. They'd done this with all the other cats. *Poke.* Whatcha doin'? *Poke.* Whatcha gonna do? *Poke.* Whatcha gonna do if I do *this*?

The calico's answer was, as ever, *delightful*. Moose poked her—a mild little swat, really. In response, the kitten rocked back on her hind legs, leaped into the air, and bonked Moose on the noggin with those same legs, kangaroo style, before twisting, midair, to land. She overdid the landing a tad—her back end overbalanced, and she ended up crashing to her side. Once there, she pretended she'd *meant* to do that and proceeded to clean her awkward foot like she'd just walked through something sticky. Yummy, of course, but sticky, because she had to concentrate on it, and that was the important part. If she concentrated hard enough on that stickiness on her paw, nobody would see that she fumbled the landing, right?

Lewis felt a little like he'd fumbled the landing, and he wasn't sure why.

He'd come in trying not to be annoyed that Killian's ex had been there and Killian didn't seem particularly affected in any way. He wasn't angry, wasn't sad—just seemed pleased to see the guy and bemused, once again, to find they were—his words—ankle-deep in another batch of kittens.

"But at least that explains it," he'd said earnestly, as though knowing *why* all the shelters were full made their own predicament *so* much easier to bear.

And then he'd asked Lewis about all the players in his little drama again, and when Lewis had told him about Jackson Rivers, Killian had chuckled.

"It's like a *sign*," he said, but he hadn't explained that either.

Of course, he *had* needed to shower and change for work, and Lewis totally understood, and it wasn't Killian's fault that his ex-boyfriend had stopped by to, as far as Lewis understood it, act as Killian's own personal Lucifer and tempt him away from the one true path.

But Killian had heard Lewis getting fractious and upset, and he'd paused in his rushing about to take Lewis's face between his palms and kiss him soundly.

"*You* have nothing to worry about," he chided. "You are exactly where you need to be." He gave a slight smile, the kind Lewis used to think of as "aloof" but now was starting to realize was a little bit anxious. "I hope you feel like that too."

And Lewis was caught, mouth open, wanting to scream, "Yes! Yes, I am *exactly* where I need to be! Here! With you! I want to send my parents Christmas pictures with *you in them*. I want them to come visit us in the summer, when it's a bazillion degrees there and only a million here, and take them to Old Sacramento and show them the places to eat! And I want them to meet *you and* know you're in my life and you're *important* and that I think we could go the distance and be together *forever and ever and ever*!"

But then the white kitten, who really *couldn't* hear danger coming if it announced itself with a brass band got pounced on by *both* Moose *and* Squirrel, and Lewis and Killian had both gone, "Oh no!" before Lewis scooped the poor baby up and cuddled her, trembling, in the crook of his arm.

Killian had ended up kiting out of the apartment, pausing to kiss Lewis goodbye and ruffle all the kittens on his way. "It's been busy," he told Lewis. "I might be late."

"I'll save dinner for you," Lewis told him. He'd been planning to broil chicken that night, steam some rice, sauté some veggies. Very healthy and also nice to heat up.

"Sounds awesome," Killian told him. He paused at the door, head over his shoulder. "You, uh—you like being here, right?"

"I love… it," Lewis had told him, because once again the rush of their lives had steamrolled right over the appropriate moment for Lewis to take charge of this romance and make sure it was on solid bedrock.

But Killian had smiled like he maybe knew something Lewis didn't, something *wonderful*, and then taken off, and Lewis was stuck back here in the apartment he was starting to consider *theirs*, wondering how many times the gods had to throw a perfectly good opening at him before he jumped through it like a rabbit down a hole.

"Kitten," Lewis murmured to the little calico, "I've got to up my game."

The kitten gave him a tired look and then curled up, right there on the floor, with one eye open. Lewis sighed and picked her up and put her in the playpen with the white and black ones. The pen was still outfitted with a clean litter box, a sleeping box with towels, food, water, and various safe toys. Killian had cleaned it out in anticipation of the last small-batch kitten leaving and then good-naturedly helped Lewis put everything back in now that they had kittens that *really* needed the shelter from the adolescent Moose and Squirrel, who saw everything that moved as a thing that needed to be pounced on.

Then he stood and looked around. Dinner was made—the chicken was broiled, the mushrooms and veggies had been sauteed with some butter and garlic, and the rice was in the steamer. He *could* start working on his new project, but given the timeline he'd seen in the specs, he figured nobody would expect him to even look at it until after Christmas.

He sighed.

Christmas. What was he supposed to do about getting Killian a present? He still had the money his parents had put in his account when he'd fled to Sacramento, but if he was going to find a place to rent, he'd really need it.

But if he was going to stay here, with Killian, who he loved—

The whole train of thought derailed.

Wasn't that the important thing?

From what he could see, Killian was about the cuddling, the kindness, the quiet, hidden ways that lovers showed they cared. Lewis could get him something basic—like covers for his couch since the furry crap machines had destroyed the leather—and Killian would be fine.

But would he be fine not knowing Lewis loved him?

From what Lewis could see, Killian had lived the last six years of his life believing he wasn't the kind of person somebody could love unconditionally, madly, without reserve.

Lewis was crazy about him. Absolutely. After less than a month, Lewis didn't want to think of a life without Killian in it. He didn't want to think of a *day* without Killian in it.

It turned out that kindness and decency and, oh my God, *sanity* wasn't just sexy—it was a life-altering, crazy-making, absolutely devastating aphrodisiac, and Lewis was *all in.*

And Lewis didn't want to wait a minute longer than necessary to tell Killian that they should move in together and raise kittens and plan hikes and plan *trips* and stay in the apartment and move out of the apartment and… and *grow* together, and be.

Together.

It's all Lewis wanted for Christmas. It's all he wanted for *life.*

Double-checking to make sure everybody was safe and accounted for, Lewis grabbed his coat and the scarf and hat Killian had produced from his drawer and headed out the front door. On his way, he met Todd and his girlfriend, Aileen, and realized that hey, this was Todd's one night off a week.

"Bro!" Todd said excitedly, giving him an unselfconscious hug. "How you doing?"

"Great!" Lewis told him. "On my way to Catches—"

"Us too!" Aileen was a medium-sized, sturdy girl with brown hair, brown eyes, and many, *many* freckles. Todd adored her, and Lewis figured that if his goofy brother could ever get his act together, Aileen could be his sister-in-law, and they could work as a team to keep Todd on the straight and narrow.

"Excellent," Todd said. He grinned at Aileen. "Little bro here got a job. Did I tell you that?"

"Nope," she said, booping him on the nose. "Because that would mean we spent an hour together in which *you* neither fell asleep nor bolted out of the apartment without your jacket screaming, 'Fuck me, I'm late!'"

Todd groaned. "God—it's awful. I like working at the movie theater, but they give me shit for hours—"

"Because it's a kid's job," Aileen said.

"And I love working at the bookstore, but they pay crap for even *fewer* hours—"

"Because it's a job for a retiree who wants to talk to people," Aileen filled in.

"And I'd love more hours as a teacher's aide, but I'm so busy with the other two jobs—"

"Because that job doesn't pay enough either," Aileen sighed.

"Babe. I'm so confused. All I know is I got tonight off, and I get to see you, and my apartment is cold—"

Aileen sighed. "Because the heat got turned off because you're broke."

Todd gave her a naked look of pleading. "Babe, if you can help me unfuck my life, I'll do anything…."

Aileen sighed and gave Lewis a beseeching look. "I know Lewis sees the obvious answer," she said.

Lewis cocked his head, careful as he stepped because the old trees here had roots that disrupted the sidewalk. "Really?"

She nodded. "Really."

"Okay, first of all, give up on the bookstore. There's a retiree there who needs to talk to friends."

Todd whimpered but nodded.

"Second of all, commit to the TA job and make yourself available all the hours, since the movie theater can give you time at night."

Todd nodded, frowning, and Lewis added, "Unless, of course, you don't watch movies, which I know you only do at Killian's place for the pizza, and you can find a night job that makes more money than that."

"Like what?" Todd asked as they drew near Catches.

Lewis nodded his chin toward the place. "Like waiting tables or bartending. People who do it regular and take it seriously make their rent all the time. Dude, Killian works five nights a week, has two days off, and can take vacations whenever he's saved enough money. He's got money saved, pays into insurance, and owns a car. Do you know why?"

Todd had to raise his voice over the crowd of people on the patio—the *patio*—in the forty-degree night. "Because the place is rockin'?" he asked.

"No!" Lewis called back. "The place is rockin' 'cause he's good at his job!"

And he was. Suzanne was working the bar with him and three other bartenders, and Lewis watched them flipping glasses almost dancelike without looking at their hands, talking to patrons, laughing at their jokes, simply keeping up with the flow of people coming up to the bar to order drinks. The waitstaff was doing its job, and Lewis assumed the kitchen was in top form. As they shouldered their way in, Lewis saw a familiar face wearing a tight black T-shirt over his amazingly huge chest.

"Oh my God," Lewis gasped. "Nicky, are you bouncing tonight?"

Nicky shrugged. "There've been some unwelcome elements in the last week. Suzanne said she'd pay me if I crossed my arms and looked intimidating and kept the assholes in line."

Lewis nodded, suitably cowed. "Well, carry on. God knows we don't want any assholes here."

Nicky rolled his eyes. "Lia's working up near the bar. You should see how decked she is when she's wearing a tight shirt—half the guys want to bang her and the other half feel their dicks shrivel just looking at her. It's great."

Lewis snorted. "Being intimidated by muscles isn't a good look for a man. Any man."

"No, but it does explain all the potbellies in the dick-shrivelers," Nicky muttered. He looked over Lewis's head at a familiar-looking giant truck with big diesel-oozing exhaust pipes standing up from the bed and a large political banner on the tailgate. "Speaking of... ew. This fuckin' guy."

"He comes in here?" Lewis asked, and his mind was churning like a cartoon animal's legs over a cliff. Where had he seen that truck before?

"Once last week. Killian's day off, thank fuck. But screw this guy—we just had a table open up. You guys go up and sit, and I'll have the kitchen comp you some appetizers. That way he's got no place to sit."

Lewis had dinner waiting at home, but Todd was perpetually broke, so Lewis ordered two appetizers for his brother and took the table, which had, in his opinion, the best view in the house.

Killian.

His hair was pulled back into that half ponytail, and his arrestingly blue-gray eyes were alight over everything in his path. He danced out of the way of a barback hustling by with a full tub, practically pirouetted around Suzanne as she pulled two drafts at a time, and flipped the two shakers—one in each hand—he'd been working on before he drained them into the ice-rimmed glasses for the specialty drinks.

When he was done, he took the cash offered for the drink and the tip, made change, and threw the tip into the jar over the register, ringing the bell above his head in appreciation. The bar cheered and someone else ordered, and Lewis grinned, catching his eye and winking.

Killian winked back, and Lewis relaxed into his chair. No, Killian was too busy right now for huge declarations of love or big gestures or anything, but seeing him in his element made Lewis happy.

And then he heard one of those big loud assholes who could fuck up the atmosphere of an entire establishment, laughing crudely.

"Man, who the fuck cares if all the shelters are full. If you can't give 'em to a shelter, drown them, run them over with cars, whatever. My mom tried to leave me her 'babies' to take care of, and I dropped them off at the vet's. For fuck's sake, the cat was *blind*—can you believe that? Jesus, people, grow up."

Lewis's head swiveled around to focus across the bar at a guy with a barrel chest, an alcohol-roughened red face, and a ball cap over greasy hair, and all of a sudden, it clicked.

He knew where he'd seen that truck before, and he knew who that asshole was, and whoa boy, did he have a thing or two to say.

Lewis had always been good about running into a fight without backup—it didn't even occur to him until he was halfway through the crowd that it wasn't just him anymore.

And until he tapped the guy on the shoulder and snarled, "How *could* you!" it hadn't occurred to him that the guy was at least six and a half feet tall, either.

"LEWIS, DUDE!"

Killian stopped, mid pour, when Todd's voice carried through the restaurant. What he saw made his heart freeze—but somehow made his body move without thought, which had *never* happened, not even in the military where everything had been done by rote and training.

Lewis stood in front of a big, rough-looking man—not muscular like Nicky, but not all fat either. His shoulders were broad, he was tall, and he had one of those expressions of someone who didn't mind hurting something smaller than he was.

Lewis qualified! But Lewis, true to everything Killian had learned about him in the past few weeks, was not backing down.

"Dude!" Lewis replied, shaking his brother's hands off his shoulders. "You don't get it! This guy threw two cats out of a moving truck and drove off! This fucking asshole abandoned Boris and Natasha— *How could you?*"

Killian didn't ask himself the same question. He wasn't even surprised. He didn't ask himself what the odds were that the guy who'd thrown away Boris and Natasha would wander into his bar or how Lewis had figured it out. He didn't *care* what the odds were, and he trusted Lewis implicitly. He'd seen guys like this. People thought sociopaths ended up in prison, but sometimes they just drank a lot and beat their wives or girlfriends, abused animals, and came to a bar to brag about themselves. The world was small sometimes, and Killian was over it. What *he* was asking himself was whether he could get between Lewis and the ugly cat-abusing asshole before the asshole killed Lewis!

He wasn't even aware he'd vaulted over the bar and had started to shove his way through the crowd until the guy snarled, "What's it to ya, ya little faggot!" and some of his spit hit Killian's face.

"Don't you touch him!" Killian shouted. "You keep your fists to yourself, you fucking cat-murderer. We don't serve your kind in this place. Get out!"

"Who in the hell are you?" The guy scowled at Killian, but Killian was taller than Lewis, and he had some muscle on him. He didn't look like an easy mark, and he'd bounced his share of rough customers before.

"I'm the guy who's not going to let you pound my boyfriend because he called you on your bullshit. You threw two cats out of a moving ugly-assed truck, and we saw you. And we found a home for the cats, by the way, but you have to give your fucking human card back for that, because Jesus Christ, what a douchebag!"

The guy laughed cruelly and then delivered the stunning and original *bon mot* of, "What a fucking faggot."

"Get out!" Killian snarled, using all the intimidation he'd learned in eight years of throwing scumbags like this out of his bar. "You are *not* welcome here."

"Let me talk to your manager," the guy snarled, and Killian was not surprised that Suzanne had appeared at his elbow.

"I'm right here," she snapped. "Get out."

"Dude, who runs the place? Chicks and fags?"

"I've called the cops," Suzanne lied—she had to be lying because Killian knew she hadn't had time. "Get out or you'll be arrested."

"For what?" the guy snarled, legitimately puzzled. "I was just standing here shooting the shit when this little punk—" He gestured to

Lewis, who was behind Killian's shoulder, straining to be let through. "—started yelling at me!"

"Nicky!" Suzanne called. "Nicky, get over here and deal with this!"

"But what'd I do?" the guy asked, still puzzled. "I was just fucking standing here when—"

Nicky was so big he didn't have to push through the crowd. They sort of parted for him on general principles. The din of the bar had died down by now, and the silence was like the tumbleweed and haunting-flute part of the western when the two big honchos were about to draw down.

"Killian?" Nicky asked, sounding puzzled and hurt. "This guy—"

"Threw away Boris and Natasha," Killian confirmed grimly.

And that's when the guy cocked his fist back and Killian's face exploded in pain.

LEWIS SAW it happening and was powerless to stop it. To a boneheaded redneck kitten-murdering asshole, the logic was impeccable. Nicky was unbeatable, and Killian wasn't expecting it. Pop Killian in the nose, and while everybody was staring at the blood, run away like the coward you were.

With Nicky on your heels like the avenging tank-engine of justice.

Lewis saw the bottoms of Nicky's cross-trainers as he disappeared out the door and into the night, and then his attention was on Killian, whose knees had gone wobbly and who needed help being borne gently to the ground.

"I'll get ice," Suzanne said, and Lewis crouched in front of him.

"Killian, are you okay? Dude, *are you okay*? What were you thinking, getting in front of that guy? Jesus!"

"He hit me?" Killian asked, like he needed to make sure.

"Yeah, buddy," Lewis said, smoothing his hair back from his face with tender fingers. "Dude. Why'd you do that?"

Killian peered at him blurrily. "'Cause I love you and I'm tired of you getting hit."

Lewis gasped, wanting to smile—more, he wanted to crow, to shout, to dance!—but first he wanted to make sure Killian's nose cartilage hadn't shattered into his brain pan and was making him say things he didn't mean.

"I love you too," he said softly, accepting a napkin from Todd to soak up the blood. "I can take a hit, baby, but I'd rather you didn't have to."

Killian regarded him soberly over a nose that was currently blossoming like a murderous rose. "Nobody hits my kitten," he said.

Lewis couldn't help the chuckle that escaped, and Suzanne got to Killian's other side and said, "C'mon, Lewis, let's get him to a seat."

Killian helped with his legs, and between the three of them, he got into a chair with an ice bag and a pile of napkins to sop up the blood. Suzanne looked at the crowd and made an instant decision.

"Todd, you're on bar," she said.

Todd stared at her. "I got no idea how even to—"

"Don't worry. I'll make it really easy for you," she said. Then she stood up and called to the crowd. "Two-dollar drafts, five-dollar well drinks, nothing fancier than soda and ice to mix. I've got a trainee at the helm, and he's stepping up to be a mensch. If anybody shits on him, they're banned for life, like the guy Nicky just chased down the street. Any questions?"

There were none. Suzanne bent down again and squeezed Killian's shoulder. "Enjoy the night off," she said before handing Lewis her car keys. "Lia will help you get him to the car. Take him to the hospital to get that set. Mercy General is right down K Street—you can find it. Tell them workman's comp, give them my name. Killian's got the bar's number." She turned and kissed Killian on the forehead. "Nobody hits my kitten. Jesus, Killian, I'm having that put on a T-shirt. You'll never live it down."

And with that she hustled Todd up to the bar, and Lewis had a job to do.

They met Nicky on their way out to Suzanne's car. His T-shirt was torn, and so were his knuckles, but his smile was bright enough to light up the street.

"Dear God," Killian mumbled through his ice pack. "What happened?"

Nicky gave a bloodthirsty grin. "Two words," he said with a satisfied nod. "Plausible deniability."

"Aw, Nicky," Lia said from Killian's other side. "We can't afford legal fees for that."

Lewis grinned back—he appreciated a bruiser with an agenda that matched his own. He reached into his back pocket and pulled out the card that Jade Cameron had shoved in it earlier that day—he'd already put the info into his phone. "Here's a good lawyer if you need one," he said. "They frickin' owe me. Let us know how the night goes!"

"Will do." Nicky got close to Killian, gently checking out his eyes and his nose under the ice pack. "Yeah, go get that set for sure or it'll never stop bleeding. And he's probably got a concussion." He gave an evil laugh. "I understand those are going around tonight."

He gave a small salute, and he and Lia strode back into Catches, his torn shirt only making him look more badass.

"Let's get you to the hospital, big guy," Lewis said, helping Killian into the car.

"This is so embarrassing," Killian mumbled. The word he said sounded like "embarbbing."

"He sucker-punched you, Killian. Totally not your fault."

"Whabeber," Killian sighed. "Sthill lub you. Sthay."

Lewis swallowed. "Stay?"

"Foreber."

Lewis's eyes watered. "I don't care if you have a concussion," he said. "I don't care if you don't remember this tomorrow. I don't care if you wake up in a month with no memory of this moment at all and ask me when I'm leaving. You'd better make sure you mean it, Killian, because it's all I ever wanted."

Killian gave a snort and sputtered blood. "I lub you. Sthay."

"I love you too. You'd better believe I'm staying."

And with that, Lewis put the car in gear and took his man to the doctor so he could make sure it wasn't some sort of broken-nose-induced psychosis.

Damn, he really wanted to stay.

KILLIAN WOKE up and groaned. He was in bed wearing last night's T-shirt and his briefs, with Lewis behind him for once, spooning him carefully.

"You okay?" Lewis asked, obviously anxious.

"Ou. Ch." It felt like the word needed more syllables than that. "Wha 'appened do my heab?"

"You got hit by a random kitten-abusing douchebag," Lewis told him. "Don't worry, buddy, I've got painkillers next to the bed."

Lewis's comforting warmth disappeared, leaving Killian with Moose and Squirrel cuddled to his chest and the heavy throbbing in his nose and face. In a moment, Lewis reappeared in front of him with a prescription bottle and glass of water.

"I warn you," Lewis said, "these made you loopy as fuck last night. You started telling me a hell of a story about you and your army buddies and some sort of small-arms class, and I'm sure it was hilarious, but I didn't understand a word you said."

Killian closed his eyes and moaned. He remembered the moment—he and Jaime had been in a small-arms class with a contracted instructor who didn't know that much and liked to throw his weight around. They hadn't been dating yet, had never kissed, but they'd made fun of the man behind his back until their stomachs ached with suppressed laughter. It had been Killian's best moment in the military, and if he remembered right, he'd been trying to tell Lewis he'd trade in that moment and every other good moment in his life if only he and Lewis could make all sorts of good moments together from now on.

"It wab thupid," he mumbled, taking the pills and giving the glass to Lewis. "I jus wanted do thay I lub you. A lob. Neber lubbed thomeone like I lub 'oo."

Lewis set the glass down on the table, eyes bright and red-rimmed and shiny. "I've never had a knight in shining armor before," he said gruffly. "You jumped between me and that truck with so much passion, Killian. And I know you think you're all calm and levelheaded, but you've got fire in your blood."

"'Oo," Killian said humbly. "Ith all 'oo."

"You make me so happy. Do you still want me to stay? It's the last time I check because the only thing I've got planned today is to call in to work and to have my parents ship my clothes. That's it. You will never get rid of me after last night. I'm like toe fungus, only prettier."

Killian managed a smile. "Tho pretty," he said. "Don' wanna get rid o' 'oo." He heard a sound from out in the front room. "The kiddenth tho—"

Lewis laughed. "We'll find homes for them," he murmured. "It's what we do. We're a team. Now go to sleep and let me do stuff before I come back and check on you again. You had a pretty nasty concussion—let's let your noggin heal."

"Work…," he began, but Lewis shook his head.

"Nope. I talked to Suzanne. You're out until the day after Christmas—doctor's orders, workman's comp. You'll need to fill out paperwork today and see the doctor again on Christmas Eve. We've got your back, baby." He kissed Killian on the forehead. "Just like you had mine last night."

"The'll be thord-thaffed?" he asked, feeling bad for Suzanne through the throbbing in his head. They'd already been short staffed before Killian had been taken out.

Lewis grinned. "Nope—Todd is apparently her new bartender. He texted at the end of last night. Said he'd put in his notice for the movie theater and the bookstore job, and the tutoring job won't take up again until after New Year's. You apparently got popped in the nose and saved his life."

Killian smiled, hopeful for Lewis's brother, and closed his eyes, floating toward sleep almost before Lewis got dressed and left the room. It was okay, though, he thought. They had each other's backs. They'd be okay. There would always be things to do together, useful things. Clothing drives. Kittens to rescue. Friends to help. A community to be part of. He and Lewis would be partners together, taking on all the weird life stuff as it came at them.

Even rednecks with fists like railroad ties.

Even a dozen kittens.

Even their own questing hearts.

He closed his eyes, feeling safety like he'd never felt it before. Lewis would be there when he woke up, and Killian had the heart of a lion to defend his mate, and there was nowhere else Lewis would rather be.

NICKY'S MOTHER-IN-LAW placed the last three kittens the day before Christmas.

Nicky showed up that morning, ostensibly to get the package of cookies Killian and Lewis had set aside for him and Lia, and another one for Lia's mom, but instead he had a plastic kitten crate and a letter from Lia's mom's Rotary president, offering to place the last three kittens with senior citizens who had an oddly shaped hole in their hearts. Apparently Lia's mom had attended two meetings since she'd adopted Boris and Natasha, and her stories of what it was like to own an "imperfect" cat had made others in the club open up their own hearts as well.

"Dude," Killian said, detaching the little white one from his shirt where she liked to cling. "That's...." He looked into her face. He really liked this kitten. Not as much as he loved Moose and Squirrel, but it could happen. "I'm gonna miss her," he apologized.

"Yeah, but Killian," Nicky said, taking her from him, "your two terrors are gonna continue to beat the crap out of her. She needs to be somebody's only baby."

Killian sighed, knowing Nicky was right and resolving not to be selfish. "'Course," he murmured. "C'mon in."

Sometime after pizza night they'd put tinsel streamers up around the ceiling of the front room, including a wreath over the computer table, where they'd stacked presents. Killian had realized that he would probably never own a breakable tchotchke again in his life, seeing as the twin terrors could be relied upon to knock anything and everything off of every shelf in the apartment at a moment's notice.

Nicky looked around the place and smiled appreciatively. "Christmas decorating a little bit different this year," he said.

"Everything is a little bit different this year," Killian agreed—but happily.

"How's Lewis?" Nicky asked.

"Staying," Killian answered. He'd been telling people that all week. It hadn't gotten any less amazing.

"Dude," Nicky said, offering him the fist bump. "You two are perfect together. It's like fate."

It was.

Nicky stayed for a cup of hot chocolate before whisking the kittens off to their forever homes, and Lewis got back from work shortly after. He had in his arms some packages that Killian hadn't been expecting.

"You said no presents!" Killian complained, embarrassed. He'd literally slept for two days after the concussion, and when he'd lamented to Lewis that he hadn't been able to find a suitable gift, Lewis had kissed him and told him that they were each other's suitable gift this year. Killian hadn't been happy about it, but he'd conceded because going out and buying something stupid without thinking about it felt wrong. Not after all they'd come to mean to each other this month.

"I said *you* didn't have to get *me* any presents," Lewis said. "You already got me two kittens, which is amazing, and you opened your house to me"—he balanced the packages in his arms as he spoke—"and your bed and your heart." With a clatter he let them fall onto the couch. "I thought I could get you some doodads that would make us laugh." He hefted another couple of bags over his wrist, this one from a man's clothing store. "Also, I needed clothes because my mom gave all my stuff to local thrift stores by mistake. Consider this Christmas shopping by convenience and enjoy opening stuff tomorrow like I'll enjoy wearing my own pajamas."

"I like you in my pajamas," Killian said with a small smile as he took the bags toward the bedroom.

"You like me out of them better," Lewis said with a certain amount of satisfaction in his voice. "Which should be the natural order of things as far as I'm concerned. Hey—where'd the other kittens go?"

Killian returned from setting the bags in the bedroom and grimaced at Lewis's dismay.

"Baby, Nicky's mother-in-law found a place for them. I'm sorry. I was going to text you and tell you, but you got here before I was expecting you. I thought you had stuff to do at the office."

Lewis grinned. "It was a Christmas party, which was fun, and my bosses loved the cookies, by the way, but I don't have any good friends there yet. Don't worry. Next year I'll stay and get drunk and have to take an Uber home. It'll be great."

"I look forward to pouring you onto the couch," Killian said, and boy did he ever. "But…." He sobered, "I'm sorry about the kittens."

Lewis moved into his arms. "I'm not," he said with a sigh. "I got two kittens for Christmas and the perfect boyfriend to boot. More kittens is really too much to ask for."

Killian grinned. "What about another perfect boyfriend?" he teased.

"Not necessary," Lewis murmured, moving in for the kiss. "Twelve kittens that I could love is possible, but there's only one you, and he's all I ever wanted."

Killian opened his mouth under Lewis's gentle kiss and then let the fire he knew was coming ignite his blood. Lewis was all the passion he'd ever dreamed of, and for a moment, it looked like they'd conflagrate right there in the living room.

Then there was a knock on the foyer door, and Killian's phone buzzed in his pocket, and he knew a friend was coming visiting for Christmas.

"Later," he said with satisfaction, pulling away.

"You bet your ass later," Lewis said, his eyes sparkling with the mischief and the joy that made him unmistakably Lewis.

Together they moved to open the door, to greet their friend, to welcome kindness and joy into their home. The world could hold all sorts of surprises—from kittens to concussions, as they'd discovered— but this Christmas Eve, they'd found they could greet all those surprises together. As a team. As their own little family.

As two people in love, with all the hope in the world.

EASTER EGG HUNT

THERE'S A lot of Easter Eggs in this one—feel free to skip this if you're not interested.

"Karcek"—Xander Karcek first appears in *The Locker Room*.

Derek Huston and Rico Gonsalves-Macias—first appear in *Bitter Taffy,* the second book of *The Candy Man* series.

Joey and Callum—Joey is part of the Fishiverse (Fish Out of Water series and all the attached books.) He first appears in *Fish on a Bicycle,* forever known as "Hurricane Joey and his nine-inch dick."

Cramer and Henderson, Attorneys at Law—Jackson Rivers, Ellery Cramer, and Jade Cameron make their first appearance in *Fish Out of Water.*

Galen Henderson joins the firm in *Fish on a Bicycle* after first appearing in *Black John.*

Henry first shows up as Dex's little brother in *Dex in Blue,* then reappears in *Fish on a Bicycle,* and finally got his own book in *Shades of Henry.*

Burton (the backer who helps pay for Lewis's project) first appears in *Racing for the Sun.* He gets his own book in *Hiding the Moon.*

Constance (the other backer) appears in *Hiding the Moon.* He gets his own book in *Constantly Cotton.*

Jaime, Cameron, and the "band of rogue accountants" all appear in *Homebird.*

So a few words about the "law firm" and the "consulting firm" that Lewis ends up dealing with at the end of this story.

Derek's consulting firm came first, in *Bitter Taffy,* which is part of the Candy Man series, and the building is one I had cause to visit— and liked immensely. Sacramento has converted Victorians that really are very cool. When I wrote *Fish on a Bicycle,* I needed a place to put Jackson and Ellery's new office, and I thought, "Hey—there's still vacancies, right?" Rico and Derek get one mention, unnamed, near the beginning of that book, I think.

So when I wrote about Lewis looking for a job, I thought, "Oh, hey—he could work for them! It would be a fun callback, and Lewis really deserves a rainbow-friendly establishment after his last experience job hunting, right?"

And then I had to figure out how these two regular guys would end up having to place twelve kittens the month before Christmas.

Oddly enough, it didn't even occur to me that I had already written the answer in a one-off ficlet on my Patreon last December. This story about Henry—Jackson and Ellery's new boy-Friday—and Dex, his until-recently estranged brother, seemed like a nice little Easter egg basket of references.

I don't know how I made the connection that the dilemma with the kitten mill and Lewis and Killian's problem finding a shelter for their many kittens could actually be related, but when I did figure it out? The ending of the book pretty much wrote itself.

If you haven't read the Fish Out of Water series or the Johnnies series, don't feel obligated. You don't need to read them to enjoy this novella. But if you *have* read them, this novella might have a little level of secret fun.

And if you want more little fiction nuggets about your favorite characters, please check out my Patreon account here: https://www.patreon.com/AmyHEALane Not everything is behind a paywall, so you should have plenty of free and fun reading if you wander around a bit.

—Amy

FRANCES'S BEST PRESENT—MERRY COUPLEMAS 3

A Dex and Kane Ficlet
By Amy Lane

THERE WAS a pounding at the door that wouldn't stop.

Kane growled and snuggled closer into Dex, grunting in irritation when he realized that—unlike himself—Dexter was not naked.

"Why are clothes?" he grunted, bucking his morning wood up against the soft knit fabric on Dex's backside. "Me no like."

Dex grunted in return. "I had to get up and pee, Carlos. The rule is no running around the house naked until Frances is in college."

Kane whimpered. "So long!" he protested, and at that moment another spate of knocking hit the front door, along with, oh God, Kane's only real in-law.

"Guys!" Henry called through the house. "Guys! Let me in! C'mon, it's Christmas Eve!"

"*Uncle Henry*!" Frances's shrill squeal zapped Dex out of bed like he'd been zinged with a wire and even had Kane hitting the floor with both feet in a solid *thunk*.

"You go let him in," Kane muttered. "I'll get dressed so I can hide the body."

"No hiding the body," Dex retorted. "For one thing, he knows all the law enforcement people. If we kill him, we both end up in jail for distributing pornography. It'll be bad."

"Not murder?" Kane asked skeptically.

"Well, I'd help ya hide it," Dex told him. "We wouldn't get busted for murder, but, you know, they'd suspect us, so they'd have to hit us with something. Now get dressed. I'll go pretend like we weren't just plotting death."

Kane felt absurdly grateful, and he grabbed his clothes from the floor, where he'd kicked them off the night before as he and Dex had fallen into bed and had sleepy, frantic sex after getting home from the Johnnies Christmas party. It had been a big night—their first real company Christmas party—and he and Dex had seen all the models dress casual/ nice and look… proud. Like they were part of something they could be proud of, and they liked their coworkers and shit. Kane was proud of that. It made the work at Johnnies not dirty—just adult. It was something grown-ups with functioning libidos could watch to enjoy themselves, and nobody had to be ashamed of that, nor did they have to be ashamed when they were ready not to do it anymore.

One of the things they'd gotten to do the night before was give a kid who'd gotten a scholarship to nursing school a car. The whole company had contributed because Cotton was much loved among all the models and the staff, and seeing him light up because they'd given him a way to get home—well, it had made Kane a little misty.

And then he'd seen how proud Dex had been, and that had made him horny, because basically everything Dex did made him a little horny. So once they'd gotten Frances from Henry's place, where they'd left her because all their friends from Johnnies had been *at the shindig*, they'd arrived home and put her to bed and, well… did what grown folks did when the kids were asleep and they were sort of overwhelmed by how awesome their partners were.

Kane had topped because Dex's ass had gotten the tiniest bit squishy in the past three years since they'd gotten together. Not so anyone who hadn't nailed him could notice, but *Kane* had noticed, and as much as Dex complained and worked out and tried to squeeze "extra steps" into his everyday work life, Kane was rooting for him not to go back to quarter-bouncing time.

Pounding Dexter's asshole when his cheeks were a little squishy was one of Kane's favorite things.

But then, so was Christmas Eve stuff, when all the packages were wrapped and the dinner was planned and all he had to do was make cookies with Frances and Dex and hang stockings and listen to Christmas music. It was just like people did it on TV, and dammit, Kane had been looking forward to getting it done with a *little extra sleep*.

So he was dressed in pajama bottoms and a sweatshirt that still stretched over his chest when he stalked barefoot out of his room, but his irritation was brought up short by Frances's delighted squeal.

"*For me*, Uncle Henry! Is that kitty for *me*!"

Oh no. Oh no, you stupid motherfucker, *no*!

Kane's footfalls made a slap, slap sound as he hurried out to the front room in time to see Dex—tall, blond, blue-eyed, and beautiful—standing, hands on hips, head cocked, brows drawn down in irritation at his shorter, stockier, but nearly identical younger brother.

"I told you!" Dex was hissing. "She can't have furry things. They freak out because of the reptiles! Her bunny…." Dex lowered his voice down beyond the subflooring—where they would have buried the bunny if they could have but had needed to settle for a soft patch of lawn in the backyard.

"My bunny had to go to a bunny place," Frances said glibly, reaching inside the pet carrier to get what Kane could only assume was a cat. "He was getting bald and not eating, so Unca Dex said he'd find a bunny place, and then one morning he wasn't moving, so Kane said he'd take the bunny to the bunny place *right now*, and now he's gone." She sighed. "But look at him! Kitty—" Her voice went a little skeptical. "Right? Unca Kane, it *is* a kitty, *isn't it*?"

Kane stared at the thing in her arms. "Uh, yeah, bunny." He wanted to curse himself for using her old nickname—they'd been going to stop calling her "bunny" after her pet bunny *died*, but it just popped out, like they were saying two different words. "It's uh…."

His brain supplied the breed—Egyptian hairless—but his mouth went somewhere unexpected.

"Beautiful," he breathed reverently. "Can I see him?" He gently tugged the creature from Frances's arms and held… him? Her? Kane checked under the tail. Her. "Her," he amended. "She's *beautiful*." He stared at Dex, not sure what was going on with his face, his eyebrows, his forehead, or his attitude, which he tried to wave around in front of Henry every so often to remind Henry to treat his brother right. But Kane couldn't retrieve the scrunchiness of his face to save his life at the moment, and his attitude was right out. He was left stroking the… the *prickly skin* of the gangly adolescent *bald* animal with a faint velvet of Siamese markings around its nose and eyes as piercingly blue as Dex's.

"Lookit her, bunny," he said to Frances, his voice pitching reverently. "Story says they were originally bred to not have any fur so they didn't make the Egyptian king guys sneeze, or shed on their nice clothes, but I think cats like her were just a happy accident."

The kitten let out a piercing, ear-shattering "Yowl!" before rubbing her whiskers up against Kane's nose and purring.

"And she likes us!" He turned to Dexter in a blissful dream. "Can we keep her, Dexter? We can keep her, right? Me and Frances, we'll set up the litter box—"

"I brought it," Henry said proudly. "And some litter, and her preferred food. Oh!" He rummaged in the pocket of his hoodie and pulled out a little plastic portfolio. "Also have her vet records and her breeding records in case you want to breed her, and her lineage 'cause she's a purebred—all the shizzle." He smiled obsequiously at his brother, who gave him a baffled look before turning that same bafflement to Kane.

"But... but snakes and geckos," he said, sounding as though he'd stepped off the wrong bus into a world where the sky was made of cheese. "You... you said yourself, Carlos. You really loved reptiles... amphibians, giant fuc—frickin' iguanas who hate me. You... you're in love with a *cat*?"

Kane held her prickly, scaly, leathery body up to his chest and took in another one of those absurdly fish-scented feline kisses. "She's so fu—frickin' ugly, Dexter. I can't even *breathe*."

Dex nodded, looking a little shell-shocked. "Uh... I'm not sayin' no," he said quickly, "but me and Henry need to have a talk on the porch, okay?"

Kane smiled happily and then sat down right next to the kitchen table with the kitten on his lap, Frances beside him, leaning her head on his bicep.

"He... he's not gonna say no, is he?" she asked, sounding a little worried.

But Kane knew his Dexter. This was the guy who'd bought him a frickin' turtle when his gecko died because he hadn't wanted to see Kane sad.

"No, bunny," he murmured softly. "Not to us. Not about this. Now what should we call her?"

Frances reached out her pointy finger and let the kitten scent-mark Frances like she'd scent-marked Kane. "I love her so much," she said, her voice as awestruck as Kane's had been. "She's my best present already!"

Kane gave an inward sigh and consigned all the pink and sparkly clothes, dolls, doll clothes, and shoes to the wind, and God knows what

Dexter had killed himself getting for Kane too. "Mine too, bunny. Who woulda thought Dex's dumbass brother could have pulled this off?"

"Be nice," she commanded. "We *love* Uncle Henry. Uncle Henry brought us a kitten!"

Kane had to—reluctantly—admit that Henry hadn't done too badly for himself. He had an exciting job as a PI in a law firm, a boyfriend that Kane sort of liked, and once he'd knocked the chip off his own shoulder, he hadn't been a bad guy.

"Yeah, bunny. Uncle Henry's a peach. I hear ya. What do we call our kitty here? Peaches?"

"No, silly!" Frances laughed.

"Then what?" Kane looked down at his niece and didn't want to know what kind of spike-laced firepit he'd walk over to keep her laughing and smiling like that. "What's a good name for her?"

She grinned and told him, and he laughed out loud.

It was perfect.

DEX MANAGED to grab his cold-weather coat as he walked past the peg by the door, so he was only freezing from his toes to his balls as he and Henry stood on the porch and talked.

"How could you!" Dex demanded, but not in the angry tones of a parent. More in the despairing cry of a brother with a knife in his back. "I thought you loved me! I helped you out when you got here, we have dinner once a week…. Is this about Thanksgiving? Because I would have done it at your place if I'd known you were so mad!"

"What? No!" Henry stared at him like he was crazy. "What are you so mad about? I-I *love* you, dumbass! I thought this would make Frances happy, and that would make you and Kane happy, and you would love me back!"

Dex wondered if his eyes were going to get stuck in that permabulge he felt coming on. "Of course we love you back! You don't need to drop scaryass deformed cats on my family for us to love you. A hug and some cookies would have done it!"

"She's not deformed!" Henry argued, seemingly stung. "In fact, she's *perfect*. She's got, like, award-winning genes—she could win cat shows. She can have billion-dollar babies if you want to get her bred. She's *royalty*!"

Dex took a breath, and then his eyes widened as he remembered everything he knew about Egyptian hairless cats. "She… she *is*," he realized with horror. "Where did you get this *super expensive royal pain in my ass*?"

Henry gave a pleased smile. "Trade," he said, nodding.

Dex gaped at him. "For what?"

"Well, see, Ellery had this case where the guy had *catnapped* all these pureblood cats, see? Because they were being taken to kitty mills, where they were getting impregnated at, like, this age. I mean, you saw her. She's way too young to be preggers, and they'd keep her that way until she died. I mean, no love or anything—she's just an incubator with a pedigree to them, right?"

Dex recoiled in horror. He hadn't had a chance to pet the creature, but thinking of the instant adoration on Kane and Frances's face made him hurt for the poor little ugly hairless thing currently getting spoiled for love in his dining room.

"They do that?" he asked, feeling hopelessly naïve.

"Yeah," Henry said with a shudder. "Our entire office—me, Jackson, Jade, even AJ, our tech guy in training, and Crystal, our psychic tech girl—spent, like, three days finding homes and reputable breeders for the cats after we busted the place. But in the meantime, we had to get our guy off for grand theft. He got a year, minimum security, but he said the only thing he had to pay us with was, well, Princess Leia Organa Lilith Persephone Caligula in there—"

Dex gave him a droll look. "If that's her real name—"

"Don't even finish that sentence," Henry told him, and pulled out the little plastic portfolio, waving it like it was the word of God. "It's her real name. Anyway, she was the cat he'd legitimately bought, and then he'd realized the people he'd bought her from were monsters, and then he catnapped a shit-ton of purebred cats, and then, well, he got caught, and Jackson and Ellery did their thing. But she's basically their lawyer fee, and, well, you know."

"They already have two cats," Dex said. He'd actually visited Jackson Rivers's and Ellery Cramer's place and had seen the two three-legged cats who did more damage than a six-legged horse.

"Yeah—they're monsters," Henry said in the indulgent voice of a beloved uncle. "I love them so. Anyway, after placing as many of the cats as we could, and filling up the shelters because not all the business was purebred, we were left with the kitten mill's most valuable asset. And since Galen and John had taken one to keep *their* cat company, the whole office was like, 'But where does this sweetheart belong?' and then, well, I thought of you!" He paused and looked a little crestfallen. "Also because I spent so much time trying to place all those other cats, I barely did any Christmas shopping. I mean, Frances I got, but you and Kane—"

Dex managed to let a chuckle escape. "Did you get your boyfriend something?"

Henry's full-out grin told Dex that yes, Henry had indeed. "I got him a four-day trip to Tahoe, in Ellery's cabin," he said softly. "Jackson and Ellery are going up tonight for Christmas Eve and Christmas day, and me and Lance get it for New Year's. We're doing office Christmas dinner in between."

Dex let out a soft smile. "What about tonight?" he asked, and Henry gave him a game smile.

"Uhm, tomorrow I've got Christmas with the flophouse guys in our apartment, but Lance is working a double, starting an hour ago, so tonight—"

"You're coming over here," Dex said with a sigh—not of resignation or unhappiness so much as it was of letting go of all his irritation and objections to being suddenly saddled with a pet that, all dead rabbits buried under the porch considered, might not have such a great chance at their house.

But look at his little brother. For eleven years he'd been stuck in a toxic relationship, under their father's thumb, and *such* an asshole. But when he'd come out of that, he'd been... well, stronger, but also *kinder*. The heart—the truly good heart—that Dex had seen in Henry as a child, well, it had grown and flourished here.

"Yeah?" Henry asked, excited. "Am I forgiven?"

Dex held out his arms and Henry went, and the hug was long and a little tearful on Dex's part—but that might have been the frozen toes.

"You're such a good kid," Dex said, a little choked up. "I'm so proud of you and how you fixed your life. Yeah. You're forgiven. I love you, kid."

Henry's smile held so much sunshine, Dex's eyes burned some more. "Love you too, Davy. Now can we go tell them we can keep the cat?"

Dex nodded. "And then you get to help us make breakfast and bake cookies and all the good things, okay?"

"Awesome! Merry Christmas to *me*!"

THAT NIGHT, Henry lay on his brother's couch and watched the Christmas tree lights twinkle as he fell asleep. His body was full and practically buzzing with sugar, and his heart was full and also practically buzzing, but this time with love and the certainty that he couldn't remember a better Christmas.

There'd been all the things promised—a good breakfast, punctuated by visits from some of Dex and Kane's friends as they wished the family a Merry Christmas and exchanged gifts. They'd made cookies—which had been part of the gift giving—and conversation and, in the evening, games. Dex's bestie, Tommy, had come by, bringing his husband and their toddler, Chance. Tommy's husband was a devastatingly beautiful, hauntingly quiet man named Chase, and something about him made Henry itch to hear his story but also aware of the fact that maybe it would never be Henry's to hear.

But that was okay. The last year had taught him that everybody had their ghosts, their demons, and hopefully, their angels. Henry got the feeling that his brother was angel to a lot of lost souls, a little like Jackson Rivers was, and that made him proud.

Finally they'd put an exhausted Frances to bed, after she'd fallen asleep listening to Dex read a few Christmas classics, including "T'was the night before Christmas...", and then Dex and Kane had come out with a special pile of gifts, wrapped in bright pink glittering paper.

Santa gifts, Henry knew, recognizing the custom from his friends' parents, although his own father hadn't been much of a fan.

His phone buzzed in his pocket right when the cat jumped on his chest. He situated the cat first and then smiled at Lance's message.

It's after midnight. Merry Christmas.

Merry Christmas to you, Galahad, he texted, smiling fondly. He and Lance had a Christmas day planned much like this Christmas Eve had been for Dex and *his* friends. He felt like he had a blueprint now, to share with his boyfriend. Something they could strive for together.

You have a good night?

Henry didn't ask about Lance's night—if it was good, he'd hear it, but if it was bad, Lance would save it and possibly cry about it, sometime when they were in bed together and the lights were out. Like he'd thought with Dex's friend, everybody had their demons and ghosts—it was his job to be Lance's angel.

One of the best, he keyed.

Did they like their gift?

Henry chuckled and petted the cat, who snuggled in a little closer onto his blanket. God, she was affectionate. As the client had said, she was so damned sweet. Who would want her for an incubator when she could flat-out give unconditional love?

Kane's in love. I think Dex is jealous, but Frances has dibs.

He got a bunch of laughing faces on his phone screen, and then, *God, I love you.*

I love you too—a whole lot.

What'd they name her?

Henry had to refrain from laughing out loud as he texted the name, and when his phone buzzed again, he could swear he heard Lance's stomach-rolling laughter.

They texted for a little while longer before Lance was off break and had to stop the conversation, but their words on the screen left a sweet little glow in Henry's chest.

T'was the morning of Christmas and all through the house, all the critters were stirring because iguanas and snakes and turtles didn't give a fuck about what time it was when they had sunlamps to keep them warm.

The kid was nestled all snug in her bed while visions of pink stuff swam in her head.

His brother and Kane were naked and fucking—Henry was making a guess 'cause they were doing it quietly, which made him super lucky.

And all the people he loved, his new friends and family, were content for once and hopefully at rest, just like Henry on his brother's couch.

With a cat named Lizard purring drool on his chest.

Still in a Holiday Story Mood?
Read on for an Excerpt from
ChrisMyths
by Amy Lane

Chapter 1: Nobody Ever Misses the Big City

"ANDY—ANDY, IT'S time to get up. Your train leaves in an hour."

Andy Chambers rolled over in bed and pulled the pillow over his head. "You can't make me," he said. "I live here, I pay rent, you can't make me."

Eli Engel, boy of his dreams, cosigner of his lease, welcome pain in his ass, smacked him on the backside.

"Andy, you have to. It's *your* family. I'm just some schmuck that's stolen you away for the last three years."

Andy groaned and eyeballed the man he loved more than life. "I keep telling you they don't think like that."

Eli's mouth—full and smiling most of the time—went crooked. "And yet they don't visit either."

"They think New York City is evil," Andy muttered. "And Brooklyn's the moon." With ill-disguised reluctance, Andy swung his feet over the edge of the bed and straight into his moccasins while he reached for the sweatshirt he kept by the end table. Their apartment in trendy Williamsburg had great hardwood floors, but those floors got chilly in December. The whole apartment got chilly in December. Mostly, Andy and Eli fought the cold by wearing layers around the apartment and by fucking like monkeys. Even though he was launching straight into the shower from bed, Andy didn't want to make the trip without an extra layer.

"Well, family is important," Eli said. "You go visit your family for Christmas, and I'll be here when you get back. Now shower. I'll go make you breakfast."

Andy watched his retreating back miserably. "Family is important," he'd said. But Eli didn't *have* any family. He'd been kicked out of his parents' house for being gay and had spent months on the streets before being taken in by Rainbow House, a shelter down in Bedford/Stuyvesant. They'd helped him apply for college and get scholarships—he'd gone to

NYU, gotten a degree in management, and turned right back around and started working at Rainbow House, doing everything from fundraising to organizing sports programs for the residents. Rainbow House was open to everybody, but it specialized in LGBTQ youth, and Eli was their biggest success story and most ardent advocate. He loved the employees there with all his heart, but when all was said and done, they all went home to their families for Christmas.

For the last three years, Andy had spent Christmas with Eli, celebrating with the residents of Rainbow House.

Having Eli tell him "Family is important, go visit yours," was painfully generous—and Andy hated it.

But his mother had been absolutely incessant.

"Two phone calls a day, Andy," Eli had told him at the beginning of December. "I mean, I get your family is super close, but two phone calls a day? Man, you've *got* to go visit them or they'll never leave us alone. We'll be answering their calls in the middle of sex into our sixties!"

Andy had snorted at that unlikely scenario, but he'd also softened.

"Our sixties?" he'd asked winsomely. "You promise?"

Eli had looked away, biting his lip. Andy had done his best to help his lover believe in forever, but Eli had a lot of damage to overcome. That was okay—Andy was up for the job.

"Just go," he'd said, not looking Andy in the eyes. "Your job practically shuts down during those two weeks. Take the time off, go visit your parents, and come back to Brooklyn."

Andy had sighed and rubbed the back of his neck. It was true that his job in a local tech firm really *did* shut down over Christmas, but that's not what Eli was saying.

Andy knew because Eli had been saying it from the very beginning of their relationship.

Back Then

"OH! HEY! You dropped your umbrella!"

Andy was the kind of guy who bought trench coats with an umbrella pocket and then had an extra spot on his waterproof briefcase for a spare. But this guy, with curly dark hair falling into brown eyes and a bony jaw covered with stubble, looked like the kind of guy who went out in the rain frequently and then wondered why he caught cold. Andy had been watching the guy on the train for the last few weeks, feeling vaguely protective over him. Andy had been rooming in Park Slope then, with a group of new hires for his tech firm. They all commuted to Williamsburg, and Andy had seen this guy getting off in Bed/Stuy and had worried for him. He'd looked so earnest, so focused on being somewhere else. Andy, who had grown up in the country, had loved the city because it meant he had to be focused on the *now*.

"Oh," said the sloe-eyed stranger. "Thank you." He gave a shy smile. "Good luck, this." He shook the umbrella Andy had handed him. "It looks like rain."

"Well, stay dry," Andy had replied awkwardly. "Maybe I'll see you tomorrow?"

For a moment he saw hope in the stranger's eyes. Excitement.

"You'll have better things to do tomorrow," the stranger told him with a wink, and then his stop had come and he'd been gone. Andy had turned to Zinnia, one of his roommates, and sighed.

"What's wrong?" she asked. "I've seen him on the train before. I think he thinks you're cute."

"I thought so too, but he seems absolutely certain I'll have something else better to do."

Zinnia snorted. "Prove him wrong!"

The next day, Andy had tucked three kinds of protein bars in his pocket—one with chocolate, one with nuts, and one that was a veganese delight. As the dark-eyed stranger stood to get ready for his stop, Andy held out the breakfast bars and said, "Here, breakfast on me."

The stranger had gaped at him in surprise. "I, uhm—"

"I bet you skip it, right?" Andy said. "I mean, you look super focused on your job or whatever, but you should have breakfast."

The subway hissed in preparation to stop, and Andy felt a little desperate.

"Please?" he said. "I'll bring you one tomorrow too!"

"Tomorrow's Saturday," the stranger told him, his wide, full mouth quirking up in a smile.

"Then I'll bring you one Saturday," Andy said, pretty much past pride. This man's brown eyes were fathomless, like the night sky full of stars.

"Okay," the man said, taking the one with chocolate. "I'll bring coffee."

"Lots of cream and sugar," Andy said, trying not to be embarrassed. Since he'd come to the city, it seemed like all New Yorkers took their coffee black.

The next day, Andy dressed casually, wearing his wool peacoat from his Vermont winters instead of his slick lined trench coat. But he still carried an umbrella—and a selection of protein bars—and took the same train as usual to Williamsburg.

This time when the doors opened three stops before Bed/Stuy, he saw the dark-eyed stranger get in, carrying two paper cups of coffee.

With a shy smile, the man came and sat down next to him, handed him the coffee, and accepted the breakfast bar in return.

"My name's Eli," he said, and Andy noted he'd tried to shave in the last twenty-four hours, but there were still patches of stubble like he'd forgotten a lot.

"I'm Andy."

"So, Andy, where are we going today?"

Andy had grinned. "I just got a raise. I was hoping to find an apartment in Williamsburg. Want to come with me?"

Eli grinned. "Sure. I work for a nonprofit—it'll be nice to dream."

And Now

THEY'D EVENTUALLY found the perfect apartment, and by then, Andy wanted Eli to move into it with him. The only problem, he realized, was that to Eli, all of it—Andy, the job he loved, the safety of the home—all of it was a dream, and he still dreaded waking up to an awful reality of being alone every morning.

And now Andy was *leaving* him for Christmas.

Andy raced through his shower and getting dressed. His suitcase was already packed, including gifts that needed wrapping. He wanted as much time with Eli as possible before he took off for the train.

Eli was already dressed when Andy got out, and he'd scrambled eggs with some toast for breakfast. Andy looked at the plate waiting for him on the counter in the kitchen and wanted to cry.

He'd been the one who'd made Eli eat breakfast for three years. Eli *never* remembered to eat—had become too used to *not* eating when he'd lived on the street or been broke and going through school. Three years of Andy stuffing his pockets with breakfast bars or getting up early so breakfast was on the table, and now Andy was leaving him and Eli was the one sending him off with breakfast. It didn't seem fair.

He'd even sliced some green onion and tomato to put on top.

"What?" Eli asked anxiously as Andy stared at the plate. "It's not good?"

Andy forced himself to take a bite. "It's delicious, babe. You're getting better."

Eli rolled his eyes. "You left enough food for an army."

As if. "The refrigerator is too small for an army. And you'll run out in a week, so, you know, don't forget to eat."

Eli shrugged. "Most of me will still be here if—when you get back." He grimaced and clapped his hand over his mouth, but he'd said it, and Andy knew he'd meant it.

"*When*. Oh my God, *Eli*. We've lived here for three years. What do you think is going to happen? I'm going to go visit my parents and forget I'm in love?"

"It's Vermont over Christmas, Andy. You've seen the propaganda. You'll go home, your parents will convince you the city was a bad dream, and I'll be the first thing you forget."

Andy gaped at him, suddenly angry. Three years? Three years and Eli didn't trust him more than this? "You complete asshole," he said, voice choked. "You think I could forget you? I'll show you. I'll come back in two weeks, and you're gonna have to eat those words."

Eli regarded him with deep skepticism. "You gonna cook them up like pizza?"

Damn him. Andy's mouth quirked. "Yes, asshole. I'm going to cook up a giant pizza that says Eli, I Love You and make you eat the fucking pizza. Two weeks. Love to Mom, a few handshakes with Dad, some bonding with my siblings while I convince them to get the hell out of Vermont, and I'll be home before you know it." His whole demeanor softened. "And maybe then we can get a pet for the apartment?"

They'd put it off because Eli didn't think it was fair to bring something into a situation that could change. Andy wasn't sure how three years didn't make a solid enough foundation to bring a pet into, but dammit, he wanted a cat!

Eli shifted. "Do you think we're ready for pet ownership?"

"Yes, Eli! I work from home three days a week. Why can't we get a cat?" He tried to remember his patience. "Baby, we live a good life. We live a *great* life. Don't you want to, I don't know, *expand* that life a little? A cat would be a good thing, don't you think?"

Eli took a deep breath and closed his eyes. "I'm sorry. I don't mean to be so insecure—"

Andy abandoned his eggs and moved to the other side of the table, breathing out, and rubbed Eli's arms briskly with his cupped palms. "Maybe when I get back from this trip, you'll see. Nothing's going to break us apart, okay?"

Eli leaned forward and rested his cheek on Andy's shoulder. He did that when he was feeling soft, and it always made Andy feel like king of the world. He wrapped his arms around the boy of his dreams and squeezed him tight.

"I've got to go," he whispered. "I'll call you every day. I promise."

"I love you," Eli offered, still taking comfort, and Andy took it as a win. Eli wasn't demonstrative by nature—too many years of having nobody had left him wary of being affectionate, even in private. But an unsolicited "I love you," from him was like gold.

Andy hugged him even tighter and then moved back enough to tilt his head up and take his mouth, softly at first, and then as he remembered this had to last through two weeks of his parents, his sisters, his damned hometown, he deepened the kiss, took more, pulled as much of Eli's sweetness into his soul as he could to sustain him for the coldness of winter in Vermont. In these moments he felt like the power of his six-foot-plus, two-hundred-pound frame wasn't wasted. His entire purpose was to keep Eli Engel—*his* angel—safe from all the harm the world had to offer.

Finally Eli pushed him away, reluctance written in every line of his body. "You need to leave," he said. "You're gonna miss your train, and then your mom's going to make you go next year!"

Triumph! "You said next year!" Andy replied, his face lighting up. "I'm bringing you crow pizza when I come back—you just watch!"

And with that he had to run. Eli was right. Between the slow elevators of their building and the struggle to get a cab to get him to the station, he really might miss the train!

And he had to go now so Eli would know he'd be back.

CHAPTER 2: HARD TO BE A SAINT IN THE CITY

AFTER ANOTHER frantic kiss, Andy dashed out the door, leaving the apartment a cold, vacant place, and Eli tried hard not to get too emotional. There were things to do, right? It was the Christmas season; the kids at the shelter needed a thousand things, and Eli was in charge of Christmas with them this year. It didn't even bother him that he was Jewish by birth. Christmas was all about the fantasy. The idea that there was a perfect day and a perfect love and that children would be cared for by magic or fate or a responsible adult were all equally unlikely in the minds and hearts of the kids at Rainbow House.

Andy had asked him to come to Vermont, but this was the one year Eli absolutely, positively could not leave. The fact that Andy understood this sort of made him the perfect boyfriend, but it could also mean Andy was totally okay with leaving Eli behind.

Argh!

Nobody kissed like that when they were totally okay with leaving someone behind, right?

In the end, that was the thought that got Eli going. He made quick work of the kitchen—but first he finished the eggs Andy hadn't eaten. Eli didn't waste food, ever. He'd known too many hard times when food was a luxury. Andy had known that when packing little homemade dinners for him, Eli noticed as he put the eggs in the fridge and took stock with a little lump in his throat.

Ten days' worth of dinners—along with a note that said there would be a food delivery on the twenty-ninth of December so Eli would have food until the third. Eli also knew Andy had stocked the freezer with frozen burritos, but Eli wouldn't let Andy's hard work go bad. Andy knew that.

Andy knew him so well.

That first day after they'd met on the subway, the one thing that had drawn Eli to him—besides his big blond good looks and country-boy smile, of course—had been his way of paying complete attention to Eli, as though Eli was his favorite subject and Andy was studying him for the big test.

Back Then

"SO YOU know everything about me," Andy said, taking Eli by the hand and pulling him off the subway car at the Williamsburg stop. "You know I'm a tech coder, you know I grew up in a tiny town, mom, dad, two kid sisters—so boring, yawn now. But what about you?"

"Nothing to know," Eli mumbled. The streets of New York were always so busy. He liked being able to tuck his hands into his pockets and keep his head down and go. Walking hand in hand with someone was harder. He had to be aware of his space and Andy's space and—oh. Andy drew nearer to him, bumped shoulders, and kept up that grip on his hand.

This was nice. Andy's body heat radiated out from the protective wool of his peacoat, and Eli felt like a lizard basking in the sun.

"There can't be nothing!" Andy laughed. They came to the real-estate agent's office, which had a small blue-and-white striped valance to protect people from the weather. Still smiling, he drew Eli under the valance and looked into his face. "You have the prettiest eyes," he murmured before bending to place a quick kiss on Eli's lips. "There's got to be a story in there somewhere."

Then he lifted his head and turned to open the door and let them into the small office, greeting Elaine Stritch, his agent, with a hearty hello. Eli was left, heart pounding, to listen as Andy negotiated the three visits they were going to do that day and introduce Eli as his new friend who was helping him get a feel for Brooklyn.

It turned out to be bullshit, of course. Andy worked in Williamsburg and had for nearly a year. He walked down the street with that shoulder-swaggering confidence that made people part for him, and Eli began to cling to his hand just to ride his wake.

The agent was competent—which meant she showed them the apartment, talked for a moment about the features, and then left them alone to decide.

But as they looked around each place, Eli started to realize that Andy was looking for more than just an apartment. He was looking for a life, a future, and that... that blew Eli's mind.

"No," Andy murmured at the first one. "No windows. We need windows to the outside. I don't care if they're in the front, in the kitchen, or in the back—there's got to be a window so we can look outside and see what kind of day it's going to be."

Eli had snorted. "So *you* can look outside and see what kind of day it's going to be."

"So me and the person of my choice can look outside and see what kind of day it's going to be," Andy corrected him. "I'm not going to live here alone. I'm going to settle down."

"Just like that. You assume you're going to settle—"

Andy had kissed him then too, until Eli couldn't remember what he'd been going to say.

"And we need a guest room," Andy said breathlessly when they came up for air. "Because my family's going to visit. And yours too."

"I don't have any family," Eli confessed in a daze. This wasn't first-date conversation. Hell, this wasn't even *date* conversation. Eli didn't tell *anybody* this. The facts of his somewhat pathetic existence were locked behind his eyes, because he hated pity.

"Well, you'll have mine," Andy offered blithely. "And if not visiting family, visiting friends. And if not visiting friends, we'll adopt."

Eli sputtered. "Adopt? You're already planning for kids?"

Andy had paused then, gazing into Eli's eyes with absolute determination. "You want kids, don't you? At least one? To open your home to a small person, someone we can shower with affection and spend time with, and love?"

Eli had been helpless then. Absolutely helpless. He'd been kicked out of his house when his parents found out he was gay. Ever since, he'd lived with the fantasy of having a child of his own, whom he swore he wouldn't let down. Someone who would be treated like a child should be—with love and care and attention and laughter. It was his pet plan, held close to his heart even as he built up his credibility and trust at Rainbow House. Someday he'd learn enough from the kids at Rainbow House to feel like he could give a child a childhood, make his house a home.

And here was this giant of a man who brought him breakfast and found his umbrella and grabbed his hand to dream impossible dreams… and they had the same dream?

He'd almost run away then, terrified by all the promise in Andy's sparkling blue eyes. But when he took a step back, he realized he was already in Andy's arms, clinging to his casual shirt underneath the peacoat, sheltered by the peacoat like a duckling under a parent's wing.

"Someday," he rasped.

"Me too," Andy murmured. "So yeah. We hold out for a guest room that can be a kid's room. And windows so it doesn't feel like a prison. And hardwood floors and arched doorways."

"Arched doorways?" Eli asked, looking around at the very pedestrian lines of the apartment they were in.

"Damned straight."

"Well, now you've gone too far."

And Andy had grinned then, blinding him with his vision, his dream for the future, the intoxicating fantasy that Eli would be in on that dream from the ground floor.

It took three more months and countless visits to the real-estate office for Andy to find the perfect apartment. By the time he did, he'd had Eli so wrapped around his heartbeat that subletting his own tiny hole in the wall to a recent graduate from Rainbow House and moving in with Andy had seemed inevitable.

But Eli had lived with him for two years before he gave up his lease and let the graduate have the apartment for real.

Award winning author AMY LANE lives in a crumbling crapmansion with a couple of teenagers, a passel of furbabies, and a bemused spouse. She has too damned much yarn, a penchant for action-adventure movies, and a need to know that somewhere in all the pain is a story of Wuv, Twu Wuv, which she continues to believe in to this day! She writes contemporary romance, paranormal romance, urban fantasy, and romantic suspense, teaches the occasional writing class, and likes to pretend her very simple life is as exciting as the lives of the people who live in her head. She'll also tell you that sacrifices, large and small, are worth the urge to write.

Website: www.greenshill.com
Blog:www.writerslane.blogspot.com
Email: amylane@greenshill.com
Facebook:www.facebook.com/amy.lane.167
Twitter: @amymaclane

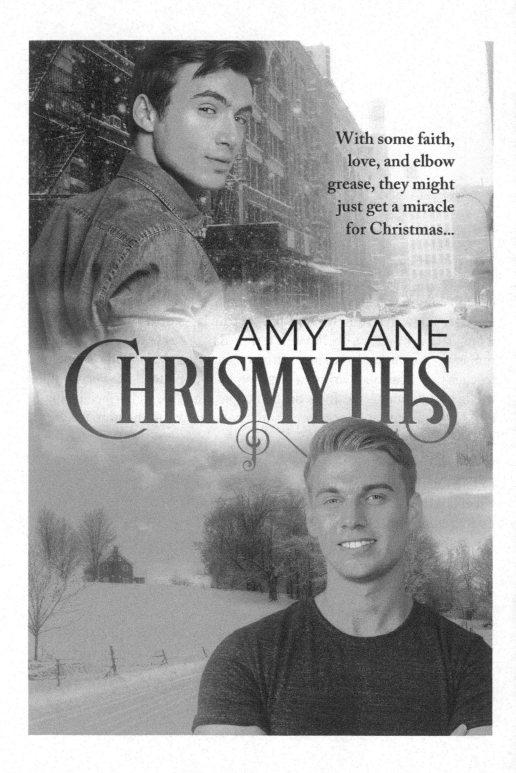

With some faith, love, and elbow grease, they might just get a miracle for Christmas...

AMY LANE

CHRISMYTHS

After courtship, cohabitation, and learning about love and each other, Andy and Eli face the ultimate test: being separated at Christmas.

Eli's seen the propaganda—the country boy goes home from the city and realizes his heart is back among the snow, trees, and chickens. A big happy family is something Eli, with his demanding job running a shelter for LGBTQ youth, can't provide. He's been readying himself for the other shoe to drop anyway—Andy's mother is a force of nature, and she wants her little boy home.

Andy may be in Vermont, but his heart is back in Brooklyn with the man who's battling basement floods and crumbling buildings to bring Christmas to sixty kids who've had their hearts broken too many times already. Holiday myths may say that Christmas means going back home to a happy family, but Andy knows happy endings don't come without a little faith and a lot of hard work. He's got an army ready to put in the elbow grease. If he can get Eli to believe in him, they might just save Christmas after all.

Cassidy Hancock hates being late—he's pathological about it. Until the crisp fall morning when he pauses to watch his neighbor's handsome son chase his dog down the sidewalk… and gets hit by a tree.

Mark Taylor sees the whole thing, and as a second-year medical resident, he gets Cassidy top-notch care. In spite of himself, he's fascinated by his mother's stodgy neighbor, and as he strives to help Cassidy recover from a broken leg, he begins to realize that behind Cassidy's obsession with punctuality is the story of a lonely boy who thought he had to be perfect to be loved.

Mark and his family are far from perfect—but they might be perfect for Cassidy. As the two of them get to know each other, Cassidy fantasizes about the family and happy-ever-after he never thought he'd have, and Mark starts to yearn for Cassidy's wide-eyed kindness and surprising creativity. But first they have to overcome Cassidy's fears, because there is so much more fun to be had during Christmas than just being on time.

www.dreamspinnerpress.com

FRECKLES

Amy Lane

Small dogs can make big changes… if you open your heart.

Carter Embree always hoped someone might rescue him from his productive, tragically boring, and (slightly) ethically compromised life. But when an urchin at a grocery store shoves a bundle of fluff into his hands, Carter goes from rescuee to rescuer—and he needs a little help.

Sandy Corrigan, the vet tech who eases Carter into the world of dog ownership, first assumes Carter is a crazy-pants client who just needs to relax. But as Sandy gets a glimpse of the funny, kind, sexy man under Carter's mild-mannered exterior, he sees that with a little care and feeding, Carter might be "Super Pet Owner"—and decent boyfriend material to boot.

But Carter needs to see himself as a hero first. As he says goodbye to his pristine house and hello to carpet treatments and dog walkers, he finds there really is more to himself than a researching drudge without a backbone. A Carter Embree can rate a Sandy Corrigan. He can be supportive. He can be a man who stands up for his principles!

He can be the owner of a small dog.

www.dreamspinnerpress.com

AMY LANE
homebird

Crispin Henry isn't an adventurer. He learned early on that the world is a frightening place and that home is rare and precious. If his friends didn't drag him to sports games and ill-advised trips to Vegas, he wouldn't get out at all—and his trip to Munich for Oktoberfest is no exception. But it's there that he meets Luka Gabriel, and he learns to take a chance.

Luka is a free-spirited world traveler, working at Oktoberfest to feed his enchantment with new places and new people. His only possessions fit in his backpack, and he depends on the kindness of strangers for a place to sleep. Crispin should know better—but he takes Luka's hand anyway, and together they turn three nights in Munich into the relationship neither of them has been brave enough to risk—and neither can let go of.

When Luka turns up on Crispin's doorstep before the holiday season, Crispin takes him in on hope alone. Yes, he knows the odds are good Luka will flutter out of his life again and leave him bereft, but isn't it worth it to see if Luka is a homebird after all?

www.dreamspinnerpress.com

Christmas Kitsch

Amy Lane

Sometimes the best Christmas gift is knowing what you really want.

Rusty Baker is a rich, entitled, oblivious jock, and he might have stayed that way if he hadn't become friends with out-and-proud Oliver Campbell from the wrong side of the tracks. When Oliver kisses him goodbye before Rusty leaves for college, Rusty is forced to rethink everything he knows about himself.

But nothing can help Rusty survive a semester at Stanford, and he returns home for Thanksgiving break clinging to the one thing he knows to be true: Oliver is the best thing that's ever happened to him.

Rusty's parents disagree, and Rusty finds himself homeless for the holidays. But with Oliver's love and the help of Oliver's amazing family, Rusty realizes that failing college doesn't mean he can't pass real life with flying rainbow colors.

www.dreamspinnerpress.com